This sum
brings to
leading Australian and overseas writers.
True to its title, it ranges over many
topics – from surfing to boxing to porn
stars to Wyatt Earp, Ernest Hemingway,
and the madness of poets – and visits
many places – from Galicia to the
Languedoc, Sark Lake to Brummana,
Whyalla to Moorollala, and
Fitzroy to Freo.

Heat 2. New series

Edited by Ivor Indyk

Fitzroy
to
Freo

The Giramondo Publishing Company from
The University of Newcastle
Newcastle, Australia

Published by the Giramondo
Publishing Company
from the Faculty of
Arts and Social Science
University of Newcastle
Callaghan NSW 2308 Australia

Designed by
Harry Williamson
Formatted and typeset in
11/14 Garamond 3 by
Andrew Davies
Printed and bound by
Southwood Press
Distributed in Australia by
Tower Books
(02) 9975 5566

Copyright in each contribution to
HEAT belongs to its author.
This collection © Giramondo
Publishing Company 2001

Fitzroy to Freo
(HEAT 2, New series, 2001)
ISBN 0 9578311 2 9
ISSN 1326-1460

All rights reserved.
No part of this publication may be
reproduced, stored in a retrieval
system or transmitted in any form
or by any means electronic
mechanical photocopying or
otherwise without the prior
permission of the publisher.

The editor acknowledges the
support given by the following
organisations:

The Department of English
and the Faculty of Arts and
Social Science at the University
of Newcastle

The Australian Government
through the Australia Council,
its arts funding and advisory body

Sydney Grammar School

The NSW Government –
Ministry of the Arts

Acknowledgements

ASSISTANT EDITORS:
CHRISTOPHER CYRILL – FICTION
LUCY DOUGAN – POETRY
ROSALIND SMITH – ACADEMIC

EDITORIAL ADVISORY BOARD:
DAVID BOYD, ANNA COUANI,
MARTIN DUWELL, KEVIN HART,
ANTONI JACH, NICHOLAS JOSE,
EVELYN JUERS, VRASIDAS KARALIS,
CASSANDRA PYBUS, IMRE SALUSINSZKY,
JOHN SUTHERLAND

Annual subscription (two issues)
$40 in Australia and New Zealand,
$55 overseas.
Institutional subscriptions
$66 in Australia and New Zealand,
$75 overseas.
Amounts are in Australian dollars.
Australian rates include GST.
Payments may be made by cheque,
money order, Visa or Mastercard

Subscriptions and editorial enquiries:
HEAT
PO Box 752
Artarmon NSW 1570 Australia
TEL. AND FAX: (+61 2) 9419 7934
EMAIL: heat@newcastle.edu.au
WEBSITE: www.mypostbox.com/heat

Contributions and correspondence:
HEAT
Department of English
University of Newcastle
Callaghan NSW 2308, Australia.

All published contributions by
academics are refereed.

Prose

9   Jessica Anderson   PROJECT! PROJECT!
21   Fiona Capp   THAT OCEANIC FEELING
35   Louis Nowra   LUST AND ADORATION
53   Manuel Rivas   WHAT DO YOU WANT WITH ME, LOVE?
63   Martin Armiger   BIFF
83   Janet Kieffer   SARK LAKE
93   Simon Petch   THE LAW, THE WESTERN, AND WYATT EARP
113   Abbas El-Zein   QUEST FOR AN INDIAN KING
129   Barbara Brooks   LIL'S STORY
147   Tom Carment   ILLUSTRATED TALES
161   David Brooks   NAPOLEON'S ROADS
171   Tim Richards   THE FUTURES MARKET
185   Antoni Jach   STRANGE HAPPENINGS ON VIA SILLA

Poetry

18   Meredith Wattison
31   Simon Armitage
49   Jennifer Maiden
58   Lidija Cvetkovic
79   Jan Owen
108   Alan Wearne
126   Jill Jones
143   Deb Westbury
158   Joanne Burns
181   James Lucas
194   John Bennett
221   Lucy Dougan

Contents

Literary Engagements

197   Mandy Sayer   THE SHORT STORIES OF ERNEST HEMINGWAY
209   Hugh Tolhurst   MANIC-DEPRESSIVE ILLNESS AND POETRY
223   Judith Beveridge   WRITING HOME: THREE NEW ZEALAND POETS
233   Brendan Ryan   THE COLLECTED POEMS OF JOHN FORBES
241   Martin Duwell   CONTEMPORARY AUSTRALIAN POETRY
249   Greg McLaren   BLOWING DANDELIONS: A NOTE ON CALYX

Jessica Anderson

Project! Project!

Jessica Anderson is the author of *Tirra Lirra by the River* (1978) and eight other books of fiction, the most recent of which are *Taking Shelter* (Viking, 1989) and *One of the Wattle Birds* (Penguin, 1994).

In the Botanical Gardens, opposite the big double doors of the old exhibition building, Ruth stood waiting for the Maidmonts.

Beneath her bronze umbrella, she stood and watched the crowd of mothers and children waiting for the double doors to open. The Maidmonts were late.

The rain was merely a gauze, a softening of the early autumn air, but now and again Ruth saw a young mother dart out from her avidly talking group to bend over her child, to pull up and settle a hood of yellow, scarlet, or cobalt blue.

Though these mothers were themselves unprotected, still in their summer cottons or supple synthetics.

The doors were opening. The crowd clustered, and was beginning to mount the steps, when in her side vision Ruth saw the Maidmonts, Clive and Stella, emerge from a narrow path, out of the darkness of tree ferns.

Ruth, shocked, stared. It was only a year since she had seen them. How, in one year, had Stella become obese, and her spine so cruelly bent that she almost faced the ground? Ruth quickly composed her face. They hadn't seen her; they were immersed in some conflict –

anyway, concerned only with each other. Clive seemed unchanged. Still a tall thin straight old man, he inclined sideways above his wife's tottering figure, matching his nibbling steps to hers, cupping with one hand her nearer elbow, and with the other sheltering her head with a small pink umbrella.

He was talking, Ruth saw, quietly but with intensity. She put down her umbrella and went forward, rehearsing a greeting. *Well, hello, you two.*

They wore the clothes they had brought home from Europe fifteen years ago, when Clive had retired from the Government Architects Office. These, they had merrily announced then, would see them out. Today Stella wore the pleated tartan skirt, the Liberty blouse, the Burberry, and Clive wore his Scotch tweed jacket and the little matching hat. But as Ruth went forward she saw that his shabby trousers disproved that old cheerful prediction, and that both wore dirty canvas shoes.

'Well hell-*oh*, you two!'

She and Stella had always been of a height, but now she had to bend at the waist, and twist sideways, to kiss Stella's cheek, while Stella stood unmoving, and Clive pulled a handkerchief from a pocket and said loudly, 'Stella's *got to sit down.*'

'I don't,' said Stella in a soft little voice, while Ruth said, 'Yes, Clive. But where? They've cancelled our exhibition.'

Clive pushed back his hat. He wiped his sweating forehead and shouted. 'She's got to rest *now*.'

'But not in this rain. And not in there, because – *listen* – they've postponed our exhibition.'

'What! But it was you – *you* who rang and suggested –'

'I know. But they cancelled. There was a little notice in the Herald, they told me. I didn't see it.'

'*Jesus!*'

'School holidays. See?' Ruth pointed to the few mothers and children still on the steps. 'They've put on something for the children instead.'

'I don't care,' said Clive. 'She's got to rest *now*.'

'The gallery isn't far,' said Ruth. 'The Magnum exhibition is on.

We could have a quick coffee first.'

'And cake,' said Stella.

But Clive thrust the little pink umbrella into Ruth's shoulder bag and strode to the exhibition building, indignantly swinging his arms, while Stella said in her small voice, 'It was you who gave us that pot of crimson azaleas.'

'Yes,' said Ruth, 'a year ago.'

'That lovely crimson. Almost transparent.'

'Yes. Just before I went to Italy.'

'I know.'

'*Chiuso, chiuso*. That was Italy.'

Clive came rushing out of the exhibition building. He leaped down the steps. 'They've put out a chair,' he shouted. 'Come on!'

The chair was just inside the entrance. After their nibbling shuffling ascent of the steps, Stella obediently sat, and at once directed her strained glassy gaze, her little private smile, at the last few children filing into the exhibition room. Ruth moved to Clive's side and said quietly, 'Stella's been ill?'

He had set back the tweed hat and was wiping his forehead again. 'Stella's never ill,' he said curtly.

'But Clive, her back – '

'Back? Her back? Well, there's a bit of trouble with some vertebrae. But it's her memory. Her memory. It just bloody well collapsed. You mean to say you didn't notice?'

'Before I went away? Oh, little things, maybe – '

'Then you're pretty bloody unobservant.'

Ruth laughed, startled. She had received the usual number of angry epithets from husbands, lovers, and teenaged children, but nobody called her unobservant before. She said, 'I gave her a pot of crimson azaleas – '

'Ah yes, and I suppose she remembers it. Random things. Things like that. Great! But that's not the point. She can never be left alone. That's the point. Or she scalds herself. Or wanders off. A police job one time.'

Stella's plaintive voice reached them. 'What am I doing here?'

Both went to her chair. Both bent to her level. 'You're resting,'

Clive fiercely told her.

'You said – someone said – cake.'

Ruth heard Clive's intake of breath, heard the soft *aaaahhh* as he rose to his height and let it out. He slightly raised his tweed hat, then pulled it firmly down. More than fifty years ago, the three of them had been art students together, at Sydney Tech. Clive now bent over his wife and said with gaiety, 'Coffee and cake in the gallery, dear. I'll meet you two in the portico. In ten minutes approx.'

In three big paces he reached the door. Ruth watched him disappear down the steps. 'I haven't the least idea,' Stella was saying, 'what I'm doing here.'

'You were resting,' Ruth told her. 'Are you better now?'

'I was perfectly all right before.'

'Then we'll go, shall we?'

'Go where? Where is Clive?'

'Gone ahead, to the gallery. You and I are meeting him there.'

'Oh yes, cake. Well, if you'll lend me an arm, as the saying goes.'

But on the steps she said, 'You're no good at this, Gwen.'

'I'm not Gwen,' said Ruth. 'I'm Ruth. Ruth Plummer.'

Lately, Ruth had begun to consider seriously the accusation of her children (and even of one grandchild) that she was selfish and egotistical, and had always been selfish and egotistical. 'I am Ruth Plummer,' she said gently. 'And this is the last step.'

'Oh look, it's raining.'

The rain was heavier. 'Never mind,' said Ruth. 'We have my big umbrella.'

She put it up. It was a beautiful umbrella, and she had expected it to be admired. 'I bought it in Italy,' she said.

'*Chiuso, chiuso.*'

'Now, we take this path.'

'Wait. I had an umbrella. Pink.'

'This one's bigger.'

'But wait – *wait* – where is mine?'

'In my bag. It's easier if we share mine. Come on, Stell, it's not far.'

But when they left the shelter of the building, they walked into a wind that whipped the rain about, so that Ruth was forced to bend from the waist, and to twist sideways, to keep them both under the shelter of her umbrella. She could and did reject the charges of egotism and selfishness, but had to admit to impatience, though adding that she had developed a method of controlling it. She would, she explained, project. She would mentally concentrate on a future where the irritant, whatever it was, was absent. When Stella tried to pull away into the rain, Ruth heard herself saying, courteously though rather loudly, as she roughly pulled her back, 'Shall we have coffee and cake first? Or see the Magnum exhibition first?'

'Mag what? What is that?'

'Magnum. It's a group of photographers.'

'But Clive said – said an exhibition of woodcuts.'

'That was the one we just left.'

'Why?'

'It was postponed. Clive will take you another day. One of yours is in it.'

'One of mine? I don't believe it.'

'True. That's why I rang and suggested it.'

'The poinsettias, I suppose. Does Clive know? Where is Clive?'

'No, the frangipani. Clive's gone ahead. And yes, he knows. I told him on the phone. If he didn't mention it – '

'He didn't.'

' – it must be because he wanted it to be a surprise.'

'The frangipani. That's good. That was my best. Someone once told me it was subtle.'

'I told you that.'

'Subtle. I was so pleased. I wasn't often called subtle. You were supposed to be the subtle one. Ruth gets those subtle effects. Remember that?'

'Ages ago.'

'Clive was always saying that.'

Clive had said that about her early woodcuts, though never about the painting that had since made her a minor celebrity. He had said it, she used to suspect, to annoy Stella. She said, 'I wish this bloody rain would stop. Try not to *pull*, Stell.'

'Yes,' said Stella, 'subtle effects.' Then abruptly she halted, and with a strong grip dragged Ruth's arm down. The spokes of the umbrella struck the path. 'Clive! shouted Stella. 'Where is Clive?'

'Let *go*!' Ruth spoke through clenched teeth, and tugged with all her strength until she could raise the umbrella into place. Anger rushed into her. It clutched at her breastbone. '*Project!*' she told herself. '*Project!*' And she brought up an image of herself sitting alone in her new silver car. There she was – soon, very soon – slowly, at peace, driving out of the Domain carpark, yes, and perfectly making the turn. 'Clive,' she was then able to say, 'has gone ahead to the gallery.' She changed the umbrella to her left hand and put her right arm firmly round the hump of those shoulders. 'Maybe there's a queue, and Clive has gone ahead to save us a place.'

'A place?'

'In the queue. What would you like first, Stell? Coffee and cake? Or the exhibition?'

Stella's voice became roughish. The young Stella had been known for this roughishness. 'You know me! Guess!'

'Coffee and cake?'

'A nice big slice of naughty rich chocolate cake.'

'In that case, said Ruth in a pleasant steady voice, 'I may have to skip the exhibition. I didn't count on so much delay. You were rather late arriving, and now – well – I'm picking up Susanna at three-thirty. Susanna? You know? My grand-daughter?'

'We have those. We have four of those. Where are we going?'

'The gallery.'

'Not that we ever see them. We don't see much of the biggies. But the littlies, never.'

'Oh, they're the busiest little creatures in the world.'

'If you don't serve them, you don't see them. That's what Clive says.'

'Does he *indeed*? Then it can only be gospel truth. Where are you two parked?'

'Parked?'

'Your car?'

'Oh wait – wait – yes, that's right, we're not. There was that fuss, you know. And Clive lost his licence.'

'He didn't mention that on the phone.'

'He doesn't. He won't. He flies into rages. He gets those now. Those rages. He never used to. Sarcastic, he was sarcastic, but always a gentleman. People used to say that. Always a gentleman.'

'Yes,' said Ruth, recalling the various inflections – of praise, of weariness, of a sarcasm like Clive's own. 'I am sure,' she said, 'that he still tries to be.'

'Always a gentleman. That's what held me back, you know, what you used to call his bloody respectability. Not that it matters, in the long run. Still, the frangipani, that's nice.'

'When did he lose his licence?'

'Not long ago. I suppose you were in England.'

'Italy.'

'*Chiuso, chiuso.* Did you paint?'

'No. Nothing. It's over. Infantile of me to imagine an Italian miracle. It's *over*.'

'Well, join the club.'

'Infantile! Stupid!'

'Oh look, Gwen, there's a nice seat.'

'A nice bloody wet seat. Come *on*.'

'Dear, I need to sit down for a bit.'

'You *don't*. Clive will be waiting for us.'

'I expect he's gone for one of his runs.'

'What runs? We are meeting him in the portico of the gallery. And listen, *listen*, we have only to get past this fountain, look, and then turn that corner, look, and we'll see the big gates.'

'The dear old garden gates.'

'Exactly. And we go through those, and then we have only that nice bit of flat road. And we're *there*.'

So they did hobble on. Ruth held Stella firmly to her side and tilted over Stella's head the big umbrella, while calculating that the time she could now spend at the gallery would be, at most, forty minutes. Again she saw herself in her new silver car, and then saw her granddaughter waiting at the door of the dancing school, her shapeless white legs emerging from her dark school uniform. She had painted Susanna once, and had had a success with those sweet silly ragdoll legs.

When Stella said, 'There they are, the big gates,' she soothingly agreed, but did not look up.

'And just look at Clive.'

Ruth did look up then. On that nice bit of flat road, Clive was running. He ran through the rain, knees high, head erect, elbows circling. First they saw him through the tall railings, then in full view as he passed the wide open gateway. Hunched together under Ruth's umbrella, they stood and with strained raised eyes watched him disappear up Art Gallery Road.

'Clivey was always a good runner,' said Stella then, contented.

'And obviously,' said Ruth in a careful, light voice, 'still in training.'

'Oh, not like in the days when they were all doing that – you know – that – '

'Jogging.'

'Yes, not like then. But he runs every day. He makes sure he does.'

'By hook or by crook.'

'Well, what *he* says is,' said Stella with her roughishness, 'that he makes *bloody* sure.'

'I see,' said Ruth. 'Well, do come on now.'

'Where are we going?'

'Cake,' said Ruth, curtly. 'Chocolate cake.'

Clive was waiting for them, not in the portico, but standing at the head of the steps, anxiously craning his neck. He saw them; he ran down the steps; he grasped Stella's free arm. Then all three of them, heads lowered, climbed slowly up to the shelter of the portico.

Here, at once, Ruth took the little pink umbrella from her bag and gave it to him.

'But hey, Ruthie,' he said, 'you're coming with us.'

In a wonderful gesture of liberation, Ruth brought up her left arm and looked at her watch. 'I think not. I am to pick up Susanna. Which hardly leaves me time for the exhibition, and certainly not for coffee and cake as well.'

'Then let's do the exhibition first.' He looked at his wife. 'Stell?'

'You know me! Cake first.'

'She needs the sugar hit,' said Clive to Ruth.

'Well, so sorry,' said Ruth.

'Clivey should take off that wet jacket, shouldn't he, Gwen?'

'Yes, Clive, you should. And look, do understand why I can't stay. We've lost so much time. I'm sorry. I could have given you a lift to your train. But there's a good bus service. And taxis. Phone in the foyer.'

Clive looked at her steadily for a moment. Then he said, 'They wouldn't have postponed that exhibition like that. Without notice.'

'All the same, they did.' Ruth reached out and touched Stella's arm. 'Stell, goodbye now. I'll ring you.'

'They didn't,' said Clive. 'They wouldn't.'

But at least she was free simply to turn and leave them. His raised voice followed her across the portico.

'They didn't! They wouldn't!' And as she ran down the steps he shouted, 'You bungled. *Bungler!*'

She could see the entrance to the underground carpark. Half-blinded by tears of anger or sorrow, she put up her umbrella and hurried downhill towards the concrete hood sheltering the steps. But the surface of the grass surprised her. Thick, coarse, wet, resilient, it made her stumble, it forced her to slow down. She was halfway down the slope when she heard from behind the shouts, the hoots of laughter. And in only a few seconds she was overtaken by five running children in brightly coloured slickers, red, cobalt blue, yellow, the hoods fallen, the wet heads exposed, and immediately following them, two young women, these running entwined under one umbrella, and shouting expostulations at the children as they ran.

In her tear-blurred vision those seven figures seemed to be hurtling, all slightly, eerily, airborne, above the slope of shining green. They disappeared, one by one, beneath the concrete hood, and by the time she herself reached that hood, she was perceiving that vision of their flight as wonderful, perfect, or exactly what she wanted.

On the steps, beneath the hood, she stopped. She put down her beautiful umbrella and stood flicking the water from its folds while rather quickly, though without panic, she reassembled them, those seven (or eight?) bright blurred hurtling shapes against that swathe of pocked and lustrous green.

Meredith Wattison
All These Stars Make My Head Go Back

They are like rain on a black velvet coat.
My son, 9, staggers, slack-jawed, says,
'All these stars make my head go back.'
My silver, sequined, bottom-half, is theatrical wetness, stars, metallic,
my top-half naked, spills like lava.
Red, rubbery (comic book) nipples float.
My tail's side zip, a train,
goes back to my hip,
goes back to my waist
for passengers,
(bites my skin like glitter)
its pleated films and gauzes (drag queen femininity, motion),
its shredded green plastic (seaweed),
are lost in the blackness.
Black-blue glass beads like thin macaroni
are sewn, drip stiffly, unsilently brush,
ended with a black ball,
cover my pudendum,
under its glitz a fairy light,
silver white in this blackness,
fractured, defused.
All these stars make my head go back.

Quarantine

And so, you have quietly died on your 87th birthday,
did not wake the next day.

I want to cut the flowers
I wrote to you about
in intimate, intimated, detail,

the pleated red poppies,
their intortions,
the torn, dark flags on the rose stems,
the golden calendulas,
their exquisite, dry grub, seeds,
the budded cornflowers,
their clenched fur.

I want to cut them
and hold them
for the 23 hours
it would take to be there,
open my hand
and let them spill onto your grave
like split light
but quarantine would not allow.

When you couldn't hear us on the phone
what could you hear?

MEREDITH WATTISON

When your sight was failing
what could you see?

When you took off your ring
what did you know?

Light found you leaving
and gone, travelling here
by intimation,
my garden a shivering clash of colour this morning.

Meredith Wattison's first collection of poems, *Fishwife*, was published by
Five Islands Press in 2001.

Fiona Capp

That Oceanic Feeling

Fiona Capp is the author of two novels, *Night Surfing* and *Last of the Sane Days* (Allen & Unwin) and a study of the surveillance of Australian intellectuals, *Writers Defiled* (McPhee Gribble/Penguin).

One late afternoon in mid-winter, when I was three months pregnant, I took some visiting French friends to the Point Nepean National Park because they were keen to see the notorious entrance to Port Phillip Bay known as the Rip. The Park was soon to close for the day so we quick-marched past the gun emplacements and the maze of underground bunkers at Fort Nepean and did not pause until the land fell into the sea. Around the corner in Bass Strait, the surf was thunderous; line after line of ragged, blue barrels shattering into foam. To my right Port Phillip Bay was shot silk with occasional white caps. Yet in this narrow strip of ocean between the Heads – this bottleneck where the Bay and the Strait collided – the conditions were perfect. I knew it was a prized surf break but it still surprised me that this should be so. During a south-westerly gale on an ebb tide, the difference between the sea level inside and outside the bay created a wall of water that broke from Head to Head. Today, a light south-easterly was blowing. Just beyond the breaking waves a small motor-boat hovered, which I took to be a fishing vessel until I saw a small figure paddling nearby in the water.

I had spent many hours imagining my way into such a moment

in my novel *Night Surfing* but I had never seen it for myself. Surfers have been coming by boat to this break they call Quarantine, Corsair or The Point for decades; but Point Nepean only opened to the public in 1988, and until twenty years ago it was regarded as a secret spot surfed only by the cognoscenti. The other times I had been here, there had not been a surfer in sight. Now, absorbed by the figure of the surfer, I did not notice a giant tanker stacked high with rusty red, orange and green containers approaching from Bass Strait. Suddenly its massive bulk loomed at the gateway of the Heads. The tanker nosed steadily forward, dwarfing everything it passed. Soon after, another tanker approached from the bay, this time in the south channel, much closer to the Corsair break. Against it, the surfer was a mere fly on an Icy Pole stick. No wave would ever loom so precipitously or darkly above him, or cast such a shadow. For a brief moment, a trick of perspective put the surfer and the vessel on a collision course until the ship slid calmly by, bequeathing him its wake.

Point Nepean was a forbidden place when I was young. Apart from the Bass Strait and Westernport coastline, it was the only wild bit of the Peninsula left. In the days when this area was an army officer-cadet training school and closed to the public, you could only see Point Nepean in the distance from the Sorrento to Queenscliff ferry. A rugged, ti-tree-covered headland tapering away to a small, half-moon beach with remnants of an old fort and the colonial-style buildings of the Quarantine Station just inside the Bay. The small incursions made by man on this tip of coast only accentuated its air of isolation. I was amazed there was a beach at all, that it hadn't been swept away by the powerful currents and surging tides of the Rip.

The other image I had of Point Nepean was taken from a postcard that was pinned to the back of the kitchen door of our beach house at Sorrento. It was an aerial shot, a seagull's-eye view of this promontory carpeted in green and surrounded by the deep blue of Bass Strait looking as benign as frozen jelly. I would often study this postcard as if it were some far-off land. In maps of the time, this end of the Peninsula appeared as an empty space. The rest of the Peninsula was a network of roads and built-up areas but all roads stopped at the beginning of the army reserve. The road through the reserve wasn't even marked – as if its existence were a government secret that could not be divulged. What intrigued me most was how this narrow arm of land separated the wilds of Bass Strait from the dreamy waters of Port Phillip Bay. I had always thought of them as two distinct worlds. The Bay I associated with childhood, with sandcastles and lazy, endless afternoons spent snorkelling or floating on my back staring at the sky. When I was about ten years old, my older sisters and older brother grew restless with this 'kids' playground' and we began to spend more time at the ocean beaches of Sorrento and Portsea, beaches which were to become the stage upon which my rites of passage to adulthood would be played out.

Sometimes we would go walking in a straggling line along the endless stretch of Portsea back beach to the crumbling arch of London Bridge. The walk always ended where the barbed-wire fence was strung across the cliff tops and signs told of unexploded shells, warning us to 'Keep Out'. Occasionally we would hear the reports of gunfire as the officers in the army training camp practised on the rifle range. Deep inside this territory we knew that there was a graveyard belonging to the Quarantine Station, and an ocean beach where a prime minister had drowned, and a rocky stretch of coast upon which an untold number of ships had come to grief. It wasn't until I was in my late teens, when all prohibitions were a red rag, that I dared sneak into this territory. And only much later than that, after I had witnessed the lone surfer riding the tanker's wake, that I dared admit to myself that I too wanted to surf the Rip.

I knew it was a crazy idea. I hadn't surfed for fifteen years. Occasionally when the subject of surfing came up in conversation, I would remark that I still had my wetsuit and board and that I intended, at some stage, to return to the water. But as I entered my late 30s, the claim was starting to sound wishful and even hollow; an expression of nostalgia rather than one of genuine intent. I lived in the inner suburbs of Melbourne 100 kilometres from the surf, I now had a young child; life had settled into a comfortable routine. And yet, when sitting in the local park watching the other parents playing with their children,

I would be gripped by a quiet feeling of panic. During holidays as I swam in the shorebreak at Sorrento back beach and played with my baby boy in the rock pools, I would find myself casting furtive glances toward the surfers out beyond the break, like Prufrock watching the mermaids riding seaward on the waves and wondering, 'Do I dare?' If I didn't make a move to join them soon, I feared I never would.

I had always known that water was my element. When I was a girl, I wanted to be a swimming instructor. The man who taught me to swim had an indoor pool in his backyard and ran a private swimming school. The pool was less than twenty-five metres long, yet in my child's eyes it was vast. Gold veins of reflected sunlight danced on the ceiling, the air was fuggy with chlorine and voices echoed strangely as if in some undersea chamber. Pools were greener then. And like some ancient shepherd, the instructor would stand at the edge holding a long pole with a crook to rescue floundering children. I loved the other-worldliness of this steamy, glassed-in realm; this place where normal boundaries seemed to dissolve. But as I grew older and my family began spending more time at the ocean beaches, I discovered the slap-in-the-face exhilaration of the surf and the call of the blue yonder. The finite world of the swimming pool lost much of its appeal. In my restless, adolescent eyes it became an oversized concrete trench, the refuge of the landlocked suburbanite. There is no yonder in a swimming pool.

When, in my mid-twenties, I gave up surfing and resigned myself to the concrete trench, the young woman I had once been remained disdainful of the life I had chosen to lead. Although I learned to tolerate the hot, deserted streets of Melbourne in late December and early January when the rest of the world was down at the beach, I could never throw off the feeling that I was only half alive when I was away from the sea. Waves loomed in my dreams. I would be standing at the water's edge or perhaps bobbing in the shore break when, without warning, a mountain range would rear up out of the ocean and advance in slow motion toward the shore. I would feel the undertow, the suction of the on-coming waves dragging at my legs as I tried to scramble to the beach before the first wall of water descended. I'd wake before being engulfed but strangely, I did not wake in fright. I was left, as always after dreaming about the sea, with a residue of hope and longing.

For many years I found a million good reasons why I couldn't take up surfing again. Then, one wintry day, when the novel that I had been wrestling with for months finally ground to a painful halt, I saw all my good reasons for what they were. A week later, I was in the car heading down to Sorrento to see if I could still squeeze into my old surfing skin, the wetsuit I had not worn for fifteen years. It hung on a hook in the corrugated-iron sleep-out behind our beach house along with all the old beach paraphernalia – buckets, beach balls, kick boards, boogie boards, hoola-hoops, deck chairs and badminton shuttles.

As I drove through the city and down the Nepean Highway lined with car yards and furniture showrooms, I thought of the moment when the Ocean Beach road swoops like a gull diving, the ti-tree parting to reveal the etched blue lines of Bass Strait and the honey-combed amphitheatre of Sorrento back beach with its rock pools and heaving dumpers and seaweedy depths. I remembered how excited I had been when I took my French friends, Nelly and Marc, to the rotunda lookout at the top of the cliff overlooking the beach. And how, as we gazed down on it all, I'd felt as proud as if I had carved those craggy, ochre cliffs myself; as if I had arranged for the waves to break in perfect, thunderous lines along the coastal shelf, leaving trails of milky lace; as if the flayed cheeks of the sand dunes and the wind-sculpted, rolling scrub and the silver coin of the bay behind us were my own creation. I wanted to tell Nelly, who speaks as little English as I speak French, what it meant to me. *C'est la côte de mon coeur*, I said, knowing it would sound corny in English, but hoping I could get away with it in French. *It is the coast of my heart.*

The suburbs of Melbourne seemed to go forever as if it were folly to try to escape them, as if this were the only kind of life you could lead. As I hit the Frankston Freeway, which in my mind marks the beginning of the Peninsula, I slipped on a CD of *The Best of The Eagles*, the soundtrack to my surfing memories. The opening, twangy riff of 'Take It Easy' sent a shiver through my body and soon I was singing at the top of my voice, silently laughing at my nostalgia yet alive with a sense of adventure I had almost forgotten. *Lighten up while you still can/ Don't even try to understand/ Just find a place to make your stand/ And take it easy.* The suburbs had turned into fields, the invisible ocean beckoned and I could hear the past rushing towards me with the explosive crackle of a broken wave.

In the 1940s, when my father was a boy, he spent his summer holidays camping amongst the ti-tree in the foreshore dunes of the Sorrento back beach with his parents and a few other families. (Now it is a National Park and camping is prohibited.) They would play in the dumpers and swim in the rock pools and go fishing off a squat monolith called Darby's Rock, but to go out beyond the break was considered pure madness. They knew how quickly these beaches could become a graveyard for unwary swimmers. Occasionally they would catch sight of a tiny figure out the back where no other swimmer dared go, riding his giant, three-ply surf-ski. They knew him as Snowy Man. He was the only surfer my father remembers seeing around these beaches when he was a boy and he cut a memorably heroic figure. Snowy's unwieldy ski made it hard work for him to get out beyond the break, and once there, he spent a lot of time paddling and positioning himself. But every wave he caught was a marvel. When he finally emerged from the water with the ski balanced precariously on his back, people would line the beach clapping and cheering.

Things had changed dramatically by the time I began surfing in the early 1980s. Although no one looked twice at the sight of a black-clad figure sliding down the face of a wave, surfers were, in many respects, a race apart. Australia liked to promote itself as a surfing paradise but surfers as a sub-culture were still regarded with suspicion and bemusement by the mainstream. They were beach-bums, drop-outs, ragged-haired louts who spoke their own *patois* and, in my parents' eyes, could not be trusted with their youngest daughter. I had always loved the sea and now I fell in love with a surfer and through him, with the thrill of riding a wave. I was also in love with the spirit of rebellion that surfing embodied, the escape it offered me from my sensible, suburban self.

The Best of the Eagles was just finishing as I pulled into the driveway, cut the engine and ran straight to the sleep-out. I lifted the wetsuit off the hook fully expecting it to fall apart in my hands. Gingerly I turned it in the right way, arm by arm, leg by leg, looking for spiders. A small one fell out and I quickly pounced on it. A handful of sand gushed from the second leg and I wondered what beach it was from. The beach of my last surf. Possibly Woolami on Phillip Island where I was reporting on a surfing carnival. I remember that it wasn't a very satisfying experience. I don't think I caught a decent wave. My surfing memories were littered with similarly frustrating experiences – surf too big or too small or too tricky for me to catch; getting stuck in the shorebreak and endlessly battling the white water; paddling out to the line-up only to be beaten to the waves by more experienced surfers; gutlessly pulling back from a wave I should have caught.

Above all other obstacles, it was fear that had held me back in surfing and later, kept me out of the water. Fear of failure, fear of being an imposter, fear of being out of control. All these fears coalesced in the tell-tale corrugations of a big set looming out the back, that unstoppable phalanx of pure, liquid energy from which there was no escape. It was my hope that this time I could begin to overcome the more debilitating aspects of this fear. And yet perversely, certain aspects of it – the awe I felt in the presence of this natural force, a force so unfathomable that it grants you an inkling of infinity – were instrinsic to my attraction to surfing. Eighteenth-century philosophers like Edmund Burke, and later the Romantic poets, called this phenomenon 'the sublime'. In Wordsworth's description of his young self wandering the mountains and lonely streams of the Wye River valley 'more like a man/ Flying from something that he dreads than one/ Who sought the thing he loved,' I saw myself out in the surf. The ocean was a source of the sublime, according to Burke, because it produced 'the strongest emotion which the mind is capable of feeling'. Burke emphasised the stimulating influence of the sublime on the imagination and so heralded a new, aesthetic relationship with the sea. 'I wantoned with thy breakers,' wrote Byron. 'They to me/ Were a delight; and if the freshening sea/ Made them a terror, 'twas a pleasing fear.'

Yet I knew that my love of the sea was not solely derived from the attraction of the sublime, the need for awe. Most surfers – apart from those driven purely by the competitive urge – talk openly about the sheer joy of being in the water and the visceral need for an intimate relationship with the ocean. Informing this kind of understatement is a whole philosophy – sometimes couched in spiritual terms – about connecting with a force vastly greater than oneself, about returning to 'the source'. It harks back to a sensation invoked by the French writer Romain Rolland in his metaphor, 'the oceanic feeling'. Rolland used this phrase when writing to Freud about an essay of Freud's that treats religion as an illusion. He agreed with Freud's views on religion but felt that Freud had not appreciated the true origin of religious sentiments. Such sentiments were borne, Rolland said, of a feeling which was always with him and which others too had confirmed; a feeling which he described as a sensation of eternity; of something boundless or oceanic. Freud did not regard this oceanic feeling as the origin of religious belief, but he did concede that it may be a residual memory of that earliest phase of psychic life when the child and the world are one.

Few images better capture this primal 'at-oneness' than that of the surfer crouched inside the crystal, womb-like tube of a breaking wave; an image made all the more exquisite by our knowledge of the wave's imminent destruction. No sooner has the surfer returned to that all-embracing amniotic realm than she is unceremoniously expelled into the harsh light of the world. In fact, this birth analogy is built into the Hawaiian word for surfing, *he'enalu*. The first part of the word means 'to run as a liquid', while the second refers to the surging motion of a wave or the caul on a newborn child.

Whenever I tried to pin down what this 'at-oneness' felt like, one particular moment in the surf always came to mind. While whole years of my life had disappeared into a hazy blur, I have never forgotten the few seconds on this wave. I was surfing with a friend at one of the many breaks between Sorrento and Rye that can only be reached by hiking through the National Park and clambering over acres of sand dunes. It was a glorious summer's day and it must have been very hot because I remember that I was wearing only a long-sleeved vest over a pair of bright red bathers. The swell was sizeable but not too big for me to handle. As soon as I began to paddle for the wave, I knew I had been waiting all my surfing life for it to come along. I remember the water swelling beneath me and how I was perfectly in tune with its rhythm. I remember a surge of energy lifting me high above the hollowing water, the thickness of the shoulder, the glowing desert-like appearance of the shore. Above all, I remember the instant at the top of the wave just as I rose to my feet to 'take the drop', poised on the brink with the weight of the in-rushing ocean behind me and the wave unfurling beneath me. The spool of my memories always froze at this last split-second of clarity and separateness before the screaming descent where mind, body and wave became one.

The wave had become to me like one of Wordsworth's 'spots of time', a moment from the past that remained preternaturally vivid, a singular memory that I could draw on for imaginative nourishment and solace whenever I felt the need. The phrase 'spots of time' comes from Wordsworth's great poem 'The Prelude', but the idea is echoed in 'Lines Composed A Few Miles Above Tintern Abbey' in which he speaks of the 'tranquil restoration' which his memories of the Wye River Valley brought him when he was oppressed by the din of towns and cities. Wordsworth's version of the 'ocean feeling', of the interconnectedness of all things culminates in his famous lines:

> And I have felt
> A presence that disturbs me with the joy
> Of elevated thoughts; a sense sublime
> Of something far more deeply interfused,
> Whose dwelling is the light of setting suns,
> And the round ocean and the living air,
> And the blue sky, and in the mind of man:
> A motion and a spirit, that impels
> All thinking things, all objects of all thought,
> And rolls through all things.

In the lines that precede these, Wordsworth has been reflecting on how his relationship with nature has changed. How he has come to accept that the 'aching joys' and 'dizzy raptures' of his youthful encounters with nature are now a thing of the past. It is the perspective, you might think, of an old man. Yet Wordsworth was, at the time of writing, only 28 years old – one year older than his sister Dorothy whom he addresses in the second part of the poem. Dorothy reminds him of his former instinctive self. He assumes that she will, in time, take the same path as he has, that her 'wild ecstacies' will inevitably mature into 'sober pleasure' – the pleasure of memory and of 'elevated' reflections on the time they spent together in this valley.

But was this path really inevitable? As I contemplated my return to the water, it wasn't sober pleasure I was after. Why couldn't the more mature understanding of nature as something we all 'half-create' co-exist with the immediacy of youthful rapture? I wanted to believe that it could. Otherwise I might as well sit back in my armchair and replay my surfing memories, and save myself the trouble of getting wet.

Cautiously I eased the wetsuit on. Apart from a tear at the base of the right leg, it remained in one piece. The cool, damp rubber over my body felt strangely familiar. I pulled up the zip and went to look at myself in the mirror. I grinned at my reflection. Fifteen years seemed to fall away. Flinging open the back door, I leapt down the steps and did cartwheels across the lawn.

Simon Armitage
Going Up

Lived in a boot.
Hand-made calf-skin, fitted dead snug.
Rolled down tongue so it was open-top.
Jehovah's Witnesses didn't know where to knock.
Not hundred per cent waterproof but good enough.
Drank beer over garden wall of ankle cuff.
Lived in a boot.

Lived in a boot.
Peered through eyelets
like a sailor coming in to port.
Picnicked outside on toe-end like it was Castle Hill.
Salt-mark – like tide-mark around bath – wouldn't come off.
No fucker visited, but so what.
Lived in a boot.

Lived in a boot.
Pulled laces tight on nights with no moon.
Kept loaded twelve-bore in hollowed-out heel.
More and more neighbours in slip-ons and brogues.
Less and less walks, stayed home to keep guard.
Lived in a boot.

Lived in a boot.
Wore down on one side – started to rock.
Scuff-marks and cracks, polish and dubbin – couldn't be faffed.
Toxocariasis from shit from dogs – owners should be shot.

Leather went saggy like an old face, nails came through.
Stitching rotted around welt, insoles went manky,
smelt.

Didn't do any more, didn't suit.
Moved out. Moved to a hat.

Working From Home

When the tree-cutter came with his pint-size mate,
I sat in the house but couldn't think.
For an hour he lurked in the undergrowth,
trimming the lower limbs, exposing the trunks.

I moved upstairs but there he was, countersunk eyes
and as bald as a spoon, emergent into the orange day,
head popping out through leafage or fir,
a fairy light in the tree of heaven,

a marker-buoy in the new plantation of silver pine.
Or traversing, bough to bough, from one dead elm
to the next, or holding on by his legs only,
or accrobranching the canopy. At lunch,

he pulled the wooden ladder up behind,
perched in the crown of a laurel, and smoked.
He nursed the petrol-driven chainsaw like a false arm.
The dwarf swept berries and beech-nuts into a cloth bag.

I was dodging between rooms now, hiding from view.
Down below, they cranked up the chipping machine,
fed timber and brushwood into the hopper.
Through a gap in the curtains I looked, saw into its mouth –

steel teeth crunching fishbone twigs,
chomping true wood, gagging on lumber and thick stumps.

Sawdust rained into the caged truck.
Birds were flying into the arms of a scarecrow

on the far hill, or leaving for Spain. I sat on the stairs
between ground-zero and outer space, thought of his face
at the bathroom window watching me shave,
his lips in the letterbox, wanting to speak.

Simon Armitage has published eight volumes of poetry: his *Selected Poems* (Faber & Faber) and his first novel, *Little Green Man* (Penguin) were both published in 2001. He has been a winner of the Forward Prize and a recipient of the Lannan Award for Poetry. In 1998 he co-edited *The Penguin Book of Poetry from Britain and Ireland Since 1945*.

Louis Nowra

Lust and Adoration

Christy Canyon and Silvana Mangano

Louis Nowra's memoir *The Twelfth of Never* was published in 1999; a new novel, *ABAZA: A Modern Encyclopaedia*, has just been published by Picador.

It is a curious sensation to hold her vagina in my hands. Made out of latex rubber, the replica is said to be made from an actual casting from her vulva. Indeed her labia are rather graphic, girdled by what the kit box calls 'silky realistic soft pubic hair.' The kit includes a vibrator, a jar of lubrication jelly and an autographed intimate photograph of Christy with her personal statistics. The prominent motto on the box is, 'Make Love to the Legend herself!' It is hard to be inspired by it however, given that the vagina seems lifeless, as if drained of blood; and the fact that it is not attached to her body gives it a decidedly peculiar appearance, not unlike that of the artist Hans Bellmer's vicious reassembling of female bodies. When I first held the replica of Christy Canyon's vagina I did stop and ask myself how I had ended up with such an object in my clammy hands. An infatuation with a porn star should have its limits, but apparently not.

My fascination with her started out as a joke. A friend gave me a porn movie catalogue which proved an amusing read, with movies ranging from the basic *Anal Babes* to parodies such as *The Woman in Pink*. What attracted me was the title *Pretty in Peach*, an obvious reference to the 1986 movie about teen angst *Pretty in Pink*. I didn't like the movie but as I read the porn catalogue description I became intrigued. 'People say the most interesting things before, during and after love making. They say things like "more". They often say "stop"'. "A little to the left" is also a favourite. But not for Christy. She quotes Sartre, Kierkegaard. And Kafka. Sure she'll make it with the pizza man – this is adult. But only if he can tell her the meaning of life, first. Join Christy Canyon, Summer Knights and Tianna Taylor as they talk about motives versus actions, the existential void, and being pretty in peach.' The video cover shows a voluptuous Christy and the words, 'When it comes to sex, you have to be a little philosophical.' I had never seen a hard-core movie but the promise of porn stars talking about 'existential void' was enough to intrigue me and I sent away for it.

Pretty in Peach is set on a country property. While all her friends are sex-obsessed, Christy is intoxicated by philosophy. This worries her friends, one of whom says, 'I don't want her to turn into some sort of philosophical freak.' Another is confident that he can turn Christy back on to sex. 'Don't worry, I know these existential types.' But slowly it dawns on them that she is not going to change. A lesbian wants to make love to her but all Christy can do is quote Descartes, 'I think, therefore I am.' Annoyed that she is not being paid attention to, the lesbian throws away *Le discours de la methode* with her novel reworking of Descartes, 'I destroy, therefore I am'. When not making love Christy takes to wandering around the farm saying things like, 'Are you the only true appearance of choice?' and my favourite, 'Would you like to see my Kierkegaard?' Of course at the end Christy finds sexual satisfaction with a stud, but even that cannot change her philosophical bent and she tells him, 'You are the embodiment of my overtly erotic desires that come from the essence of my being.'

The sex is graphic with penetration and ejaculation, and is highly arousing. The mixture of pornography with pseudo-philosophy is essentially a one-joke idea that gets less amusing as the film continues. The acting is wooden and the actors largely forgettable except for the very attractive Christy Canyon. I had bought the movie for the corny plot and silly dialogue but was unprepared for her impact on me. Every time she appeared on screen all the other actors vanished. Her presence was neither slutty nor imperious. Her amiable manner, her ingratiating smile and the casual ease with which she made love seemed at odds with the frantic couplings of the others. Of course the stunning first impression is her Junoesque body: Tall and, as they primly say, well-endowed, she resembles those curvaceous 1950s stars Jayne Mansfield and Marilyn Monroe, and when she is naked it is not far-fetched to say that her figure resembles Titian's *Venus of Urbino* or Velazquez' *Venus at her Mirror*.

The odd thing for me is that I had never been attracted to such voluptuous, earthy women – but it was not only her body, there was something else about her that attracted me. She had a naturalness that was riveting. While the other women groaned too loudly or obviously faked erotic ecstasy Christy seemed to be genuinely enjoying it, in fact, one female critic described watching her sex scenes as almost a personal embarrassment because they seemed so uninhibited. Yet for all her sensuous body and performance – and indeed I did find her very sexy – my added attraction to her had nothing to do with sex. She had what I can only call 'star allure'. This allure has as its main ingredients, energy, beauty, sensuality, but also something unclassifiable and ineffable. It is as if through an act of alchemy the camera transforms an actor from a living person into an object of contemplation so that they end up becoming the subject of mute adoration. Their cinematic personalities are too individual and large to inhabit a character: instead, they merely assume the name of the character, which we never remember, only the star's name. We come to worship such stars to the exclusion of all the others. It's hard to define exactly what this 'star factor' or 'It' is. Whatever it is, Christy Canyon has this 'It' factor.

What I had to know was whether *Pretty in Peach* was a unique video. Maybe she was dreadful in others. As I discovered, she was even sexier and more charismatic in the next movie I bought called *I Dream of Christy*, the plot of which ventures into the metaphysical. As the video catalogue trumpets, 'What if dreaming about Christy Canyon was somehow to bring her to life. Right in front of you. Hot and ready to do anything you want. Well, you're in luck...'

I was hooked. I began to collect her videos and magazine pictorials, in fact anything that she had acted in or been photographed for. I found myself buying *Penthouse* and *Hustler* for her picture spreads.

Soon I had many of her videos including *Play Christy For Me* ('Christy is your own private eye and she's more than willing to work overtime to do some undercover investigating. You'll feel completely secure in her hands knowing that she's best at cracking hardcores.'); *Crazed 2* ('She's part Bonnie, part Clyde with a little bit of Thelma and a lot like Louise. She's Christy Canyon and she's tearing up the road in *Crazed 2.*'); and *Sex Asylum 4* ('Christy reprises her smash hit with a return engagement as the nurse who caused a fever that hasn't let up in five years.').

Given that she has made over fifty movies (not including her brief appearances in such early films as *Attack of the Monster Mammaries* and *Bitches in Heat*) there is a huge range to choose from. And yet, for all the different characters she has played, she always remains Christy Canyon, as if the costumes and plots were interchangeable, with the one constant that holds the movies together being her presence. Her light Californian 'valley girl' voice doesn't attempt a pseudo-sexy huskiness like other actresses, she appears more comfortable naked than wearing clothes (which is good given the inelegant and corny 1980s frocks she had to wear), and there is something old-fashioned about the sex. Yes, she does have group sex, men ejaculate inside her, and over her breasts, and she gives good oral sex, but there is nothing too outrageous if you compare her films to contemporary porn. In fact she makes it quite clear in interviews that she refuses to do anal sex, golden showers or fetish films.

For a short period she only did lesbian scenes in a series called *Where the Boys Aren't*. You can tell how obsessed I was becoming with Christy because I bought those videos, even though I find lesbian sex as erotic as watching croquet. I became like a train-spotter, desperate to catch even a glimpse of her in an old compilation video so poorly recorded that literally I couldn't make head or tail of her as she was reduced to a vague outline in a dense scratchy fog. I also set out to find out as much as I could about her. She is half-Armenian, half-Italian. Born 17 June 1966, she is what her video covers call 'a sensual dark beauty'. She has long brunette hair, deep brown eyes and a sumptuous 36DD-24-36 figure. She has won many 'Best Female' awards in adult films, and has had several names throughout her career including Tara

White, Tara Wine, Linda Daniel, DeeDee and Missy. She loves French food and the trashy novels of Jackie Collins and Danielle Steele. In her private sexual life she prefers the missionary position. After a dozen videos I knew her litany of orgasmic cries off by heart and I assume they are from the heart given that the moment of orgasm is probably unscripted. There is the 'Harder, harder,' said with a breathless urgency, 'Oh, yes, yes, yes,' groaned and moaned like I imagine Molly Bloom's affirmation of life should sound, and 'Oh, my God,' a phrase that has a rising inflection to the moment of orgasm when at the climax the name of the deity collapses into a downward spiraling moan. If I frequently felt she was mine and mine alone then there would be the occasional sober realisation that across the world hundreds of thousands of men were masturbating to her on video or in a picture-spread believing she was also theirs only.

I tried to watch other porn actresses but none had anything like Christy's fabulous figure and star allure. Yet, an unforeseen thing happened to me and my relationship to her. After so many videos and magazine pictorials Christy become less sexy to me. It was as if she had grown less real and had made the transformation from a voluptuous woman to an icon. The more I saw of her, the more unreal she seemed to become. It's as if I felt I could mentally possess her in the beginning of my infatuation, but in a peculiar way the more I saw of her, the more I knew her orgasmic cry, the more I saw men ejaculating over her breasts, the more I saw her urgently masturbating, the more mysteriously distant she became.

In becoming the embodiment of sexuality she had become less tangible. Everything she did, her laugh, her sexual groans, became less personal and more of a trademark. Her bountiful breasts became a trademark, as did her vagina, so it did not surprise me when I saw that replicas of it were for sale. There is even a Christy Canyon sex doll that is as strange as the rubber cast of her vagina. The advertisements call it 'the most realistic doll ever developed'; and describe it as 'made from actual castings of Christy's face, breasts and vagina'. 'Explore her entire body and enter her vibrating, pulsating mouth. Feel her supple, soft skin next to yours. Comes in designer can for Easy Storage.' The sex doll has to be blown up. Made out of light cloth material it has long brunette hair, a mouth identical to Christy's with a battery inside for oral sex, rubber breasts taken from a mold of her bosoms, and a vagina which is an exact replica of hers.

The doll is an eerie even disturbing sight because the sexual organs are made to look as realistic as possible, yet the rest of her body has an amorphous shape as if it existed only as a vague outline on which to attach her sexual orifices. The sex doll and rubber vagina continued a further dismantling of her so that she evaded a complete definition and became only the sum of her sexual parts. I found myself watching her videos with little sexual arousal, in fact, I just enjoyed her presence on the screen. If the ejaculation and moaning became monotonous Christy never did. She once said that she had been offered work in 'legitimate movies' and she could have been successful. There is a self-mocking tone to her acting and she might have gone the route of Jayne Mansfield, who used her voluptuous figure in a comic sardonic fashion and, incidentally, made a porno film loop when starting out on her acting career. This is not to say that, if you cut out the sex scenes in her movies, you can see enormous acting potential. Porn films that have been edited into 'soft' versions (no ejaculation, no erect penis) are profoundly unsatisfying. I remember being stuck in an LA hotel room, working on a film script. I watched her in a soft version of *Oral Arguments* ('The sexy defendant is raked over the coals...and in the judge's chambers, the robes are off'), and realised that without the 'money shot', the moment of male ejaculation which most porn films build up to, the movie becomes a curious tease with no point to it. Who wants to watch sixty minutes of foreplay? Even Christy's performance, which is funny and tongue-in-cheek, seems to have no *raison d'être*. Yet, of course, this did not stop me watching it constantly, which intrigued my room-service waiter who, on seeing Christy on the television screen, immediately recognised her. 'Gee, I used to watch her as a kid. Great hooters, aren't they?' he said, with a touch of the nostalgia of someone who had been sexually weaned on her videos. I was glad he didn't say anything disparaging because I would have been forced physically to defend her.

Once the room-service waiter left my room I wondered how I had reached the state of being prepared to defend the reputation, talent and sensuality of a porn actress. It was curious but the only other film star that had had the same effect on me was Silvana Mangano. And it seemed that the two women couldn't be any more different.

When I was in my early twenties and very unsure about my sexual orientation I came upon a book called *Pasolini by Pasolini*, a series of interviews with the Italian film maker by Oswald Stack. I had never seen a Pasolini movie but bought the book because of a photograph in it. It was of the beautiful Italian actress Silvana Mangano. It is a still of her as Jocasta in Pasolini's movie *Oedipus Rex*. It shows her with her hair up revealing a high forehead, her lips are half open, her makeup mask-like and pale and her eyes afraid. Why this image haunted me I still do not know. I had a blow-up of the still pinned to my bedroom wall for years trying to discover, for want of a better word, its essence, so I could rid myself of my fascination with it, but I never have. Her exquisite unearthly beauty defies rational analysis. I used to stare at the blow-up for hours, and even filmed it with my Super 8 camera, trying to bore myself, but the obsession survived every test. I tried to weary myself with the image because I knew that while other people my age were brooding about Marx and Lenin and the problems of the working class, I was so facile that my main interest was an Italian actress rather than an Italian Marxist like Gramsci.

As luck would have it, when the first R-certificate movie opened in Melbourne it was Pasolini's *Teorema,* and starred Silvana Mangano as the housewife who is seduced by the Dionysian figure of Terence Stamp, and as a consequence takes to having sex with schoolboys. I went to the first session and was disconcerted to see an audience only of men, all of whom were sitting by themselves. The film is pretentious and densely symbolic and through its early sections there was the sound of seats slapping shut as irritated men hoping for tits and arse fled. This was fine by me because I thought I could have Mangano's beauty all to myself. When a topless Silvana Mangano lay on her back I was shocked by two things. One was the enormity of her nose. I had never seen her in profile and the contrast with her beautiful face unsettled me. The second thing that took me aback was a man across the aisle with his hand under a jiggling shopping bag on his lap. He was jerking off. At first I was puzzled as to why he would think that she was remotely sexy (a goddess like her is above any thoughts of lust), then I was offended. As far as I was concerned it was as sacrilegious as someone masturbating in front of an image of the Virgin Mary.

I wasn't the only one who thought like that. The two homosexual directors Pasolini and Visconti used her in several films as the epitome of grace, style and maternal beauty. Pasolini made her dress like his own mother in *Oedipus Rex*, and in the *Decameron* had her play the part of the Virgin Mary. Visconti used her as the glamorous mother of the handsome boy desired by Dirk Bogarde in *Death in Venice*.

Italian films were not that popular during the 1970s and I spent much of my time travelling to obscure cinemas watching bad, scratchy prints of Mangano. Yet no spoiled reel of celluloid could erase her beauty. I even grew attracted to her prominent nose, viewing it as a human flaw in the unearthly beauty of her face, as if beauty were as mysterious and incomphrensible to me as quantum mechanics, but her nose had the reality of practical geometry which made her a creature of flesh and blood.

As would happen with Christy Canyon I sought out everything I could find about Silvana Mangano. She was born in Rome in 1930. She was trained as a dancer and worked as a model before winning the Miss Rome beauty contest in 1946, which brought her into movies. Her first starring role was as a migrant farm-worker in *Bitter Rice* (1949). The film was a hit; an American critic called her 'the Italian Rita Hayworth, with an extra twenty pounds'. It was the extra twenty pounds that made me uneasy. I only saw the stills of *Bitter Rice*, and was amazed at how different she was from the slim, chic, *soignée* woman of Pasolini and Visconti's films. She must have also been disturbed by her appearance in it because as the film critic Elaine Mancini said, 'Mangano quickly moved beyond the stereotype of the earthy sex symbol, lost weight and developed her skills as a dramatic actress.'

Her transformation was radical. She now appeared graceful and thin, and minus her eyebrows. She was the gorgeous dancer in *Mambo* (1954), and the haunting, ethereal Circe in *Ulysses* (1955). She married the Italian producer Dino De Laurentiis and had four children. If Hollywood beckoned she didn't deign to reply. She didn't much like being an actress and Pasolini said that she was contemptuous of her great beauty. It was a haphazard career. The occasional film she chose to act in had nothing to do with the script but her admiration for the director. And what a strange career it turned out to be. If in *Bitter Rice* she was the most physically substantial she ever was and gave her most energetic performance, in her later performances she either seemed apologetic, as if she were in the way of the other actors, or else she seemed resigned to her relegation as an exquisite ornament in a beautiful corsage. Only in Visconti's *Conversation Piece* did she tackle a role with a recognizable exuberance. She excelled in playing a *nouveau riche* bitch with new and expensive designer clothes in every scene. But this role was an anomaly. She seemed to drift through most of her films as insubstantial as she was once substantial. Towards the end of her career she seemed possessed by a dreamy melancholy, and her characters had a profound sadness as if haunted. In an article about her in *Parkett* (1991), Richard Flood writes of how with every film the actress seemed to be saying good-bye, as if 'removing herself even further from the intrusive vision of the camera. The elegiac isolation increases from role to role until inevitably, she must disappear.' In her last film, *Dark Eyes* (1987), she plays the faithful wife to Marcello Mastroianni's adulterous husband. Mangano's performance has a chilling aloneness to it. She doesn't scream or rant at her husband or play victim, she floats through the film, only anchored by her character's loneliness and her own.

By the time Laurentiis divorced her and her son was killed in a plane accident, Mangano seemed to drift through life as she drifted through her films, roaming the world, staying with her children wherever they were living, and finally dying of cancer in 1989 after a lifetime of cigarette-smoking.

Canyon's porn career was caused by the confluence of two things, chance and video. Before the advent of video, porn was shot on film, which was costly and time-consuming. Films or film loops were expensive to copy and you had to have the equipment to show them. But in the late 1970s early 1980s the adult film industry underwent a change as profound as talkies taking over from the silent movies – video had arrived. Video was cheap. The camera was easier to use and the lighting didn't have to be as finicky as for celluloid. It was also easier to make copies of videos. Most importantly there was the invention of the

VCR. Sales of videos grew phenomenally. Couples now watch adult movies in the privacy of their homes. It is said that in the United States alone, the adult film market is worth seven to ten billion dollars. Porn no longer has a stigma attached to it, and has moved from the underground of 'stag' films to the forestage of popular culture.

Christy's introduction to a movie career seems similar to the Hollywood cliché of the lonely girl arriving in Los Angeles who is seen by a talent scout in a drugstore and is catapulted to stardom. She was a seventeen-year-old runaway who was broke and wondering where her next penny would be coming from when, in a chance encounter, she was discovered in 1984 by Greg 'Rocky' Rome, who was in the adult entertainment industry. He ran into her outside her apartment and told her she would be a great model. Not long afterwards she started nude modelling and first appeared in an issue of *Velvet* in 3D. As she said later, 'It was pretty cool to see myself in the first layout, no less in 3D glasses.'

After several weeks of soft-core magazine shoots, and having just turned eighteen, she arrived at a shoot only to find that instead of still cameras there were video cameras and they were there to film live sex. I've always wondered just how big a decision this jump from nude stills to having sex on video must have been, but in a *Hustler* interview she's quite practical about it: 'There was no way I would have done the video shoot if I had known about it. I thought to myself, Okay, I'll give it a try. $500! Gosh, I can pay this off and that off.' But the shoot was a nightmare. 'Everything on the set was really dirty and afterwards I felt really dirty.' And here we have a clue to her personality. Other girls would have fled but, even after the first dreadful experience, she decided to do it one more time. If she didn't like it she would leave. The second time was 'like 180 degrees different. It was great. All the really good people were there: Traci (Lords), Ginger (Lynn), Peter North, Tom Byron. I found myself really getting into it. And the rest is history.' In talking about the first time she is always consistent: 'Nothing was ever as bad as the first time.'

Soon she became one of the most famous porn stars, thoroughly acclimatized to the demands of making porn movies, which she viewed with professional pride. 'The first thing I think about on the set is the camera angles. Of course I love to get into the sex and enjoy it and not think about the ten camera people around me. Okay, I'm attracted to the guy and it's going to be fun, but this is work. You can't do exactly what you want in this. You have to be aware that there's a camera there and they have to shoot you in the best way possible. So my first concern is to visualise how the scene is going to turn out and make sure the cameraman can shoot the film well, and then I can enjoy the sex.'

There is no doubt that there is an element of the prima donna to Christy Canyon. She has walked out of adult film award nights when she didn't get the prize, and she has grumpily retired from the industry several times only to return. After starring in *Savage Fury* (1985) – 'Poor Christy's about to pay dearly for avenging the attack she and her girlfriends suffered but the judge has given her one chance for freedom – to go undercover and pose as a sultry, salacious and seductive sex model so the FBI can trap a ring of foreign white slave lords who supply girls for a price' – she stopped making films at the request of her then boyfriend. In 1989 she returned in *Hot in the City*, perhaps one of the few films she made where she seems uncertain and slightly inhibited. She wears a mask of makeup so thick that it resembles that of her sex doll. But practical as ever she signed a contract with Video Exclusives to produce her own line of porn movies. The arrangement didn't work and in 1991 she signed with Vivid Video. It's obvious by her comments that she regards Vivid Video as the classier act. As she said of their *Portrait of Christy*, 'It had a 35-page script. Video Exclusives only gave ten-page scripts, all sex.' In 1993 she left the X-rated movie industry for the third time. Two years later in 1995 she returned in *Comeback*.

She is retired from making porn movies now and makes much of her money in the more lucrative exotic dancing circuit. At the end of her act she poses for Polaroids and signs autographs. She runs her own fan club which has a joining fee, and among the many videos she sells is one only the fans can buy – a prolonged bout of solo masturbation. She also sells 'Officially worn Christy Canyon collectibles'. For $100 Australian you can buy a used bra, undies (red/black/white) for $50, and high heels shoes for $80.

Christy's career started off at a crucial time in the industry, and her retirement from films was also made at the right time. Some aficionados consider the 1980s and early 1990s as 'The Golden Age of Porn Movies'. Porn actresses were promoted like Hollywood stars. Names like Seka, Marilyn Chambers, Ginger Lynn and Christy Canyon were extremely bankable. But by the early 90s the adult movie industry had begun to fragment. In order to make money the industry began to branch out into wilder sexual territories, anal films became extremely popular, as did bondage, S&M, and golden showers. It seemed that nothing was taboo. Women became porn-viewers and there was a huge market for what was labeled 'couples movies'. It's said that nearly a quarter of male homosexual rentals are by women. Women producers and directors moved into the industry, although as porn director Nina Hartley said in an interview in the *San Franciso Examiner* (quoted in the study of porn movies *Skinflicks*), 'Women have different tastes. Women will get into the hottest sex if they believe it's honest. Women just want a reason for sex to be there. It can be revenge, anger, and not just romantic. But it has to have a level of emotional authenticity.'

In the 1990s many young women considered porn films to be a proper step to becoming legitimate Hollywood actresses. If Traci Lords could move from porn into mainstream films, then why not others? In fact so many women wanted to be in X-rated movies the industry was transformed. As far as the producers were concerned, there was no need to build up the career of a porn actress, as happened in the 80s, when they could use any pretty girl on the cheap – the supply is unlimited and in turn the actress can use the few porn movies she has made as a launching pad for the profitable exotic dancing circuit.

In fact, just to indicate how long the adult movie industry has been going, there has developed a sub-genre of mother-and-daughter videos. Former adult movie stars act in porn videos with their daughters. Jamie Summers and Sabrina Dawn starred with their real-life mothers in *Bringing Up Brat* and *Grandma Does Dallas*. Tami Lee Curtis also acted with her own mother in *Naked Truth About Tami*. Veteran adult actress Lee Carroll reunited with her long-lost daughter after fifteen years and they immediately celebrated the union by doing an adult movie together. Recently there has also been the trend of porn actresses trying to outdo each other in filmed gang-bangs, with Annabel Chong taking on 251 men in one session the most notorious, at least until actresses began to take on 400 and then 500 men (events organised with such military precision that 'fluffers' are employed to enliven the long line of men by orally or manually bringing them to an erection, so they will be ready to have sex in the limited time alloted to each). But perhaps the biggest change has been the rise of amateur videos which account for thirty per cent of sales. It seems like America is becoming a nation of exhibitionists and voyeurs. Compared to the perverse eroticism of fetish movies Christy Canyon's basic heterosexuality seems almost quaint and old fashioned. Indeed, compared to the best-selling amateur videos, her movies with their plots, sets, costumes and makeup artists seem from a bygone time. Her large natural breasts also seem a throwback to an innocent era. Now porn actresses seek larger and larger breast implants. Even though these enormous breasts look grotesque it doesn't matter. One actress calls her gargantuan silicone bosoms 'Cash' and 'Flow'. We have come a long way from Christy Canyon repeatedly being voted by adult magazines as having 'the best breasts in adult movies'.

Except for a small group of fans in Italy and two coffee table books on her, for which I learnt Italian in order to read them, Silvana Mangano is relatively forgotten, especially outside of Italy. So it came as a surprise to me recently to open up the entertainment guide in the Melbourne *Age* and to see her photograph, a still from *Teorema*. It was advertising an opera based on the film. Composed by Giorgio Battistelli it is described as 'an opera without singing' and follows the plot of Pasolini's film. The image of Mangano the opera company chose has her wearing thick white makeup and much black eyeliner, so that her beauty seems almost an alien's disguise. In the film she seduces schoolboys, but the boys' lovemaking is not so much sexual as a physical prayer of adoration to her alien and preternatural beauty.

It was only this year that I saw *Bitter Rice* for the first time. The film is in a neo-realist style but has salacious overtones every time the camera focuses on Mangano, whose curvaceous figure was to pave the way for such Italian stars as Gina Lollobrigida and Sophia Loren.

Although I much prefer her later films there was something unsettling about my reaction to her, as if this earlier version of Silvana Mangano was the echo of someone else. Reexamining the stills from the film it suddenly struck me: Mangano in *Bitter Rice* was almost a template for Christy Canyon. It is not only their voluptuous bodies – even the colour of their hair and the shape of their eyes is similar. In a way they could be related. And just as parts of Canyon's body attracts its worshippers so did Mangano's in *Bitter Rice*. Film projectionists would remove the scenes where she showed her breasts and keep them for themselves or for private showings where she was reduced to a pair of magnificent breasts. As I was puzzling over the resemblance and my blindness in not noticing it before a friend sent me a recent issue of *L'Espresso* magazine. On the cover was a photograph of a semi-naked Mangano and inside were other nude shots taken before she starred in *Bitter Rice*. It was confirmation, if I needed any more, that Christy Canyon and Mangano of the late 1940s were, for me at any rate, disturbingly alike.

This revelation caused me to rethink my adoration of the two women. For years I had thought of them as entirely dissimilar women; one earthy and sexy and the other asexual and ethereal. Was the separation of them in my imagination a perfect example of the Madonna and Whore syndrome? Why else would I refuse for years to watch *Bitter Rice* or look closely at its stills? Surely my early upbringing as a Catholic wasn't to blame? It's possible that I divided them in my mind because, for all their similarities, they served two different purposes. When I was in my early twenties I was sexually much more interested in men than women, and yet from a young age both my mother and I were obsessed by female beauty. Silvana Mangano, perhaps one of the most beautiful movie stars there has ever been, fulfilled my desire for beauty without sexualizing it. By the time I became fascinated by Christy Canyon I was firmly heterosexual and so she served both as an object of adoration as Mangano did for me, and also as an object of lust. Even though I realise that both women are the same woman, I still separate them in my mind. I cannot sexualise Mangano even when she is a replica for Canyon in her early films. She exists for me as the graceful, sophisticated dreamily melancholic actress of later films, while Christy Canyon remains the epitome of earthy sexuality.

Jennifer Maiden
Children's Workshop at Lewers Gallery

                Outside in the courtyard sun,
the blocks stamp down with a heartbeat's
square and wooden emphasis. The brown
big river pebbles in the garden pond
have a look like that sound but their own sound
is plashy, smooth and grinds. Indoors,
woodcuts fill three rooms, Chinese with contrast:
a sheer mountain doubled in size
in the lake it dwarfs. Town streets where
a young girl cleans her long sheer hair
in a bucket, the firm ink looks
like a noise of water, heartbeat, slippery stone.

JENNIFER MAIDEN

Close as Velvet

Sapphires aren't like the sky, unless
an Australian nightsky, close as velvet.
Once my daughter half-decided
to do the praying mantis for a Nature
Project, before deciding on the Monarch
Butterfly, with a flutter of wings.
                      Its name
is 'The Wanderer', its chrysalis
is a jewel, a mantra, which she painted
in gilded peridot. The mantis's
eating habits appealed to her, the clean
elimination of the mating male, but
the Monarch seemed more sensible. I am
a Pre-Raphaelite and believe that beauty
is about use, and pre-supposes both
a user and observer, like this other
mantress of a sapphire on your finger, which
like a Mapplethorpe flower entreats
the most exquisite sexualness from stillness,
petal after petal's icy limits
as deliberate as a crystal drill, as true.
The light is rationed and the light shines through
objects as if they were icons, though
each nightsky shut, remote as velvet, too.

Cave

          Night misery
is our point of entry.
First the rain drives down like nails
for an hour and then briefly
and much quieter
the thunder like a low surf
hunches over the roof
on haunches,
like a storm man with his arms around a child.

Download

I look down often at my hands.
The frost in a diamond remembers
the spiralling porcupine spines
of a snowstorm falling at me
on a windscreen, dismembers
my memory into curving lines
like women's necks or swans, long
loops in a helix or the over
and over of downloaded cybersong.
I look down often at my hands.
Both have been broken at times,
have been gnarled luminescent and square
like the coat of a snowgum, for years
weathered wiry from ease or defiance
in the infinite winter dance,
                therefore
as the breath blacks the air
I often look down at my hands.

Jennifer Maiden won the 1999 Christopher Brennan Award for lifetime achievement in literature. Her most recent collection, *Mines* (Paper Bark Press), won the Kenneth Slessor Prize for Poetry in 2000.

Manuel Rivas

What Do You Want with Me, Love?

Translated from the Galician by Jonathan Dunne

Manuel Rivas was born in 1957 in A Coruña, Galicia. His novel *The Carpenter's Pencil* was published in English translation by Harvill Press in 2000. His collection *Vermeer's Milkmaid*, from which this story is taken, will be published by Harvill in 2002.

Love, I have come to you to complain
about my lady, who sends you
to where I sleep always to wake me up
and makes me suffer great pain.
If she does not want to see or talk to me,
what do you want with me, Love?
FERNANDO ESQUIO

I dream of the first cherry of summer. I give it to her and she puts it in her mouth, looks at me with warm, sinful eyes, as she possesses the flesh. Suddenly, she kisses me and gives it back to me with her tongue. And I'm hers forever, the cherry stone rolling up and down the keyboard of my teeth all day long like a wild, musical note.

That night, 'I've something for you, love.'

I place the stone of the first cherry in her mouth.

But, in fact, she doesn't want to see or talk to me.

She kisses and consoles my mother and then leaves. Will you look at her, how I love the way she moves! She looks like she's permanently got her skates on.

Yesterday's dream, the one that brought a smile when the ambulance's siren cleared a way to nowhere, was that she was skating between plants and porcelain, in a glazed room, and ended up in my arms.

I had gone to see her first thing in the morning at the hypermarket. Her job was to keep the checkout girls stocked with change and to relay messages around the different sections. To find her, all I had to do was wait by the Central Checkout. And up she came, skating gracefully along the waxed aisle. She did a half turn to brake, and her long, dark hair waved in time to the red, pleated skirt of her uniform.

'What are you doing here so early, Tino?'

'Nothing.' I acted vague. 'I've come for food for Perla.'

She would always caress the dog. Needless to say, I had studied it all very carefully. Perla's night-time walk was rigorously timed to coincide with Lola's arrival. They were the most precious minutes of the day, the two of us in the hallway of the Tulipáns building, Flores district, caressing Perla. Sometimes she would fail to appear at 9.30, and I would prolong the dog's walk until Lola rose up in the night, clicking, my heart, her heels. On these occasions, I would get very nervous, and she was like a lady to me (where had she come from?) and I was a snotty-nosed boy. I would get very angry with myself. Looking back at me in the lift mirror was the portrait of a guy with no future, no job, no car, lounging on the sofa, digesting all the crap stuffed into the TV, scratching around the drawers for coins to buy tobacco. I had the sensation then that it was Perla holding the leash to take me for a walk. And if Mum asked why I had taken so long with the dog, she got a spiel delivered to her on the spot. That she might know better.

So I'd gone to the hypermarket to see her and draw strength.

'The dog food is next to the babies' nappies.'

She skated off, rhythmically swaying her long hair and skirt. It reminded me of the flight of those migratory birds, cranes or herons, that appear on documentaries after lunch. One day, for sure, she would come back and alight on me.

Everything was under control. Dombo was waiting for me in the hypermarket car park with the car stolen that night. He showed me the weapon. I weighed it in my hand. It was an air pistol, but it looked impressive. It commanded respect. People would think I was Robocop or something. We had hesitated in the first instance between an imitation pistol and sawing off the hunting gun that had belonged to his father. 'The sawn-off shotgun is more intimidating,' Dombo had said. I had given the matter a great deal of thought. 'Listen, Dombo, it's all got to be very calm, very clean. With the shotgun, we're going to look like a couple of space cadets, junkies or something. And people get very nervous, and when people are nervous, they do strange things. Everyone would rather professionals. The motto is each person does their job. No song and dance, no mess. Like professionals. So let's leave aside the shotgun. The pistol creates a better impression.' Dombo was not too convinced about being barefaced either. I explained it to him. 'They have to take us seriously, Dombo. Professionals don't make fools of themselves with tights on their head.' The confidence big old Dombo always showed in me was touching. His eyes shone whenever I spoke. If I had had the same confidence in myself that Dombo showed, the world would have bowed down at my feet.

We left the car in Agra de Orzán market and picked up the sports bags. At midday, just as we had calculated, Barcelona Street, pedestrianized and lined with shops, was full of people. Everything was going to be very simple. The door to the bank opened for an old woman and we followed her straight inside. I had rehearsed it all over. 'Ladies and gentlemen, please do not be alarmed. This is a hold-up.' I gestured calmly with the pistol and all the customers formed an orderly and silent group in the corner that I had indicated. A very helpful chap insisted on offering me his wallet, but I told him to keep it, we were not pickpockets. 'You, please, fill the bags,' I asked an employee with an efficient air about him. He did so in a flash and Dombo was infected by the civilized climate in which all this was going on to the point that he thanked him. 'Now, since we don't want any problems, please do not move for ten minutes. You've all been very kind.' And so we went, as if from a laundry.

'Stop, or I'll shoot!'

First of all, remain calm. I continue walking as if it had nothing to do with me. One, two, three more steps and off like a shot. Too many people. Dombodán doesn't think about it. He barges his way through like a rugby player. And there's me in a different film.

'Stop, you bastard, or I'll shoot!'

I take the pistol out of the open bag and turn around slowly, aiming with my right hand.

'What's wrong? Is there some problem?'

The guy who had offered me his wallet before. Standing with his feet apart and the revolver pointing straight at me, held in both hands. Now, that's a professional. A security guard in civilian clothes, I'll bet.

'Listen, boy, don't do anything stupid. Drop that toy.'

There's me smiling, saying uh-uh. And I throw the bag in his face, all the money in the air, falling in slow motion. 'Take that, you bastard!' And I break into a run, the people frightened, standing aside, what a disaster, the people standing aside, opening a cursed corridor in the street, a hole, a tunnel up ahead, a hole behind. It burns. Like a wasp sting.

The ambulance's siren. I smile. The male nurse looks at me confused because I'm smiling. Lola skates between miniature roses and azaleas, in a room with big windows. She comes towards me. Embraces me. This is our home. And she wants to give me the surprise, on skates, her pleated, red skirt swaying together with her long hair, the cherry's kiss.

That night, through the glass in the door, I can read the Funeral Parlour's illuminated sign. 'You are kindly requested to adopt a moderate tone in the interests of everybody.' Dombo, gigantic, loyal Dombo, was here. 'Please condole my acceptances,' he said to my mother with remorse. Now, don't tell me that's not funny. It sounds like a line from Monty Python. It's enough to make you cry with laughter. He looked at me with tears in his eyes. 'Dombo, you fool, get out of here, go and spend the money on a house with a room with big windows and a massive, Triniton telly.' But Dombo keeps on crying, with his hands in his pockets. He's going to soak everything. Tears like grapes.

Fa's here, Josefa, from the flat opposite. She for one always knew what the score was. Her look was an eternal reprimand. But I'm grateful to her. She never said a word. A good one, or a bad one. I would greet her, 'Good morning, Fa,' and she'd mutter something under her breath. Anything cooking in the world, she knows about it. But she wouldn't say a word. She'd help Mum, that was all. She'd smoke a Chesterfield with her at night and they'd drink a Lágrima from Oporto, while I played with the remote control. And now here she is, supporting Mum. She turns towards me from time to time, but she's stopped scolding me with her look. She crosses herself and prays. A professional.

Not long to go now. I can see the burial times on the illuminated sign. 12.30, in Feáns.

Lola says goodbye to Mum and heads for the door of the mortuary. The way she walks! Even with shoes on, she looks like she's flying. A heron or something. But what's this? She suddenly turns around, skates over in my direction with her pleated skirt and comes to land on the glass. She looks at me in amazement, as if noticing me for the first time.

'Impressed, eh?'

'But, Tino, how could you?'

She has warm, sinful eyes, and her mouth is half-open.

I dream of the first cherry of summer.

Lidija Cvetkovic
Sour Cabbage, Roses & Lies

After a decade of absence it's the crumbling
facades that strike me — chunks of paint split off
like states on the map of former Yugoslavia.
In the tenement flats everyone is spring cleaning —
tapestries, quilts, rugs, expel the odours of winter months.

Uncle Uros, not uncle by blood but by virtue of his age,
welcomes me the traditional way: a teaspoon of preserved
quince with a sip of plain water, a shot of plum brandy,
and a cup of Turkish coffee. Dark sediment shifts invisibly
as we talk. To close the ritual we turn over our cups.
Fate unfolds before us.

He orients me on the city map
marking crosses where bombs fell, following with pen
the 'charred alley-ways' of his beloved Belgrade.
He'll be off at dawn to queue for sugar —
The worst thing's the company in these queues
the fools who swear by Milosevic to the grave

while he pockets their pension.
I too had a chance to emigrate, but the state offered us
this flat...then my wife died. It was then he planted
the mass of roses by the wall. Over the years
he's guided them to cover the cracks.
April now. The wall exposed; mere buds.

Next day uncle Uros's knee is bleeding –
something about a slope and rain and a neighbour who
was supposed to help and the son who hadn't called –
Liars the lot of them! I ask about the opposition rally
while dabbing yellow on his flowering knee –
A mere two thousand, if you believe in the Politika.

And the familiar smell I cannot place – *Sour cabbage*
(of course!) *from the basement where we packed in
round chess on pickling vats when the blasted sirens
wouldn't let you sleep. One good thing, young Slobodan
learned to play chess; I let him have my king now and then.
I'll be damned if I let his namesake win in September.*

He is finished! Traitor to his own name. We'll pickle him!
When his knee stops bleeding, he pours us sljivovica –
To clean the blood from the inside. In unison we sink them –
To life! And he totters off to tend the roses, while I
feel the blood rush, my cheeks bloom.

Slobodan: from *sloboda* (slor-bo-da) n. freedom

Sole Refuge

When a man is grateful
to a river for his life
she carves her bed in his skin –
her undertows will always
pull him off his course.

It was a dandelion that did him in
when its cluster head of seed blew up.
He still flinches watching horses
step across the paddock.

His sole maps the escape.
Fear sharp as a tamarisk thorn
lodged in the tender arch of a foot;
even now he checks his tracks
for blood on the bitumen.

Inconceivable:
here he can walk for days
in a single direction
without crossing one checkpoint
border control. He walks

and finds himself yet again
at some river's edge, not knowing
what has happened in between
only that the moon has risen
water lapping at his knees.

Life Support

I've left all my belongings, all that resembles me behind:
the cat's needy meow, your callused grip on my hand;
I've left the blocked pipe, the poinciana in the yard
whose roots threaten like the unspoken between us.

The flowers here are scentless, and I hygienic
as the wash basin, as this motel linen, free of my clothes,
my hairstyles, my name – stripped to my sheet-white bones.
In sleep roots weave round my ribcage, push into my throat

when I go to speak an owl's hoot, a flutter of wings.
The coiled ear of a spring listens from the mattress' insides:
heartbeat amplifies…on the ceramic basin a hair uncurls itself…
I awake to left over dreams, the familiar taste of your earlobe –

I rinse out my mouth at the tap. In a laundromat
amid the din of spinning, someone is peeling a mandarin's inner skin.
An old drunk with a gripe against the government
mumbles something about polio and war. A single shirt whirls

now and then the sleeves fold round, mimic an embrace.
In the distance through the glass a man hooked like an ibis
roams beneath the strangler figs. He is looking for something
he has lost; his walking stick supports him.

I collect armfuls of sea waste and stones for him
seaweed's interlaced geometries, bones of birds long dead.

Exiled by the ocean blue bottles dry on the shore line
sprawl like suicides or porno stars, trail their blue veins.

At the airport you wait for me. Your freshly shaved face
shocks me. I've brought you the elegance of stones
I go to say, but you touch my hand, and I ask instead
about the pipe, had the cat been fed…

Lidija Cvetkovic's first collection, *War Is Not the Season for Figs*, was published in 2001 by Vagabond Press.

Martin Armiger

Biff

Martin Armiger's first novel, *The Waiters,* was published by Text Publishing in 2000.

The last time I saw my marriage counsellor was at the boxing. By 'my' marriage counsellor I mean the fellow is a marriage counsellor and when my last marriage was falling apart I went with my wife to talk to him. It didn't do any good. We still broke up. But I remember thinking at the time that marriage counselling as an occupation couldn't be much fun; watching two people tearing each other apart day in day out, every hour another couple destroying itself. Compared to which the boxing must have seemed a relatively harmless entertainment.

Anyway he was definitely in my wife's corner during our little bout and I probably harboured some small resentment towards him because of that fact. He might deny that he liked my wife more than he liked me. I can't even blame him if he did because she has a very attractive personality. I remember him murmuring to her, between rounds, 'You're very good, aren't you...' That didn't, from my point of view, help define him in the role of referee. Perhaps he saw himself as more than that. Perhaps, wild thought, he was at the boxing that night to watch the referees, to study their technique, though that's doubtful. I think he was there for the same reason we all were, to watch the fights.

I hate fighting. I get dry in the mouth whenever violence threatens. I lost every physical fight I was in all through school. I remember clearly being knocked sideways by David Weataway, a raw-boned redhead. We were twelve. He apologised afterwards and explained that I had insulted him in some way, for which I then apologised.

But for years I kept blundering into fights, either in myopic carelessness or just from being often out at night too late too young. I told myself that I was a lover not a fighter, but it wasn't true. I was a losing fighter.

At fifteen I was punched to my knees by a lout at a bus stop. He got me in the solar plexus and I was winded and scared. I didn't want to get up but his jeering friends shamed me into making some response. When I was on my feet the boy told me that he had hit me with an 'average' blow, one of many he had dished out that night, one, in fact, no harder than many he had received. Then he gave me another one as if to demonstrate more precisely the angle and velocity of the perfect blow to the stomach. I had my fists up but I couldn't protect myself, let alone hit him back. I couldn't seem to move my feet.

I felt sick. I wondered whether if I started vomiting they would go away. I wanted them to go away. I wanted it to be over.

I sometimes see a boxer lying on the canvas with glazed eyes and a look on his face that reminds me of that night.

There is the question of nicety. People hitting one another without good reason is generally considered by civilised societies a failure of some kind. Opinions and customs vary on what constitutes a good reason. I have been attacked in a night club for dancing with a particular girl, and once in Elder Park by a fellow in a check shirt who took exception to my haircut. Both these assailants felt wholly justified in their attitudes. Different countries and different age and social groups allow various degrees of freedom to the individual regarding the right to hit. But for adults in this country there is some kind of consensus that the defence of oneself or loved ones (or of those unable to defend themselves) is the only justification for inflicting personal violence on another. Because we don't like bullies, and we excoriate the perpetration of violence against women and children. Yet still the history books and the business and sports pages of newspapers love a 'fighter.'

There is a recognition within us that if you don't have the heart for a fight you shouldn't be in the game, whatever the game is. That the fighting spirit is an essential, even a desirable distinction. It's a national characteristic, the reason we win at cricket.

The awful folk wisdom has it that every single human interaction is, at bottom, either a fight or a fuck. That's the blunt reduction of personal politics that we cover over with a veneer of social routine, but which demands to be acknowledged whenever those routines are for one reason or another put aside.

It is not just the folk who think that. Philosophers each have their own version of the simple truth. In Hegel's world every interpersonal exchange is a contest from which one will emerge as a Master, the other as a Slave.

(Say it's not so, we protest. Reassure us that life is not like that. Love is not like that.

Love more so than anything else, he replies...)

All sport is a distillation of this contest, a coding of the power relationships between individuals and groups. Boxing is just the most naked statement of the underlying truth about people, stripped of nearly all the artifice that society imposes.

Roland Barthes called boxing a 'Jansenist' sport, 'based on a demonstration of excellence'. Jansen, influential in Catholic France since the seventeenth century, taught that the human will is naturally perverse. We have no innate tendency towards goodness, he said. Good only comes from the love of God and God chooses only those he wants.

Is this what Barthes means when he calls boxing 'Jansenist'?

The best known Jansenist in literature is probably Julien Sorel, Stendhal's hero in *The Red and The Black*. Julien is an outsider, almost an 'existential' character, but unlike the heroes of Camus, Sartre or Beckett, he is driven by a need to succeed, to get on, to claim his deserts from society. He fails. After a short life full of passion and intrigue he finds himself condemned to death. He faces this prospect with calm acceptance and a dispassionate analysis of his own culpability. He refuses to apply for a reprieve. In his own estimation he has met an appropriate justice.

'What shall I have left,' Julien asks his confessor, 'if I despise myself? I have been ambitious, I am not going to blame myself for that; I acted then in accordance with the demands of the time. Now I live for the day, without thought of the morrow.'

Two days before the execution he tells his friend, 'As to what my feelings will be, I cannot answer for them... But as for fear, no; not a soul shall see my cheeks grow pale.'

'On the day on which he was told he had to die,' Stendhal goes on, 'bright sunlight was making all nature gay, and he himself was in the mood for courage... There now, he said to himself, everything is going well... My courage isn't failing me.'

And at the end Stendhal tells us: 'Everything passed off simply and decently, with no trace of affectation on his part.'

As Cus d'Amato, the famous trainer, taught the young Mike Tyson, heroes feel fear just like cowards. It's just that the hero will get on and do what has to be done. 'Not a soul shall see my cheeks grow pale.'

'A boxing match is a story,' says Barthes, 'which is constructed before the eyes of the spectators.' An epic story of conflict. The boxer is Achilles, the hero we all look to for deliverance. Or one boxer is Achilles, the other must be Hector, the noble loser, no less worthy. How does boxing help us deal with the ultimate metaphysical problems? By simplifying them to the personal test of courage. You either stand up to your problem (your nemesis, your enemy, your fear) or you don't. That is all that counts.

This might seem like a sideways solution. But Wittgenstein argued that most of the problems of philosophy are in fact problems of language. The insoluble dilemmas of metaphysics merely need to be restated in precise terms. When you do that, he said, you find these famous contradictions and paradoxes simply disappear. In similar manner, the utter immersion of the boxer in the physical world reduces the metaphysical to nothing, which is, after all, according to Wittgenstein, the aim of metaphysics.

A.J. Liebling, writing his years of columns for the *New Yorker*, often noticed the curious preoccupations of the boxer, from the odd jargons of training arcana through strange superstitions to full-blown mystical dementia. With Floyd Patterson you got all three. Liebling called it, 'Patterson's project of increasing the percentage of himself that he would get to be.'

When Patterson was asked, 'How you coming along?' he replied, 'I'm a little bit off but I'm hopeful. If he gives me a good fight, I'll be sixty per cent of me. Then I'll take five days off, and before I drop under fifty-eight I'll go right back into hard training. The time to catch it is when you come right off a fight. Like when I started to train back in November – I was no more than forty per cent of me. Starting at fifty-eight, I might hit seventy-five or eighty for Johansson. Once I find my whole self I'll be satisfied.'

Champion fighters are all more or less loony, we know that from listening to them when they are interviewed after a fight, but we know it too from a moment's reflection on the sheer lunacy of fighting for a living. Who in their right minds would do it? What would make you submit yourself to the pain and all that work?

Ernest Hemingway in 'Fifty Grand' tells the story of Jack Brennan, an out-of-condition heavyweight champion who is persuaded to lose a big fight. As he expected to lose anyway he goes along with it and bets against himself. But the wise guys who have organised the fix double-cross him. They arrange for the other fighter to hit Jack below the belt. If Jack goes down, gives in to the pain of a low blow, he will win the bout and lose his money. Through the final tortuous rounds the reader's sympathies are entirely won over to Jack and the awful, inescapable way he solves his problem. His triumph is to successfully lose the fight.

Hemingway liked the idea of a toughness beyond what is measured by referees or a ten-count. He was a boxer himself, but it's hard to know how good he was because most of the people whom we read about going up against him were other writers. You somehow don't imagine F. Scott Fitzgerald or Ezra Pound being able to put up much of a fight.

Hemingway was a Jansenist in the same way as Stendhal. He had a thoroughly determined view of fate and destiny which he articulated in those famously terse sentences: 'Life will break you if it can. If you are so strong that it can't break you then it will kill you.'

It is the warrior's credo.

The warrior is the type who will be a fighter. He's in the army or works for a security company or else he is in gaol or selling protection. What makes a warrior? Is it the desire to inflict pain, to triumph by force? Or a more-or-less noble sense of duty? Or are these two (sadism/self-sacrifice) successive stages in the same character? What does it mean to live like a warrior? Is it a state of mind or a career path?

The mythic type that is a warrior is constantly celebrated in fiction, and particularly on film. The American Cinema is founded on the lone hero who through massive violence triumphs over the evil world. Dirty Harry. Die Hard.

In boxing writing 'warrior' is the term of highest praise. The Russian-born Australian Kostya Tsyu, we are now told by American commentators, is a warrior. Like Roberto Duran, Roy Jones Junior, Marvin Hagler. These are fighters who, though they may be beaten, are somehow indomitable. Perhaps it's just hype. Roberto 'Iron Fist' Duran was better known for the one time he quit a fight (saying 'No mas,' to Sugar Ray Leonard in the sixth round of their second bout), than for the two-hundred-odd times he won. But then he came back to fight the flashy Leonard for a third time and Duran proved himself worthy. Thomas 'Hit Man' Hearns and 'Marvelous' Marvin Hagler were certified warriors despite losing to Leonard. Yet though Leonard defeated the three toughest middleweights of the 1980s, he was never called a warrior. Mohammad Ali won the respect of the older boxing coaches not with his fourth-round knockdowns or his dancing feet and lightning hands, but by letting himself get horribly punched around for ten rounds by George Foreman in Zaire before recovering to put him down. He lost God-knows how many brain cells that night but he became a warrior.

There are elegant boxers who can't put an opponent away. They look good but the killer instinct is missing. There are fighters who can't really box, ugly-looking sluggers that nobody wants to face. (Television commentators have a favourite call: 'Here we have a fighter against a boxer.')

Then there are boxers who are fighters. These are the warriors.

After years of writing about war and warfare John Keegan concluded that there will always be wars because there will always be warriors, a special genetically-determined sub-group within the species.

The flesh has depths. Within the mysterious processes of the body are those infinitesimally small transformations that bring thought to action – by which the word is made flesh. To live inside those transformations is to live at the speed of your body. This is both a speeding-up and a slowing-down process. The man or woman who understands the secret life of the body, lives within its rhythms, lives therefore totally within the moment, is here now, as the western Zen school used to say. The boxer is here now.

1963. My family lives in a comfortable house in a small town on the northern edge of London. Sitting in the lounge room with my father on a summer's night I watch the television broadcast of the stoush at Wembley Stadium between Cassius Clay (as he was then) and the Englishman, Henry Cooper. Henry is the British and Commonwealth heavyweight champion, a cockney, well liked (as they say) but suspect for having a glass jaw. Commentators don't think he has the class of his opponent.

The American, on the other hand, is a brash loudmouth who strikes most British observers as not behaving as a sportsman should. He seems to lose control of himself at his various press conferences, shouting crazy threats and promising (in rhyme) to murder our Henry. Sportsmen, in this place at this time, are expected to behave with a certain amount of decorum. There is a widely-held ideal of diffidence, as if to say: Yes, we won the war but it was just a bit of luck. Yes, we lost the empire but we don't want to go on about it. The affected humility is supposed to conceal, and at the same time reveal, a quiet self-confidence. Clay is a stranger to these behavioural subtleties. He is so sure of himself that people find him a bit off; so contemptuous of such conventional *moeurs* as 'respect for one's opponent' that the public sympathy is united against him, and the national affection (a misplaced pride) flows in a surging wave onto Cooper.

Then there is style. Clay does not box as a heavyweight is expected to box. He doesn't lumber out of his corner, doesn't 'control the ring' or throw his weight around, not at this stage of his career. Worst of all, he refuses to 'take the fight' to his opponent. Instead he seems to be constantly moving backwards, staying out of reach of Cooper, skipping away from trouble, hardly throwing a punch.

My father is disgusted at the exhibition.

'That's not boxing,' he says.

I wonder where his expertise on boxing comes from. He was in the army but I am unaware of his ever having climbed into the ring. The person with whom I see him most often in physical conflict is me, and against that opponent at least, I can attest that he is of the 'never a backward step' school. Whether from having been shelled in North Africa or from marching about on the South Downs carrying sticks for rifles, he brought out of the army experience an uprightness of bearing and an air of knowing more than anyone else about anything you care to name. Now he pours himself a scotch whisky with a little water in it. Every one else in the house is in bed. We are sitting together watching a fight, but he doesn't offer me a drink.

He now expresses the opinion that Clay is clinically mad. He is not the only one who thinks that. Some six months later even Clay's own doctor, after examining the fighter before the first Liston bout, announces, 'He is emotionally unbalanced. He acts like a man in mortal fear of death.'

Is this fear or madness we are watching, I wonder, or something else again?

I am hoping that Henry will catch up with Clay and land one on him. In an early round he does just that, though it hardly seems to hurt. My English heart is pounding with fear and anticipation. As someone who could never fight his way out of a paper bag I admire those who can. These men have so little truck with fear. They are so good at fighting that they have transformed it into an art. They play with it! I relate to boxers much in the same way that teenage girls relate to characters in a television soap opera: impossible role models. They (the boxers and the television characters) do the things that we (me and the girls) only dream about. We want the best for them, or, in some cases, we want them to get their come-uppance.

The braggart and the bitch we want to see fail. And the ones we like, we fear for.

My father writhes on the sofa in annoyance. He points out the deficiencies in Clay's technique, bewails the inability of Cooper to take advantage of the situation. Strangely, despite the sentimental hope attached to the Londoner, I find myself fearing for both of the fighters. It will be painful to see either of them humbled, though one of them will surely be so.

Clay is still dancing, still moving backwards. Cooper is doggedly following him around, occasionally throwing out a jab, when suddenly, 'out of nowhere,' Clay hits him with two punches, a left and a right, and Henry goes down.

(I recall the image on the little black and white TV; still remember, allowing for the distortions of time, the snarl on Clay's face, my father jumping as if he had been hit himself, the groan of the BBC commentator, the shock we all feel, shared in that instant; a catharsis, the recognition of defeat.)

Cooper never gets back in the fight. In the next round, the fifth, he is hit again and it's over.

The pity replaces the pride. The next morning's newspapers recognise Clay's unconventional skill, celebrate his burgeoning greatness. I read these stories in snatches, folding them up to put through letter boxes, sliding them under doors on my paper round. Henry was brave, they say, but he never had a chance. All day at school I think about this event, what it means. At length I sort it out. Cassius Clay wins by not playing the game of being a fighter. He does not 'act tough.' He acts like a madman and talks more than any fighter has ever talked. He is not on the same planet as Henry Cooper. The 'nowhere' that his punches come out of is the place of 'not-fighting.'

We still have myths: narratives which strike us with an ineluctable 'rightness'; unshakeable beliefs that are not really provable. The warrior is important in that belief system. So important that men get nervous about women boxers or women in the army. Ever since the Amazons men have had problems with the idea of women as warriors. *Xena The Warrior Princess* is a good joke, but despite the almost domestic character of what modern armies actually do, particularly the peacekeeping functions at which, theoretically, women should be as good as men, most of us believe that an army without warriors is asking for trouble.

Some women like to fight and some of them are good at it. Fighters like Mischa Merz and kickboxer Rebecca (The Wrecker) Russell are stylish and graceful and can take care of themselves. But I don't particularly want to watch them and I can't quite work out why that is. When women fight, especially when they get emotional about it, I feel the earth shift on its axis, the heavens rent. In the same way, and despite all I learned from feminists in the 1970s, I cannot help but feel an obscure pity for those men who elect to stay home and look after the kids. That's not to say we should stop anyone doing what they want to do. But watching women fight I am like that boy watching Clay and Cooper on television. I don't want to see either of them get hurt.

Women don't like boxing, mostly. They find it primitive, atavistic, needlessly harmful. Irrelevant to what they think is important. The atmosphere at a boxing match is not one that appeals. The uninhibited way that men hoot and whistle at the Round Card girls. The very existence of these girls, parading around the ring, holding up their cards. They are usually skimpily dressed, except in Wales where they wear Welsh national costume, ankle-length, amply cut. Other countries have their own way of dressing Round Card girls. It is considered polite to allow some acknowledgment for the trouble these girls have gone to with their appearance. Some men hoot and whistle. Others lean back in their seats and murmur to their companions an agreeable witticism or a small word of appreciation. Some women at the boxing also share a witticism or two, others do no more than narrow their eyes. There is a sexual undercurrent that is not just to do with the card girls or the half-naked fighters. Nor is it about dominance and submission. Mike Tyson reportedly once had (consensual) sex with twenty-two women at a party. Is it possible? Sonny Liston supposedly said that the blowjob was the white man's greatest invention. A recording engineer told me that he took a girl to a fight at the Hordern Pavilion. This was in 1982. 'I didn't think she liked me,' he said. 'But she gave me a knee-trembler in the car-park afterwards.' He thought that the excitement of the event had 'warmed her up,' and recommended the venue to anyone on a first date. 'We didn't even get out of the car-park,' he said again, looking at me with calm wide-set eyes.

Boxing is for men about men by men, said Joyce Carol Oates. And the reason is that it gives pleasure to men. Organised sport has become such a soulless pursuit – the work ethic, the Protestant influence, the fetishisation of all activity in advanced economic society – that it's easy to forget that sport comes out of games. The people who like running like it because it's fun and part of that fun is seeing who is fastest. Kids like kicking a ball around because it's a gasser to do so, not so that they might one day play for Essendon or Arsenal. My dogs chase each other round the porch to see who is top dog. It's more fun to do that than to lie around watching TV. Or it is for dogs, at any rate, and for some poor low stumbling fools of men too. The great thing about boxing-gym culture is it allows men to play with the idea of fighting, it reminds them of the warrior code without putting them in too much danger. Mild men practise fighting just to keep in touch with a deeper reality.

Most of us (readers, desk-people) are not going to be physically threatened in everyday life. If it ever did happen we would most likely be too surprised at the event itself to do anything about it. So to spar in a gym at least gives us an idea of what a fist aimed at the head looks like and feels like. The true warrior will take a punch to give a punch. The gym bunny doesn't have to.

But some men don't like the whole thing; they genuinely feel a revulsion for organised combat, for the spectacle of two men hitting each other to see who is best at it; they despise those who take pleasure in watching one man beat up another man. Doctors, for example, don't seem to like it.

The hard part to deal with in boxing is the harm that it does to those who make a career out of it. Sugar Ray Robinson (whom some call the greatest-ever boxer) suffered from Alzheimer's disease for the last few years of his life. He suffered in private, unknown to his fans. Mohammad Ali's struggle with Parkinsonism is more public. Wherever he goes he is applauded. The way he has dealt with his affliction has finally brought the brattish youth into a near universal affection. (The exception to that universality being, of course, Joe Frazier.)

Boxing is not the most dangerous sport on a fatality count. You can die driving fast cars. More people get killed every year falling off horses than in or near the ring. But in those other sports there isn't someone following you around trying to hurt you, bent on causing you pain. That brutal fact, the essence of the sport, makes each contest a primitive event. A boxer can toughen up his body, but the many blows to the head that he incurs over the years do irreparable damage (or perhaps it is just one blow, one time) making the boxer in effect a human sacrifice.

Thom Gunn in his book of short stories *The Pugilist at Rest* is relentless in his detailing of the things that happen to boxers. The 'black lights of oblivion' (a phrase made popular by Thomas Hauser in his book about boxing), the broken ribs, the constant headaches, the pissing of blood for weeks at a time, the fever, delirium, and finally the left-temporal lobe epilepsy.

How can we tolerate a sport that treats its practitioners so harshly? Aren't the rules there to stop that happening? Or do we accept that boxing is actually about self-destruction?

'He fell down almost before he was hit.'

When Joe Frazier got knocked down by George Foreman he jumped in the air like a vaudeville enactment of a man being knocked out. It looked, from a distance, as comic as the actor Joe Pesci looked getting knocked on the floor in *Raging Bull*. But what Frazier was experiencing was, one supposes, more awfully real. He wanted it to end.

Virginia Woolf noted that the pleasure of reading Sir Thomas Browne is made somewhat keener by the realisation of the gulf that separates the Elizabethan sensibility from our own. She quotes Browne's casual witnessing and reporting of an episode of torture, notes the way the writer can watch a person being torn to pieces without appearing to feel any sympathy, nor expecting any in his fellow witnesses. This marks them off from us, she says. She cannot imagine any writer from the twentieth century, in the presence of pain, failing to identify with the victim of violence.

Perhaps boxing for us is like torture or public execution for the Elizabethans. Perhaps future generations will class us all as primitives, we who take pleasure in a primal contest that involves the deliberate infliction of pain on the one hand, on the other the boxer's abandonment of himself, the offering of his own body as a gift to ruin.

We share a pleasure in observing these fights that already borders on the illicit. The pleasure perhaps of watching what we shouldn't watch.

Stendhal: Everything can be acquired in solitude, except character.

'He walked into it.'

The really big fights happen somewhere else, in Las Vegas or Atlantic City (or maybe Tokyo or even Zaire) and we watch them on a big television at a local pub or one of the clubs. World Championship bouts: Chavez or De La Hoya or Lennox Lewis or Mike Tyson. I was always surprised at how many people actually liked Mike Tyson. Men in Sydney pubs in the middle of a Sunday afternoon would cheer the television screen as he walked (thousands of miles away) from his dressing room to the ring. Tyson had learned from Ali that the important battle to win is the mind game. But Tyson put an unfortunate slant on it. When he said he wanted to kill his opponent he had nearly every other fighter in his division believing him. It got boring. Personally I was rooting for Evander Holyfield and was delighted to watch him humiliate Tyson. Typically this great triumph, a feat of courage and skill, was followed up by a bizarre post-bout interview in which Holyfield raved about God and His Purpose and seemed incapable of dealing with any other thought. I suppose it's asking a bit much to expect fighters to do what they do and then be amusing. (Athletes, said Richard Ford, are people who are happy to let their actions speak for them.) But some do well enough. Kostya is always modest and natural. Barry Michaels, the champion middleweight, was asked after a fight in Melbourne how he felt. 'Alright,' he said, 'But Jeez, mate, it's a hell of a way to make a quid.' Shannan Taylor ('The Bulli Blaster') is quite insane, grabbing the microphone and shouting at the audience about how misunderstood he's been, what a hard life he's had, thanking the people who've stood by him, imagining, for some reason, that any of us want to hear about any of that stuff.

Marrickville Town Hall has fight nights every couple of months, which is where I met my marriage counsellor again. I say 'met' but I might as well say 'saw', because he didn't speak to me apart from saying hello. This was a pity, because I wanted to talk to him. I had just been reading about Ted Hughes and Sylvia Plath and had been struck by the way they described their marriage. 'A fight to the death,' Hughes called it. 'One of us,' Sylvia remarked more darkly, 'is done for.'

The prescience of poets. She died and he came undone more slowly. I wanted to ask my counsellor about the marriage-as-fight-to-the-death analogy. I wanted to test my positive notion of 'not-fighting' against his critique of 'passive aggression'. I thought he might have acknowledged that it was okay for me to have messed up my marriage, to tell me, in this male environment, that everyone does it. I suppose I wanted him, in some way, to forgive me. But he kept ducking away and I didn't chase after him.

I was with a couple of friends. The three of us usually go if there's something on. Marrickville is close to where we live but the boxing there is of a variable standard. Parramatta Stadium once had Kostya Tsyu (January 20 1996 v Hugo Pineda in the pouring rain). Another time we drove to Newcastle (again for Tszyu – though that was the first time we saw the great talent of Lovemore Ndou), and once to Wollongong for Shannan Taylor. We are fight fans.

One night we go to a club in Newtown.

When we arrive there is a fight, an unscheduled one, in the ground-floor bar. The bouncers (who normally break up these things in fairly expedient fashion) are all upstairs watching the boxers. We skirt the mayhem, climb the stairs. The room where they have the fights, when we get there, is relatively calm.

A local notable, Tom Domican, a 'colourful identity' with the reputation of a thug, walks into the club, a smile on his smooth square face. He moves through the crowd with a proprietary air like a country squire in his vineyards. This is his turf.

Some of the younger boxers from early bouts are brought up and introduced to him. He speaks to them in a kindly knowing fashion, the old warrior, the brother in arms. He encourages them and gives them a tap on the head. The gesture of a confident man. It is not enough to be a good fighter. You also have to be connected.

Boxing is indivisible from the marketing machinery which surrounds it, just as the art world, the literary world or the world of pop music contain within themselves both the nobility of the enterprise and the crassness of its exploitation. Indeed their nobility is framed within and defined by the structure of reward and recognition bestowed by their respective milieus.

Both Mohammad Ali and Mike Tyson are forever linked with Don King. The blatant manipulation of the market by which King boosted his own dominance (and that of his fighters) is no worse than the tactics of corporate warriors or the hypocrisies of politicians. But we resent the machinations of King Promotions even more than the meanness of bankers, perhaps because of that feeling which fight fans share (one to which Oates refers in *On Boxing*), that boxing is the truest of sporting contests, that it is somehow more real than life itself. In this most fair of sports we want fairness to rule. We want to see the best fighters matched against each other, not watch champions spend years avoiding their challengers.

The last thing most of us want is to see someone get beaten up. Sport has rules to determine exactly how you get to win, to make it equally possible for anyone to win, and to protect the losers. When things get too rough, when one brawler is punishing the other and the other has lost the ability to defend himself, the referee is supposed to jump in. The marriage counsellor, by way of contrast, can send you to your corner, can even force a round break, but he can't stop one combatant hurting another. He can't stop the fight. That's the difference between sport and life.

'He didn't see it coming'

There is another brawl in the audience just before the feature bout at Newtown. A couple of the flimsy chairs we are sitting on get thrown around. Under the hot lights in the gilt- and red-lined room there is an atmosphere of anticipation and apprehension, which only settles once the contest begins. When one of the boxers goes down – it is Mick Beattie, a local favourite – he goes down hard and he doesn't get up. Not for a long while. The fellow that knocked him down is an honest bruiser from South Australia called Garth Cussion, and he knocked Beattie down with a good solid hook that bashed the senses right out of his head. Garth is wandering round the ring in a state of suspended exhilaration. He has just won the Australian Light-Heavyweight Championship with that punch, but the other bloke doesn't get up. The referee can't make the announcement. It should be Garth's big moment but all anyone can think about is the fighter on the ground.

When Beattie finally manages to raise himself and leave the ring the whole room breathes out together, a collective sigh of relief. We are all guilty if he dies. All of us share the responsibility for putting the boys in the ring, exposing them to this danger. If we are not there, don't buy tickets, are not interested then it wouldn't happen. Would it?

Jan Owen
The Flask
translated from the French of Charles Baudelaire

There are some perfumes so potent they can pass
through anything – they'll even penetrate glass.
Open an antique oriental box
which creaks and balks, barely unlocks,

or a wardrobe in an empty house –
black dust, the acrid odour of loss –
and there'll be some old flask which holds it all,
the living, leaping spark, the returning soul.

A thousand dormant thoughts, chrysalids of gloom,
softly stirring in the shadowy room
are disentangling their wings to lift and soar,
gold-spangled, glossed with rose, brushed azure-clear.

Heady memory turns in the troubled air;
your eyes close; vertigo's overwhelming power
seizes your very being, you're tossed
back through the mist towards the abyss

and pinned down over the edge of the years. Ahead,
like Lazarus ripping open his shroud,
a ghostly body wakes and moves –
your old love, rancid, seductive as the grave.

And when I too am lost in the memory of man,
from the sinister cupboard corner where I've been thrown,
an abject filthy old flask cracked through and done,
listen, my lovely, I'll have you again.

I'll be your coffin then, sweet pestilence!
The witness of your force and virulence,
beloved poison distilled by angels, tart
liquor corroding me, living death of my heart.

Café

At Starbucks
on Orchard Road
green umbrellas frenchify the kerb,
red straws tilt at the orange juice
and the coffee of the day is Guatemala.
It's Saturday, early
and the balloon man's come
with a jostling brood of
eight tugging colours incarnate.
Miss Pert, three, claims a pink,
and a back-packed girl and boy
lead in lilac and blue, late Valentines
with a short uneasy motion.
The man in the purple shirt is sipping
Sun Tzu's *Art of War*. And the air
the air – pungently, velvety clear:
balloon weather,
wistful and aromatic.
A plump teenager in a tunic
brings in the gold and ties it to her chair;
it sways, full-bodied as the
espresso's one ounce shot coming
through like a waterfall clearing its throat.
The steaming fragrance is free
as the crystals Miss Pert is spooning
over the cloth to her mouth.
To the left, Ms Caffe Americano

handphones Seattle – 'My God, he would!',
stirring and stirring.
Outside, a red balloon and a white,
let up into the crown of the end umbrella,
are kissing the canvas,
philosophers latched to Being.
Everyone's holding a string now, even Sun Tzu.
The vendor is selling the last one. Green.
Going, going. Gone.

Jan Owen was the winner of the 2000 Gwen Harwood Poetry Prize, and currently has a residency at the Paris Studio of the Australia Council.

Janet Kieffer

Sark Lake

Janet Kieffer was winner of the 1997 BBC World Service Award for the Short Story. Her stories have been published in the US, UK and Canada. She lives in Colorado.

My mother and father, Amanda and Lou, went in one canoe, my mother trembling like a dragonfly and pointing out rocks in the riffles and chutes between the lakes. Their Gruman was loaded with duffle bags, boxes and tents that were haphazardly shoved under the gunnels. When they got to the big Vs in the water in the faster chutes, Amanda pointed and cried out: '*Lou?*' and big Lou adjusted his paddle in the stern to avoid a rock suspected below the surface. The water up there got frothy sometimes, and you could never really tell where the rocks were – but the Vs were practical canoeing theory, or at least that's what Corky told me. It wasn't only that the rocks were there; it was the fact that you didn't know if the canoe would sail right over them or if the rocks would bend the boat like a spoon.

I rode in the other canoe with Corky. I paddled bow, or was supposed to, but most of the time I just rode there, my Keds soaking up an accumulation of cloudy water in the bottom of the boat. The canvas duffles and tents were usually moist due to spray from an errant paddle or a sprinkle of rain, and they smelled like rotten eggs when the sun beat down. A red-bereted guy from Ely (one of the first real hippies I ever saw) had talked us into buying some red tarps, saying that they were good for getting rid of black bears, and that all you had to do when a bear was in camp was to wave a red tarp at it. Corky questioned this, but Lou and Amanda bought the tarps anyway. They said we could throw the tarp over my canvas tent in case I was stupid enough to touch it from the inside and let the rain come rushing in.

'Paddle, Astra,' Corky said sometimes, when the water was static, when we were in the middle of a vast void of water so still that the only ripples were from the startled slap of a beaver's tail. An ear-brushing wind, a hum of insects, some eerie bird song, and the rhythmic plunge-and-drip of paddle into water were the only other sounds. Water spiders skated frantically in the inlets. Corky was somehow related to my mother. He was my uncle, but he was not. He lived in a dilapidated stucco house a few blocks away from ours in St. Louis, was much younger than my mother, and was missing a few front teeth. He smoked a pipe, and sometimes only his two man friends were around, exchanging food stamps and beer. One of them was large and hairy. The other one was small and had the teeth of a beaver. The hairy one tried to finger my underpants one night and I ran away. Amanda didn't allow me to visit Corky's house alone because he was often pickled. 'His parents were a little too *nice* to him,' Amanda said, and the way she said 'nice' didn't sound nice at all. I once saw Amanda block Corky from passing through our front door one hot St. Louis night, her flowered house dress sticking to her sausage legs, and she said 'Damn you, Corky, you are pickled and you are not coming in.' And he did not; he vanished beyond the flower clusters on the locust trees and staggered on in the direction of his house, whistling a sophisticated tune. Amanda slammed the door. At random times after that, I noticed brief glimpses of his wild-eyed and grizzled face looking in through the screens of the house. It was said that my grandparents, Amanda's parents, and their parents were farmers in Arkansas who raised cattle and soybeans and fished in the rivers. There was a picture of my grandmother as a little girl sitting in a clear stream just beyond a gravel bar in Arkansas, holding up a crawdad with an expression of wonder and terror. We didn't have many vacations from Corky or from work, but we weren't planting soybeans either.

Corky shook and sweated as he paddled. He had black sandpaper stubble on his face, and he wore a rumpled khaki fishing hat with jeweled and furry flies speared into the brim. Sometimes he pulled out a tin cup and raked it into the lake for a gulp of water or he splashed a web of water across his face. And occasionally, when we went around a bend of a riffle before or after Amanda and Lou, he took out a flask and sampled what was in it. On one such occasion the riffle turned into a chute, the water started churning, and I began to see Vs all over. I squealed to alert Corky: *'We're going to crash! We're going to crash and drown and die!'* but when I looked back his paddle wasn't even in the water; his chin had tilted skyward with his flask. The chute was like a roller coaster. The inch or so of water in the bottom of the canoe sloshed back and forth. Monstrous rocks appeared everywhere, like animal heads. I hit one with my paddle to push the bow away from it. When I looked back again in panic, Corky had his paddle in the water. He ruddered us on a zig-zag course through the rest of it. The water finally stilled itself, and he said 'Relax.'

At times we floated through shallow waters with swaying green grass, and then just after that we'd find segmented reeds of wild rice that I snapped off and pulled apart to rebuild as necklaces for Amanda, Lou, and Corky. In late afternoons we'd pitch our tents in a mosquito-infested area with a rise of flat land near, or in a cradle of sweet pine needles and deer droppings with a breeze, water rushing over large rocks nearby. Twilight was the time for fishing, and I had my cast reel with a worm I'd pierced in bloody spurts on the hook, or some white pieces of pork rind, but Amanda, Lou, and Corky had fly rods. Corky fished with grace, his line like a melody or a poem, his fly barely touching the water. The shrieking loons began to sing.

Amanda pan-fried bass, northern, and walleye in the iron skillet in the evenings. I watched Corky clean the fish precisely, with the long blade of his hunting knife, after some steadying swigs from his flask. He first cut the spine of the wiggling fish, right behind its head, and he cut the head off. I was free to use the walleye heads as puppets, and I did, because the eyes on the walleyes could see in all directions. They talked to each other from my hands.

One day there were no riffles or chutes between lakes. We had some kind of destination the whole time, and I didn't know what that destination was, but we were headed there. We spent a lot of time hauling the gear. We came to a swamp. Corky and Lou had to consult maps to figure out where to go. Amanda looked at it, but they waved her away.

'Goes north,' Lou said.

'A portage through a swamp?'

'It goes north, and here we are, and we have to go through it. That's what the map says.'

'Fuck,' Corky said. He sighed and hoisted the canoe over his shoulders. A loud, complicated bird song echoed all around us. Amanda said it was a hermit thrush.

Amanda lurched behind Lou through the swamp. I followed her in my cutoffs, the water up to my knees, and Corky followed me with the other canoe, looking like a surreal and stretched out snail. We had to haul boats, shelter, stinking fishing gear, and Bisquick. The trees in the swamp were skinny and deciduous, without the striped bark of the birch. No watercress existed in the swamp, and I wasn't allowed to drink any water there. It was a nasty and mysterious place, and I half expected to see white-dead, bloated bodies surface or the Creature come. Amanda's calves sluiced against thick water, water full of life in its green and mouldy parts. Minnows pelted my ankles. Amanda looked back beyond me with the dark rolling eyes of a horse.

To get through a swamp, you have to pick your legs up very deliberately. I hauled my legs up out of the muck on the bottom, but it only revealed little dark worms that had attached themselves to me in the water. I couldn't brush them off. Corky set his canoe in the swamp water and put his canvas pack into it. The water had only reached my knees, but his cold hands inched up to my thighs and squeezed them. 'Get away from me, Corky!' I said, and I fell back into the rancid water.

'Whaddya mean?' he said. He looked hurt and helped me up. He took out his flask and poured some whisky or whatever alcohol on the place where each leech had attached itself to me, and they were easy to pull off this way, though they stretched like rubber sometimes before they relented. He smiled his missing-tooth smile at me, and I thanked him. Ahead of us, Amanda and Lou had stopped to deal with the leeches, and the four of us continued on among the skeletal trees of this murky womb.

We escaped this place and were supposed to portage around a beaver dam, but we were so tired that we got out of the canoes and hauled them over it, my feet cracking the scrawnier sticks of the dam and my legs sinking into it.

It was almost dark when we reached our next dot on the portage map. We couldn't see much, but this was supposed to be Sark Lake. We didn't build a fire and we didn't eat. Corky, Lou, and Amanda pitched heavy tents and unrolled the sleeping bags. Lou raised our enormous food duffle, with its can of beans, oil, iron skillet, and Bisquick, up to a high branch of a tree. I had my own pup tent, and Corky helped me pound in the stakes and tighten the lines, his lips sucked in where his front teeth were missing. 'This should make a fine little place for a girl like you,' he said.

Sometime during the night there came a crunching of rock and needle outside my brown tent. In half sleep I could have sworn that someone actually parted the flaps and looked in, but I couldn't be sure. I remember sitting up, listening without being entirely awake, and lying down again. I can't remember if I was fully asleep or not before I knew it was Corky, but I sat up again and saw the shadow of him peering in at me through the parted flaps. The shadow disappeared. After that I couldn't sleep, even though there were no more footsteps outside.

Pretty soon I had to pee and I crawled out of my tent with the flashlight. I relieved myself behind a little pine tree near the water, and something splashed in the water of the lake, beyond the water fall; that is, you could hear it over the waterfall, and I wandered, following the gold illumination of the flashlight. A sound like Corky's whistling came from the other side of the lake, but I was tired and I couldn't be sure if that's what it was. In spite of this, I found myself exploring, and when the path of the flashlight hit a series of stones going up a mossy bank, up I went. It was a ladder of rocks. You had to use hands and feet to climb it. When I got near the top, I tossed the flashlight upward, and the wide beam of light landed on a moose skull somebody had wired to a tree. I crawled up to a plateau on my knees and stared at it.

The flashlight revealed other wonders. Crude rock pews sat before a stone altar, the dark eye sockets of the moose skull overlooking everything. A loon wailed from a distant part of Sark Lake. Then there was a noise like the slight bending of a wicker basket, the snapping of soft pine needles, and Corky emerged from behind the altar. He sat on one of the pews. 'Interesting place!' he said. He was pickled. 'Come on over here, Astra, and sit with me.'

I had no intention of sitting there with him. I pointed my flashlight at the moose skull one more time to look at it before climbing back down the rocks.

The morning brought a great fracas to our Sark Lake camp. Amanda banged a pot and the iron skillet with a spoon in front of a black bear who hung its head like a shamed dog. Somehow the bear had gotten to the duffle bag in the tree, and some remaining Bisquick lay scattered on the ground. Flakes and dust of Bisquick clung to the bear's paws and mug. Amanda was too close to the bear, I thought, but like those animal enthusiasts who join animal rescue shelters and really don't know what they're doing, she decided she should approach the bear with a banging of pans and shame the animal as you would shame a dog. 'Get out of here!' she shouted, and she whopped the spoon against the pan. At times I wanted to rescue Amanda the way she would not rescue me.

When I first saw Corky that morning, in the middle of all of this, Corky hung his head in the same way the bear did. I looked back at Amanda, who was still shaming the bear, and at my father, who joined her by shouting at it. It was an amazing creature, and it reacted to my mother, but not very quickly. It languidly pawed the air. I remembered the red tarp, found it in the packings of my parents, and shook it wildly at the animal, who pretended to meander before high tailing it through the woods, into the water, and toward the protection of a distant shore. We watched its head bob as it swam away, the remnants of Bisquick on its body no doubt dispersing to feed the tiny, special organisms in the virgin waters of the Quetico.

This was a dramatic beginning to any day. We didn't have much in the way of Bisquick left, with which Amanda had hoped to fry up some sugar doughnuts in hot oil over the fire, but we still had bacon from the cooler, and we had our fishing rods.

We caught a lot of fish that day. I don't even know why Amanda, Lou, or Corky bothered with fly fishing; anything you threw into the chute between Sark Lake and whatever lay beyond would yield some fish – I could cast with my live bait and fish would bite at every fifth cast or so. I tried to cast into the quiet and hidden places; this is what Lou had taught me in Missouri and it worked in Canada also. As the treacherous rocks lay in hidden places when we traveled the waters, our food lay there too; but our food moved around as the rocks did not.

The fishing was so good, in fact, that we decided to stay for another day. I was secretly enamored with this idea since I wanted to climb the steps to the sanctuary again sometime when Corky was busy doing other things, or at least when he wasn't pickled.

It wasn't long before I thought I could control the weather. The Quetico was like no place I'd ever been before, and I had some kind of special bond with it and all of its creatures and plants, even the frightening ones. Proof of this lay in the fact that my breasts had started to puff out a little – only on the ends, and I knew damn well that the Quetico had something to do with it. I could bid the skies to offer rain or snow, and after lunch I jumped from rock to rock on Sark Lake, begging the skies to be kind, remembering the immortality of the Moose near the altar. I yearned to explore a small, misty island that graced the middle of the lake. I was an idealist, albeit a dirty one, and Amanda interrupted my dances and told me to take a bath. She gave me some Ivory soap and a towel. I asked her if I could have an empty canoe to practice with (as long as I was down there in the water) and Lou brought me a canoe and a paddle, shaking his head. He walked back up the trail to our camp. I stripped, my young girl belly sticking out, and I hesitated. The water was cold. I waded into it, naked, climbed into the canoe in the shallows, and paddled stern like an expert, I thought, heading for the middle of the lake. I dared myself to paddle to the fairy island and back again, and naked at that. The Ivory soap dirtied itself in the bilge on the bottom of the canoe. When I was halfway to the island, I heard the thin and paltry voices of Amanda and Lou. When I looked back, I saw their bodies, stick men on the shore, and I also saw Corky gawking at me over an expanse of weeds or brush, away from my parents, like an evil character from a picture book. I kept paddling, imagining myself a sort of female Viking with a horned hat, my blonde hair flying in the breeze. My arm muscles and back felt good. Plop, stroke, feather (drip); plop, stroke, feather. I was doing pretty well. I was going in a straight line toward the island. When I got close, a baby bird caught my attention. It was yellow and fluffy, but spotted; the closer I came to it with the canoe, the harder it cranked its webbed feet to get away. You could tell it had webbed feet by its speed in the water. A gull circled my canoe from above, pelting me with dung. The fuzzy bird disappeared into an inlet or crack in the island, and I was left to find something else to do. So I threw my paddle on the shore and rocked the canoe until it tipped over, and then I swam under it and went inside. Water light lines reflected on the inside of the canoe, and any noise I made resulted in a metallic, echoing, chamber sound. After a while the canoe wanted to tip itself back upright, or so it seemed to me, but this was fine since the air was getting thin. I got the uprighted canoe into the shallows of the far side of the island and found Corky there, soaking wet, holding my paddle, staring at me. I went back into the water until it was up to my neck, and his eyes trailed my body. His mouth was open.

'Give me my paddle, Corky,' I demanded.

He looked as if this wasn't the reaction he expected. He said, measuredly, 'A little girl should not paddle so far away like that. It ain't right. Anything could've happened to you.'

'Give me the damn paddle!' I liked saying *damn paddle* at that moment.

He didn't say anything for a second. Then he said, 'Only if you paddle back right now.'

'Did you swim out here?' I asked.

'I can swim back.'

'No, Corky,' I said. 'You can paddle the canoe. I'm the one who's going to swim back.'

He took off his sopping shirt and tossed it into the water. When I put it on, the hem of it hit the bottoms of my knees. 'Paddle back,' he said. 'I'll swim.'

Somebody had been using my casting rod. When I got back, after I'd gotten chewed out by Amanda and Lou, I thought I'd toss a few lines into the chutes and try to catch a big northern. If they wouldn't let me paddle where I wanted to, at least they ought to let me fish. I also considered using my wiles at controlling the weather to get even with all of them, but that wouldn't have helped. A raging thunderstorm wouldn't benefit anyone, least of all me if I happened to touch the inside of the tent, inadvertently, in my sleep or something.

The reason I knew someone had used my rod was because there was a lure on the end of the line. As I said, I didn't use lures; I used worms or pork rind. The lure was a treble hook, but that's not what I found alarming: the terror came when I found that the red and white flashing spoon lure actually had a drawing of the Devil on it. It was a classic Devil rendition, with pointy horns and a goatee, stamped on the red and white side of the lure. I snapped the line with my teeth and took the lure up to the Moose Skull Church for further examination. It wasn't until I'd climbed the rock ladder and sat on a cushion of pine needles behind the altar that I wondered if there was any connection between the Devil lure and the Moose Skull Church itself. Maybe the very place in which I sat had some cultish and Devil aspect. It was right around this time that I heard Corky and Amanda and Lou, below, involved in some kind of argument. It turned out that Amanda had found Corky's flask, or found Corky drinking from it, or some such thing. I spied on them from my elevated position, but I could only see Lou through the pine trees. His fat arms flailed wildly in the air. Voices echoed around rocks and trees, and you could only make out certain words, but *booze* was one of them, and *Astra* another. This outburst had stilled even the birds; it had stilled me, until I saw Corky move into view, heading toward my father with the long hunting knife he used for cleaning fish. Then they shuffled behind some trees again, and I could hear them scuffle, shout, and swear, and Amanda swore too.

'Corky!' I shouted. 'Corky, come on up here!' The noise below stopped. I saw Lou come into view in the gap in the trees, stand with his hands on his hips, and look in my direction without knowing where I was. And soon the hard sound of boot on rock came, and Corky's head, with the jeweled flies of the crown-like fishing hat, rose over the bank where the stone ladder was. A red creek of blood ran on his face. I'd planned to run when he approached, but he wouldn't look at me, and for some reason I stood, riveted, staring at the sparkling flies on his hat. Then I stepped toward him and gave him my bandanna.

We'd only planned on a few more days of this Canada business, and I wanted to keep going, but I had my doubts as to whether Amanda, Lou, and Corky would feel the same way. They couldn't smell the pines the way I could smell them, and they couldn't control the weather.

I went to the top of a bluff overlooking the lake. The sun was starting to go down. Near the shore, two bears nuzzled each other, and one bear jumped and pumped on the other bear; the bear who got jumped on seemed oblivious. It was motionless and looked drugged. The bears stayed entangled for some minutes, and then they parted and went their separate ways into the trees. A moose visited the shoreline like a shadow puppet. It sniffed and pawed at the water.

A thick beaver dam held the body of lake-water back, and a round beaver house hulked on the opposite shore. If you squinted in the needled sunset, you could see beaver heads gliding through the stillness of the water – but just as soon as you spotted them, they quietly disappeared, leaving their ripples. The water was a long way down from where I was standing, maybe fifty or sixty feet. I kicked off my Keds, took a breath, and dived.

Simon Petch

The Law, the Western, and Wyatt Earp

Simon Petch teaches literature in the Department of English at the University of Sydney. He was the first president of the Law and Literature Association of Australia. An earlier essay, on Norman Mailer's legal poetics, appeared in HEAT 3.

When the American historian Francis Parkman set out on the Oregon trail in 1846, in anticipation of the physical and moral hardships ahead he 'bade a long adieu to bed and board, and the principles of Blackstone's *Commentaries*'. William Blackstone's *Commentaries on the Laws of England* (1756–69) had formulated the legal principles on which civil society rested in the English-speaking world. Parkman, heading for the frontier, imagines a journey beyond the limits of the legal world.

The American frontier for which Parkman was bound is most familiar to us from the Western film. In the Western, the frontier represents not an absence of law but a zone of heightened conflict between radically different, even opposed conceptions of law: between positive law, or the dictates of civil society, on the one hand, and natural law, a higher but unwritten code of moral authority, on the other. This ideological frontier between positive law and natural law is seminal to the Western, where it is patrolled by figures whose position is defined in relation to law; usually the lawman, and his alter ego the outlaw, or occasionally by someone who conflates both roles.

The legendary frontier marshall Wyatt Earp is just such a compellingly unstable figure. In John Ford's *My Darling Clementine* (1946), Earp, played by Henry Fonda, is a paragon of justice and integrity, but in *Cheyenne Autumn* (1964) Ford revised this agenda, and his later Wyatt Earp, played by James Stewart, is more interested in gambling and women than in law and order. The mode of Ford's Earp films is comic, but in the two Wyatt Earp films made by John Sturges the legend acquires a decidedly tragic tone. In *Gunfight at the OK Corral* (1957) Burt Lancaster plays Wyatt Earp as a conscientious officer of the law, subtly aware that this status, symbolised by his gun and his badge, alienates him from the community he serves. And a decade later, in *Hour of the Gun* (1967), Sturges dug deeper into the legend to find a still more troubled Wyatt Earp, a United States Marshall transformed by vengeance into a compulsive killer. An influential film – the pathological Wyatt Earp it discovers is central to Lawrence Kasdan's *Wyatt Earp* (1994) – *Hour of the Gun* is distinguished from other Earp films by the ways in which its plot brings conflicting conceptions of law into focus. Caught between the laws of nature and those of society, Wyatt Earp here becomes the hero of a revenge tragedy, and also its victim. This essay is concerned with the representation of law in *Hour of the Gun*, and explores what that may tell us about the contemporary political culture of the United States.

The concept of natural law, or natural justice, entered Western jurisprudence from Cicero via Thomas Aquinas. In natural law theory, law is determined by a notion of morality which is based on an idealist view of human nature as fundamentally honourable. Accessible to the individual conscience, natural justice is a profoundly and essentially egalitarian ideal; in Cicero's words, 'We cannot be freed from its obligations by Senate or People, and we need not look outside ourselves for an expounder or interpreter of it.' Positive law, in contrast, is authoritarian, emphasizing law as rule or command, and takes a pragmatic view of human nature as in need of occasional correction. The following definition of law from the Victorian English jurist Fitzjames Stephen is firmly in the positivist tradition: 'Law is a collection of rules, or, more properly, of commands, prescribing the application of certain principles to particular classes of circumstances, with inflexible rigidity and precision.' The key distinctions in comparing natural and positive law are between individual and social morality, between nature and civilisation, and between the idea of justice and the reality of law; natural justice gives moral authority to the individual, whereas society and civilisation are given their authority by positive or civil law.

The potential for conflict between the two conceptions of law is forcefully emphasised by Samuel Johnson, speaking (in 1773) about the prescription of murder in Scottish law, whereby a crime could not be tried after twenty years: 'If the son of the murdered man should kill the murderer who got off merely by prescription, I would help him to make his escape; though, were I upon his jury, I would not acquit him. On the contrary, I would bid him submit to the determination of society, because a man is bound to submit to the inconveniences of it, if he enjoys the good: but the young man, though politically wrong, would not be morally wrong. He would have to say, "Here I am amongst barbarians, who not only refuse to do justice, but encourage the greatest of all crimes. I am therefore in a state of nature; for, so far as there is no law, it is a state of nature: and consequently, upon the eternal and immutable law of justice, which requires that he who sheds man's blood should have his blood shed, I will stab the murderer of my father." '

This case suggests the archetypal revenge plot of the Western, in which natural justice supplies the remedy for the deficiencies of positive law. Such plots are directly based on the constitutional foundations of the United States. The American assertion of unalienable rights in the Declaration of Independence was an assertion of natural rights in response to the British abuse of positive law, and, in rejection of British positivism, the American republic was based on a fusion of natural and civil law. It was the disjunction of positive law and morality (as exemplified in the case described by Johnson) that Thomas Jefferson wished to overcome. Jefferson's political vision was grounded in the writings of European legal philosophers – none of them English – who argued that positive law should be built on natural law. Jefferson was Lincoln's pre-eminent political father, and consequently Jeffersonian axioms of natural law determine the language of Abraham Lincoln's most famous speeches. Lincoln opened his address at Gettysburg in 1863 by referring to the Declaration of Independence: 'Fourscore and seven years ago our fathers brought forth upon this continent a new nation, conceived in Liberty, and dedicated to the proposition that all men are created equal.' And in his Second Inaugural Address in 1865, Lincoln laid to rest the natural injustice of slavery by envisioning a new union of states based on an inclusive notion of natural justice: 'with malice towards none; with charity for all; with firmness in the right, as God gives us to see the right, let us strive on to finish the work we are in; to bind up the nation's wounds…to do all which may achieve and cherish a just and lasting peace among ourselves, and with all nations.' As Jefferson was to Lincoln, so Lincoln was to John F. Kennedy. A century after Lincoln, Kennedy's speechwriters resuscitated a version of Lincoln's political rhetoric that similarly grounded legislative policy in natural justice. In his Inaugural Address, Kennedy based what he called the New Frontier of the 1960s on the pledge that his administration would 'pay any price, bear any burden, meet any hardship, support any friend, oppose any foe to assure the survival and the success of liberty'. This alternative to the rhetoric of Cold War pragmatism that Richard Nixon (Kennedy's opponent in 1960) inherited from Truman and Eisenhower appealed to Americans precisely because it spoke to a political dream life that had been there from the start.

This political idyll of the harmony of natural and positive law is questioned, or even subverted, in some canonical texts of American literature. For example, Melville's *Billy Budd* is a study in the natural injustice produced when moral innocence and legal guilt coincide. Billy, a young sailor aboard an English man-of-war in the late eighteenth century, strikes out at, and unintentionally kills the man who is plotting to destroy him. At Billy's court-martial his commanding officer, Captain Vere, argues that while Billy may have acted from natural justice, he must be held accountable to the letter of the Mutiny Act for the consequences of his action. Vere's appeal to his fellow-officers' uniforms invokes the full power of positive law – 'But do these buttons that we wear attest that our allegiance is to Nature? No, to the King.' – the sovereign power, that is, from which positive law, as represented here by the martial code, derives. Melville's historical fiction replays the legal quarrel of the American colonies with Britain, for *Billy Budd* is a tale told by an American of an incident on an English warship in the war with revolutionary France, and the rich political implications of the Anglo-French war (Billy is press-ganged from a merchantman called *The Rights of Man*) are focused by the narrative on the conflict between natural justice and positive law. This conflict is dramatically manifested in the scene of Billy's execution, where the narrator's description of the dawn is suffused with a transcendent sense of natural justice: 'the vapory fleece hanging low in the East was shot through with a soft glory, as of the fleece of the lamb of God, seen in mystical vision'; and this stark juxtaposition of natural law and positive law charts the division within which Melville's 'inside narrative' is written. This division is also typical of the Western, where characters and stories gather along the fault-line between natural and positive law. The 'frontier justice' that is integral to so many Westerns configures a space in which natural law and positive law are problematically related, where the laws of nature do not sit comfortably with the dictates of civil society, and where a geographical frontier symbolizes an ideological tension between natural law and positive or civil law.

The plot of *Hour of the Gun* is driven by such conflicts, and its characters are riven by such tensions. 'This picture is based on fact. This is the way it happened.' The film disclaims nothing, taking us straight to Tombstone, Arizona on 26 October 1881, and plunging us immediately into the event with which the previous films about Wyatt Earp invariably concluded: the gunfight at the OK corral, in which Morgan, Virgil, and Wyatt Earp, with John Henry ('Doc') Holliday riding shotgun, attempt to disarm Ike Clanton and his gang. In all Wyatt Earp films but this, the gunfight is given extended, loving, and almost balletic treatment. *Hour of the Gun* dispenses with such choreography; the gunplay is merely a prelude to the film's play with the law. The shooting – in which Morgan and Virgil Earp are wounded, and Billy Clanton and Frank and Tom McLowery are killed – is barely done before the legal talking starts. 'I swore to something,' says Holliday (Jason Robards), in response to Wyatt Earp (James Garner) asking if he has been deputised: 'Then wear the badge,' says the Marshall, his stress on the word introducing the issue of legally-constituted authority on which the drama turns. 'Can a County Sheriff arrest a City Marshall?' ponders Sheriff Behan (in the Clanton camp), before Wyatt Earp tells him that he doesn't have jurisdiction in Tombstone, then adding – ominously – that even if he did he couldn't make it stick.

    The plot's dramatic momentum is driven by two trials. First, the Earps and Holliday are prosecuted for the murder of Billy Clanton and the McLowerys. In his defence Wyatt Earp claims that the Clanton gang had made threats of death and violence against himself and his brothers, and that it was their duty as sworn peace officers to disarm those who threatened them. It is a matter of principle: 'I would disarm and arrest General Ulysses S. Grant if he appeared on the streets of Tombstone under those circumstances.' The judge agrees: case dismissed. This verdict provokes an attack on Virgil Earp, running for re-election as City Marshall, that leaves him crippled for life. The sole witness to the attack is a waiter, who is collared by Wyatt Earp when he arrives at the scene of the crime. Unwilling to talk, for obvious reasons, the waiter is threatened by Earp – 'You've got just as much to fear from me as you do from Clanton' – and then agrees to tell him who he saw on the condition that he doesn't have to testify. 'You've got my word', says Wyatt Earp, pledging himself to withhold evidence, and thereby complicating the legal conflict. In such circumstances the city prosecutor in this second trial (for the felonious assault on Virgil Earp) can produce neither evidence nor witnesses against the four accused, for whom alibis are provided by six defence witnesses, all in Clanton's employment and power. Case dismissed.

Now Morgan Earp takes Virgil's place at the ballot, but is killed by the same four men who had attacked Virgil. Federal warrants are issued for the four suspects, Wyatt Earp is appointed a Federal Marshall, and he begins his vendetta with the full authority of the law. At Tucson station, in a charged melée of roaring locomotives, clattering railroad cars, and steam-stained darkness, Earp kills Frank Stilwell (who has been sent by Ike Clanton to Tucson to kill him). The question of whether Earp intended to kill Stilwell is impossible to determine. While Earp is going through the motions of a formal arrest, Stilwell grabs the barrel of his revolver, but by moving close enough to make this possible, Earp may be inviting Stilwell to take just such a chance, and, holding his gun firm, he shoots and kills. A murder warrant is now issued in Tucson for Earp himself, so there are warrants on both sides. Earp is given a posse authorisation, but Pete Spence, a suspect in the murder of Morgan Earp, and now (as runner-up in the election) City Marshall of Tombstone, swears in deputies to constitute what is in effect a legalised Clanton gang. The Tombstone Chamber of Commerce, supporting Earp, raises reward money for the arrest and conviction of the suspects, while the city elders try to invoke a vigilance committee. But Earp will not agree; and, in a graphic display of the mess he is getting himself into, he even supports Spence's disarming of the vigilance committee by drawing an analogy with his brother Virgil's attempt to disarm the Clanton gang at the OK corral. 'You're not defending Spence?' asks a bewildered citizen, to which Earp replies, 'Just the law.'

Such structural parallels map the legal hinterland into which Wyatt Earp now drifts, in pursuit of the men who shot his brothers. All four of these suspects are killed, in circumstances where Earp's intentions cannot be determined, even by slow-motion replay. After Stilwell – the first of the suspects – comes Spence, probably lured into making an unwise grab for a shotgun, but Earp is well positioned to shield himself in a doorway, and he then coolly shoots the man holding an empty gun. After Spence comes Bill Brocius, shot by Earp, from a distance, in semi-darkness, as Holliday is in the process of trying to arrest him: how good, or bad, was the Marshall's aim? When Earp shoots the last of the four suspects, Andrew Warshaw, with his posse looking on, the reward money (which has diminished with each death) has disappeared entirely, and no arrests have been made. Holliday is blunt: 'I watched you keep your word to that waiter back in Tucson. You thought it was your honour that stopped you from making him testify, but it wasn't. You couldn't get a conviction in a federal court, or a lawful one, and you never intended to try. You just didn't want to be cheated out of this. Those aren't warrants you've got there. Those are hunting licences.'

Holliday is the wild card in the Earp legend. Originally from Georgia, Holliday graduated from the Pennsylvania College of Dentistry (hence the 'Doc') before drifting west, where he turned to gambling and to whiskey, where from time to time his path crossed with that of Wyatt Earp, and where he died of tuberculosis at the age of 37. A doomed (because consumptive) alcoholic who was both handy with his gun and careless of his own life, Holliday has plenty of romantic and tragic potential to tempt a script-writer or a director, but the Holliday-Earp friendship was mythologised well before Hollywood got to it. Bat Masterson, who knew both men in Dodge City, said: 'Damon did not more for Pythias than Holliday did for Wyatt Earp.' In *My Darling Clementine* John Ford cleverly focuses the tragic aspects of his story on Holliday (played by Victor Mature), who dies in the shoot-out at the OK corral. The recent Wyatt Earp films have used Holliday as a contrasting figure to Wyatt Earp's 'hero'. The execrable *Tombstone* (1993) is redeemed somewhat by Val Kilmer's baroque Holliday, but the price is that his dramatic presence (he is almost a Southern Hamlet) eclipses Wyatt Earp, played by Kurt Russell; and in *Wyatt Earp* (1994), the truly wooden central character, played by Kevin Costner, is similarly exposed by Dennis Quaid's more interesting Holliday. John Sturges treats Holliday more cautiously by keeping him close to Wyatt Earp. In *Gunfight at the OK Corral* Burt Lancaster, as Wyatt Earp, and Kirk Douglas, as Holliday, are virtually interchangeable figures (I once saw the film billed, at a revival house in Oxford, as an 'All-Tooth Performance'). In *Hour of the Gun* Holliday is almost an honorary brother in the group who face the Clanton gang, but he is closer to Wyatt Earp than his brothers are, for this film – radically – casts him as Wyatt Earp's conscience. His sardonic dialogue points the increasing imbalance between law and morality that characterises Earp's actions, and it is as if the self-professed outlaw, Holliday, tutors the U.S. Marshall, Earp, in the intricacies of the legal culture represented by his badge.

Garner's Earp is a man of few words, but as he becomes more and more compromised his habitual taciturnity deepens into introverted withdrawal, and by the time he shoots Warshaw, Earp is – as Holliday has told him – in difficulty with himself. It is a crisis of self-sovereignty, in which his authority as Federal Marshall has been subverted by his own behaviour, just as his sense of self has become complicated by his institutional identity. His authority comes from Washington, of which Arizona (as a territory rather than a state) is an outpost. The frontier communicates with the capital by telegram, and by transcontinental train; and Tucson, where the transcontinental trains meet the local railroad that shuttles Earp between Tucson and Tombstone, and where his vendetta begins, is the point of intersection and stress in the conflicted network of local and federal law. There is a strong local move to get Wyatt Earp appointed Adjutant-General of the Territory of Arizona, and his indecisiveness about whether or not to accept this appointment concentrates the question of how his authority is constituted, both morally and legally.

In the film's only remotely comic moment, Earp is watching Holliday play cards with the town doctor. Holliday, who is winning, says he's a good enough player not to have to cheat, but that he'd cheat if he had to. Earp smiles at the good-humoured banter, then chips in: 'I don't think the correct word is cheat. The house rules fix the percentage, the regulars know the odds.' The doctor says that he'll stay for another hand, and do a little rule-bending of his own. The analogy between playing the rules and playing the law is loaded with social meaning, for the legal institutions in which the film is absorbed are exclusively positivist. (The badge that figures so significantly in the

Holliday-Earp relationship symbolises the prescriptive social authority that characterises positive law.) But Wyatt Earp needs natural justice, to find closure for the death of one brother, and to remedy the assault on another. This is precisely what the legal system he represents cannot supply, and 'justice', a word scrupulously omitted from the script, is beyond the world of the film. The moving principle of this revenge tragedy is that the legally-determined world in which Wyatt Earp lives and has his being is the source of his self-alienation, and his disintegration symbolises the incompatibility of natural justice with positive law. Ironically, the most legally determinate presence in the film, the arch-spokesman for legal positivism, is Earp's nemesis, the devious and hypocritical Ike Clanton (played by Robert Ryan). 'If this were back East I could make law, the way they do', he says. 'The best I can do here is buy law.' Clanton the businessman is a would-be robber-baron, a manager of crooked lawyers, a manipulator of social systems and a self-proclaimed social Darwinist: 'If we're to corner the railroads and the stockyards and ranges, we're going to have to grow bigger and faster than nature intended.' Earp's alarming affinity with Clanton is symbolised by gloved hands. Early in the film, Clanton is seen putting gloves on and taking them off, but by the time Earp kills Spence, the second of the suspects, he too is wearing gloves. Clanton's cynical exploitation of law is simply the inverted image of Earp's reverence for it.

As Earp and Holliday close on Clanton, Earp tries to come clean with his friend who, it has become clear, is a very ill man. He admits that Holliday was right about the killing of Warshaw, and then adds that he's going to be right about Clanton. Holliday excuses the earlier killing as having been done in anger, but continues: 'You're planning this one without the law. You're throwing away all the years you've lived by the rules.' 'I don't care about the rules any more,' replies Earp, 'I'm not that much of a hypocrite'; to which Holliday responds: 'The whole thing's hypocrisy. The rules they tack on say unless you're wearing that badge or a soldier's uniform you can't kill. But they're the only rules there are, and they're more important to you than you think. Play it that way, Wyatt, or you'll destroy yourself. I know you. You can't live like me.' In response Earp tells Holliday to go back to the hotel and take care of himself. Mutually offering advice that won't be heeded, the men are displacements of each other, and Holliday's physical deterioration is a metonym for the psychological crisis that Earp can't articulate.

Throughout this discussion of hypocrisy and rules, Earp thoughtfully fingers his badge, putting it in his pocket at the end of the conversation. Before shooting Clanton he flips the badge to Holliday, making clear that this one is outside the rules. The logic of the plot requires that Earp kill Clanton, but it's a fairly cursory showdown, only a prelude to the final scene, in the sanatorium in Colorado, where Earp and Holliday part for the last time. Earp reassures Holliday that he is returning to Tombstone to take up the post of U.S. Marshall, then Holliday produces the badge from beneath his blanket, and tosses it back to Earp. This act ratifies his significance as Earp's conscience: it is as if he has held the badge in trust for its true designate. But Earp has lied. 'I'm through with the law', he tells the doctor, outside. The film ends with the men poignantly bonded in mutual betrayal. Holliday is clearly drinking himself to death at the expense of Earp, who is paying the sanatorium bills; and Wyatt Earp, whom Holliday thinks is going back to Tombstone and the law, is also headed for the Big Nowhere. Done with the law, he has no place to go – as he says, 'I don't know where I'll be' – and the film's final shot is of Holliday, drinking and playing cards with one of the orderlies, watching Earp drive into an empty expanse.

'Without women a Western wouldn't work': so said Anthony Mann, director of some great Westerns, including *The Naked Spur* (1953) and *The Man from Laramie* (1955), both starring James Stewart, and *Man of the West* (1958), starring Gary Cooper – all films with pivotal female roles. Most of the Wyatt Earp films get themselves in a tangle over women, either Earp's women, or Holliday's women, or both. *Hour of the Gun* precludes the problem of women by not having any. The only female roles in the film are the subservient ones of nurses or saloon-girls, and the closest the film gets to a marriage is the Earp/Holliday relationship, a legal bond in so far as it is symbolised by the badge. Nevertheless the feminine speaks silently but eloquently, in a single shot of Morgan Earp's widow and child on the platform of a railroad car at Tucson station. This image of widowed anguish – it is almost a still – is an iconic portayal of the victims of the ethical vacuum that is the masculine world of this film. The 'most salient fact about the Western,' according to Jane Tompkins, is 'that it is a narrative of male violence.' This is a truism. It would be more useful to say that, in its exploration of masculine conflict, the Western analyses the institutional dynamics of a masculine world. For the violence here is systemic, the effect or consequence of a dysfunctional legal system. The American legal philosopher Lon Fuller, a true believer in natural law, has said that 'the most we can expect of constitutions and courts is that they save us from the abyss'. Perhaps; but not in this film.

In this most cerebral Western, the representation of the legal culture of the Territory of Arizona in the eighteen-eighties refracts the political culture of the United States in the nineteen-sixties, when the film was made. At his trial for the killings at the OK corral, Holliday foreshadows his later point about the arbitrariness and hypocrisy of the law: 'I killed a lot of men I didn't know between 1861 and 1865, and nobody said anything about it.' In the later sixties the Civil War became a displaced or indirect term for Vietnam. By the time *Hour of the Gun* was released in 1967, Kennedy belonged to the ages, and his New Frontier, like Lyndon Johnson's Great Society, had been shattered by the war in SouthEast Asia. The Democratic administrations of the 1960s committed themselves to legal positivism while they spoke the language of natural law: conscription – like the impressment of Billy Budd – is itself a formidable embodiment of legal positivism, in Fuller's formulation 'a one-way projection of authority, emanating from an authorized source and imposing itself on the citizen'. Significant fissures developed within political discourse in the United States, the first manifestation of which was what became known as the 'credibility gap' – the gap between the casualty figures publicised by the Johnson administration, and those claimed by the Vietcong. The phrase took hold in the press, and came home to roost at the Democratic Convention in Chicago in 1968 – 'the siege of Chicago' – and the subsequent trial of the Chicago Seven. President Nixon privately put his own credibility gap on tape, and publicly gave it his own spin; besieged by Watergate, Nixon revised his version of events on an almost daily basis by getting his press secretary, the hapless Ron Ziegler, to label his previous statements 'inoperative'.

In 1987, long after Nixon, the novelist E.L. Doctorow wrote of the Reagan administration: 'Its lack of reverence for law and contempt for language seem to go hand in hand'. Doctorow was primarily referring to the Reagan administration's refusal to enforce Federal civil rights statutes, but he also had in mind the Iran-Contragate affair, which involved the Reagan administration's contracting out to lawless private hands foreign policies that had been outlawed by Congress. In the terms I have used in this essay, this is to say that in acknowledging the need to free U.S. citizens who, contrary to all the rules and conventions of diplomacy, had been taken prisoner in Iran, the Reagan administration spoke the language of natural justice, while at the same time cynically ignoring or circumventing the dictates of positive law. And, as a contrast to 'an age in which the meanings of words are dissolving, in which the culture of discourse itself seems threatened,' Doctorow recalled the 'community of discourse' of the constitutional convention of 1787 which resulted in the 'sacred text' of the Constitution of the United States. What Doctorow perceived in the Reagan administration was the culmination of a process, in modern political life, that begins in the legal culture which *Hour of the Gun* analyses. Wyatt Earp's pursuit of natural justice puts him beyond the pale of positive law. Trying to hold to the principles of both philosophies of law, he falls between them as they prove politically incompatible; his internal conflict and his subsequent alienation from the law symbolize a fundamental division between law and morality in modern American political life.

John Sturges had a reputation as a good action director, but *Hour of the Gun* isn't an action film. It attracted respectable reviews in 1967, and gets generally favourable mention in film books, but it has emphatically not become a classic as have *My Darling Clementine* and (to a lesser extent) *Gunfight at the OK Corral*. The obvious reasons for this are that it is an unusually abstract Western, that it deals uncertainly with the conventions of its genre, and that none of its competent cast was a box-office drawcard. But it was an integrated production that sacrificed nothing to the star system. Magnificently photographed by Lucien Ballard (the greatest Western cinematographer of the sixties), and with its bleak tone established from the opening sequence by Jerry

Goldsmith's foreboding score, this literary film is held together by a carefully understated script from Edward Anhalt (who had recently adapted Anouilh's *Becket* as the Oscar-winning screenplay for another drama of masculine relationship). Paradoxically, the film was an anachronism, for its explicit socio-political concerns ran against the grain of other late sixties' Westerns. Its reflective sombreness is alien to the self-congratulatory melodrama of *The Wild Bunch* (1969), Sam Peckinpah's brutal elegy for the west (and indeed the Western). And *Hour of the Gun* hardly seems related to the same genre as the spaghetti Western, in which substance is sacrificed to style, and script to music and visual technique. Still, the nameless, amoral, non-verbal character of Sergio Leone's films, the character that made Clint Eastwood a star, later evolved, through Eastwood the director, into the complex portraits of Josey Wales and William Munny. *The Outlaw Josey Wales*, released in the bicentennial year 1976, revisits the American experiment by gathering together a bunch of exiles and outcasts who, at the end of the film, declare their independence from a corrupt and immoral society, and commit themselves to a new, alternative community. And *Unforgiven* (1992) deliberates, primarily in the character of English Bob (Richard Harris), on the comparative worth of English and American systems of sovereignty. In these films Eastwood returned the Western to its great tradition of constitutional commentary. *Hour of the Gun* may not be a neglected masterpiece, but it is a landmark film that kept the Western on track.

Bibliographical Note
Philip French's *Westerns: Aspects of a Movie Genre*, No. 21 in the Cinema One Series (1973; revised edition Secker and Warburg, 1977) is still the best book on the Western. Although its distinction between 'Kennedy' and 'Goldwater' Westerns belongs to an earlier era, French's book is infinitely more informative than Jane Tompkins' *West of Everything: The Inner Life of Westerns* (Oxford University Press, 1992), and significantly more imaginative than Lee Clark Mitchell's *Westerns: Making the Man in Fiction and Film* (University of Chicago Press, 1996). French's book is my source for the apocryphal statement on women in the Western here attributed to Anthony Mann, although Mann is on the record with his theory of the Western as primitive legend, and with fascinating information about the female roles in some of his own films: see the interview by Christopher Wicking

and Barrie Pattison in *Screen*, 10, 4-5 (July/October 1969). (I owe this reference to Philip Horne.)

The gunfight at the OK corral, the tensions between the factions that led to it, and its aftermath, have been exhaustively researched by Paula Mitchell Marks, *And Die in the West: The Story of the OK Corral Gunfight* (1989; University of Oklahoma Press, 1996). I have relied substantially on this book for factual information, and it is my source for all otherwise unattributed quotations. The gunfight is still being debated, and indeed fought, on the internet: see www.wyattearp.net and www.clanton.gang.com.

The sentence from Cicero quoted here is from the *Republic* (Book III). Fitzjames Stephen's definition of law comes from an essay he wrote for the *Cornhill Magazine*, 31(1861). Lon Fuller's statements are here quoted from *Law and Morality* (1964; revised edition, Yale University Press, 1969). A succinct account of natural law theory and its relevance to modern jurisprudence can be found in Julius Stone's *Human Law and Human Justice* (Stanford University Press, 1965).

Johnson's remarks are recorded by Boswell (22 August 1773) in his *Journal of a Tour to the Hebrides*. Parkman's *The Oregon Trail* as quoted here was first published in 1849, and is edited by Bernard Rosenthal for World's Classics (Oxford University Press, 1996). Robert A. Ferguson discusses Jefferson's legally-informed political vision in *Law and Letters in American Culture* (Harvard University Press, 1984). The rhetoric of the Gettysburg Address has been analysed by Garry Wills in *Lincoln at Gettysburg: The Words that Remade America* (Simon and Schuster, 1992); and the language of Lincoln's Second Inaugural Address gets detailed consideration in James Boyd White's *Acts of Hope: Creating Authority in Literature, Law, and Politics* (University of Chicago Press, 1994). E.L. Doctorow's essay 'The People's Text: A Citizen Reads The Constitution' was published in *The Nation*, February 21, 1987.

This essay owes a great deal to my wife, Roslyn Jolly – a soul that has 'toiled, and wrought, and thought with me'.

Alan Wearne
Saturday Girl

        (i)
My game is up!
              For here's yours truly: rooted-flushed,
a dressing gown this side of the nuddy,
opening his door to... Yum Yum's understudy;
who gapes, winces, and seems to be heading crushed.
(Yes Petal, something's afoot, just don't even guess, right?
And I'll offer an explanation, tomorrow, over a nice hot cup of tea
how *This may seem 'unnatural' but it's sure natural to me.*)

        (ii)
But oh the explanations!
             – It's light opera Sweetpea, emphasise the *light*?
– Tears, maybe, but tantrums never become our little flock.
– I'm up-to-date as 1958 (now this one bordered on the cruel)
aren't you?

        (iii)
'That was?' asks Jim
             'A friend in shock,
a kiddo from the chorus, one little maid from school
at the most...'
      Well pardon my malice
but who'd she think she was, Tebaldi? Callas?

Walking The Night Alone

    'Not right,' Mum growled, 'this late your being out…'
but, Queen's Birthday Weekend home, you amble down
Dunne St, at midnight, re-learning nothing's about
in Victoria's Biggest-Hearted Little Town.

    'She's in Melbourne, singing…' and good reception might catch
you on IMT, more regular than guest.

    Thanks to Gra-Gra the planet knows your patch:
'Here's Nola,' he grins, 'our girl from Woop Woop West.'

    'Mum…' you could try, 'I've Jerry…' (but you won't)
and how, if you're both not fighting, he's keen
enough, wanting those kids you don't.

    With life still juggle-poised, shaded all-between,
at twenty four, not quite quite-on-the-shelf,
maybe there's time to make yourself yourself.

ALAN WEARNE

I Go To Rio

If ya got it flaunt it
LIBERACE

    Since everything old is always turning neo: g'day Peter (this is Alan, chum,
songwriter manqué, author of these stanzas)...future Oz icon from Fitzroy through to Freo,
with bodytalk more pirouette than scrum, and freckled with chutzpah, see him, off he prances
(as if born under Samuel Goldwyn's Leo) straight to the daughter of Frank and Ethel Gumm
(the world knows Judy, who remembers Frances?); then playing Antony to her Liza's Cleo
(after you'd been half-courted by the mum) and, finding what a boy might do, took chances
in all that Seventies turning Eighties brio, high kick both legs, twirl round and shake y' bum
with lines of Radio City rockette dancers; or entertaining on your *O sole mio*
in cabaret, bath house, that land of Kingdom Cum, which face it wasn't Tenterfield or Kansas;
only to cop one slow ugly cheerio, like when, in a Carioca slum,
a hit squad advances, and they (as you) need miracles worthy of Padre Pio...
and still it snares with relentless taraa-tarum, and all that's feared is death has the only answers.
Maybe. But, at the Maracana, when I went to Rio, we saw that the players could march to this:
    their banner's differing drum:
PARE DE POR FAVOR MATAR NOSSAS CRIANCAS

On The Road To Gundagai

... heading straight for home
JACK O'HAGEN

After church the drive, the singsong: Dad in tenor mode
winds the Vauxhall down Mount Dandenong Rd.;

lulled, Mum's glad, these patterns still keep:
Janet reading, Carol pulling faces, Margie asleep.

Till, beyond such certainties, each arrives
(stride-, stroll- or stumbling-through their lives)

out of those soul-on-sleeve
days, with what was/ is/ might be something to believe.

So Dad dies, Mum re-marries and shifts,
Janet lectures, Carol designs, Margie drifts.

Oh millstone/ loadstar
(that time of faiths/ a Sunday in the car)

behold your future, its, by extension, splendor:
welcome, ladies to The Age of Gender!

Ever Lovin' Man
(for Alan Wayman)

    Winter Saturday arvos in Bocky South:
tippling Drambuie, listening to un-bet-upon races,
her throat still gagging with traces
of the flu, she coughs them up and wipes her mouth.
    No she isn't younger, but has begun
taking an interest in 'the charts',
itemising each entry to every friend (in fits, starts,
stops and fits again) of her embarrassed son.
    Yes she loathed Scotland, but wants to return. For all that's crass-
cum-tragic must pay out with happiness
one day: life's not even hp, it's lay-by.
    So, when David's out, she tip-toes to his 45s
for 'The Loved One' or 'Sad Dark Eyes'…
och aye, this is the now scene baby.

Saturday Girl: Show-stopper ballad from the 50s musical *Lola Montez*. In this a somewhat camp performer recounts his pursuit by a rather ignorant young lady.
Walking The Night Alone: In the early 60s a young female singer visits her home town in country Victoria. She has been appearing on *In Melbourne Tonight*, a television variety show hosted by Graham 'Gra Gra' Kennedy.
I Go To Rio: The world of Peter Allen, plus a bit more. The Maracana is Rio's famous football stadium. The Portugese – 'Please Stop Murdering Our Children'.
On The Road To Gundagai: A family saga, the late 50s to the present day.
Ever Lovin' Man: A Scots migrant tries to cope with life in 60s suburbia.

The first volume of Alan Wearne's verse novel *The Lovemakers* was published by Penguin in 2001. These poems are from a new collection *The Australian Popular Songbook*.

Abbas El-Zein

Quest for an Indian King

from *Dislocating Dreams*

Abbas El-Zein's first novel, *Tell The Running Water*, whis is set during the Lebanese civil war, was published by Sceptre in 2001.

One of the more exotic stories – half truth, half legend – in currency among my extended family and the El-Zein clan, relates the adventure in India of one of our ancestors around the end of the eighteenth century. Ali El-Zein was among those who had marched from the Shi'a village of Sh'hoor, east of the city of Tyre, in the south of what would later become the republic of Lebanon, onto the castle of Tibnine, less than twenty kilometres away, defeating its Ottoman garrison of two hundred men and killing the *mutassalim*, the representative of the Ottoman governor Ahmad Pasha Al Jazzar also known as the Butcher. A few years later, Al Jazzar, with the help of the English fleet, was to halt the advance of Napoleon Bonaparte at Acre, as the French armies moved north from Alexandria into Palestine, overrunning Ottoman defences. The Ottomans, we had been taught at school, were a dynasty of Turkic people who had inherited the vast Muslim empire back in the fifteenth century, reuniting it, expanding it with new acquisitions in Eastern and Central Europe, moving its capital to Istanbul and aligning themselves with its Sunni Muslim orthodoxy. They consolidated the power shift within the empire from the Arabs of Damascus, Baghdad and Cairo in the south, to the Turks of Anatolia in the north, a shift which had already started by the thirteenth and fourteenth centuries when the Turkish Mameluks finally evicted the Crusaders from their fortified towns on the Eastern Mediterranean.

The rebels of Sh'hoor, including my ancestor, were minority Shi'a Arabs and had undoubtedly many reasons to dislike the imperial Sunni Turks. They were angry at the slaying by the Ottomans of their feudal overlord, Nasseef Annassar, in what is likely to have been an episode of violent local politics rather than religious, ethnic or ideological tension. Istanbul, long satisfied with decentralised government of the empire's outlying territories, with their colourful mosaic of religious and ethnic minorities, was now attempting more direct rule, and facing fierce local resistance. It had finally managed to overthrow the dangerously powerful leader, Thaher Al Umar, based in Acre, and had installed Al Jazzar, as a strong, ambitious and more accountable governor. Al Jazzar was attempting to secure the loyalty of the local population. He put down local resistance with an iron fist, and levied more taxes. The power of the *Ulama*, or religious leaders, was severely curtailed and, according to some history books, their manuscripts burned as fuel in the bakeries of Acre. The nineteenth-century bid by the Ottomans to re-structure local government occurred largely in reaction to their growing awareness of British, French and Austrian military superiority, as well as economic and demographic changes in the region. It would become a defining element of the politics of the Levant, the Balkans, North Africa and the Arabian Gulf, right through to the First World War.

Al Jazzar sent an expedition to avenge the fall of the castle of Tibnine and punish the rebels that my ancestor had joined. His troops sacked the village of Sh'hoor and impaled at least one of the rebel leaders, Sheikh Hamze. The El-Zeins were a clan of *Woujahaa*: they possessed some wealth and power and acted as intermediaries between the far more powerful feudal leaders on the one hand, and the peasantry on the other. Ali El-Zein, who had been in the service of his slain overlord Nasseef Annassar, ran for his life with Annassar's sons, first to Damascus, whose governor was a rival of Al Jazzar then, when Damascus proved unsafe, to Iraq. From there he found his way to the Indian subcontinent. In India, he was received and honoured by a king and became his minister. He re-married, and fathered a few children before returning to his home village some years later. His return, according to one version of the story, was hastened by the rise of British power in India. It is also rumoured that one of his Indian descendants came to Lebanon as recently as the 1970s, looking for his roots and his fellow El-Zeins. The story, as told by my father and relatives, carries an unmistakable trace of pride at this intrepid ancestor of ours, fighting and outsmarting empires, travelling through Muslim lands and spreading the El-Zein genes as far away as India!

What I found fascinating about this story, I now realise, is its fairy-tale quality, combined with its seeming authenticity. It was a fable which had *really* happened. Even when I sought it in books rather than family hearsay – there are brief mentions of it in historical records relating the Tibnine battle – it did not lose its 'magic realism'. To get to India from the Eastern coast of the Mediterranean, one must cross nearly half the Asian continent, including today's Syria, Iraq, Iran and Afghanistan. Huge distances and years of travel, hardship and adventure are delivered in a few sweet story lines, like condensed milk at the breakfast table, the product of a mysterious process of concentration.

But the fairy-tale quality, like the sweetness of condensed milk, was also what made the story suspect. The further east my ancestor went, the less tangible the events felt to the listener, the less real they seemed. How long did he stay in Damascus and how long did it take him to get to India? Where did he stop on the way? What kind of Indian king gave him refuge? Where was he in India? The ratio of words to duration declined considerably, the story starting with a specific battle which must have lasted a few hours or a few days, and ending with years of exile and finally return.

My ancestor had been, at once, a soldier, an adventurer, a politician, a womaniser and a happy refugee. His adventures took him to exotic lands. Gracious hosts gave him welcome. His needs, including his sexual needs, were attended to. And when the threat that made him into an exile expired and the threat of another tyranny loomed in India, he returned to his family and reunited with his wife, whose faithfulness was so unquestionable, it did not even get a mention in the story. Ulysses must have moved in his grave!

Whichever way I looked at my ancestor's story, I could find bold deeds and fascinating events. The fact that we were related by blood made him more valuable to me since, as a teenager, in my more self-indulgent daydreams, I would bask in his glory and claim as mine some of his heroic qualities. When I looked at my relatives, with their rivalries and petty quarrels, I could see that very few, if any, of these qualities had survived. But this did nothing to diminish my ancestor in my eyes, or make me less willing to identify with him. After all, heroes are like rare stones: their scarcity does not make them any less precious or real.

Almost 200 years after Ali El-Zein's adventures, his Lebanese descendants were to know less happy experiences of exodus. During the civil war, from 1975 to 1990, many families had to move from one place to another, one city to another, as the war ebbed and flowed. The war, like a mad fairy, kept shifting location and changing in intensity; there were times when it even appeared to have expired, only to re-erupt a year or two later. Although we were far less adventurous than our ancestor, the dangers we were fleeing were no less real. To be burnt or torn to pieces by a shell or a missile was no more pleasant a prospect than to be impaled on a pointed stake.

In 1982 – I was nineteen years old – the Israeli army invaded Lebanon, in an attempt to crush Palestinian guerrillas, adding its own distinctly superior contribution to the civil-war violence, with bombardments by land, sea and air. West Beirut was about to be besieged by the advancing Israelis and their Christian-militia allies. As the bombing intensified, my family moved to the small house of my eldest brother, who lived in a relatively safe area of West Beirut. Then, a week or so later, with the prospect of a long and painful siege looming, my father decided to take the family out of the city. On the appointed day we drove out of West Beirut through winding sand fortifications, into Christian East Beirut. We were made to wait for a few hours at a road block and our identification cards were temporarily confiscated. After some hesitation about the best place to seek refuge, and a brief stay in a small hotel near Tripoli in the north, we headed south again, and ended up in Brummana, a predominantly

Christian Maronite town in the mountains, forty five minutes to the east of the city. We had joined scores of middle-class refugees who could afford to pay guest-house rents.

Our means of transport were faster than our ancestor's horse, the car seats more comfortable than his saddle and, once we were free of the clutches of militiamen, the ride altogether smoother. But, although we headed east just like him, we could not travel far, and our range of destinations was limited. Leaving the country, conceivably to Damascus, was out of the question because it would entail crossing the Bekaa valley which, were the Israelis and the Syrians to confront each other, could have become a battleground. Besides, crossing the Lebanese-Syrian border was an enterprise laden with bureaucracy, never an experience to look forward to. Cyprus was too expensive and foreign a destination. We spoke neither Greek nor Turkish and had never been a sea-faring family. The best option by far was Brummana, merely fifteen or twenty kilometres from Beirut.

A summer resort that had been protected from development by its single-minded municipal council and wealthy locals, Brummana was both idyllic and lively. Its red-tiled houses, its sandstone churches and schools and its leafy town centre happily co-existed with vibrant cafés and nightclubs, crowded restaurants and stylish shops. Its population always became swollen, between June and September, by Beirutis escaping the summer heat. In 1982, Beirut's heat combined with war, and there were many more people around than usual.

Every day, from late afternoon onwards, the old and the young, women and men, took a stroll through the town centre, moving between restaurants, take-away shops, ice-cream vendors and hotel bars. Young men with sunglasses and wooden crosses hanging over their half-buttoned shirts and curly chest hair proudly drove their sports cars through town, and parked them off the road before strutting into a café or a club. The more glamorous men and women – by virtue of beauty, wealth, blood or class – kept the rumour circuit alive.

With my medical eyeglasses and my shy disposition, I stood no chance with the girls. Even though I had managed to drive my motorcycle out of West Beirut – the nearest equivalent to my forebear's charger I could boast – I could not compete with the more impressive motor-vehicles on display. Besides, it wasn't long before I had an accident which, not only immobilised my motorcycle, but gave me a cut eyebrow, putting me in bed for a couple of days and landing me, once again, in my mother's caring hands, an undignified experience for a nineteen-year-old who was keen on his manhood, and rather insecure about it.

Friends came to visit, to console and chatter away. We lived in a single spacious room, all five of us, my father and mother, my younger brother, my older sister and myself. Sometimes we played cards. Sometimes we argued and quarrelled. We were safe, bored and despondent. It was a deadening form of safety, twice removed from life, the safety of a hospital bed in the midst of an epidemic. Beirut was being pounded with explosives. People were dying by the thousands. We had become impotent spectators, and had no idea what we would find when we got back to Beirut, if we ever did.

The room where we stayed overlooked a major road. Confined to bed with a mild fever, I listened to the passing cars, the way would-be-travellers in sentimental novels watched ships come and go. Occasionally, a pastoral silence erupted, as if Brummana had secretly kept, from times past, a residue of rural bliss with which it indulged itself every now and then. But the silence never lasted more than a few moments and the traffic returned. In any case, I found silence depressing, especially in the afternoon, because it brought me face to face with my unhappiness. Noise distracted and kept introversion at bay.

The upbeat, sometimes jubilant atmosphere of Brummana — as the new *pax-Israeliana* started to take shape, promising Christians total victory in the civil war — was not something the refugees could step into. We were outsiders, largely unable to take part in the social life of the trendier part of town. We could only watch and pray that things did not take a turn for the worse. Nor would we admit that we were refugees — the word was somewhat pejorative and had come to designate exclusively those Palestinians who had arrived in Lebanon in 1948 and 1967 and were living in squalid camps in all the major cities.

At the guesthouse there were other families from West Beirut, mostly Muslim middle-class, middle-aged men and women, who suddenly (and conveniently) discovered how uncomfortable they had been with the radicalism of West Beirut and how much they had in common with their more politically-conservative Maronite brethren. We knew that it would be the end of the war – how wrong we were! – but we also knew that the new order was not very good for our creed.

Brummana had stunning views of the city and, from the right spots, Beirut could be seen, sprawled and shimmering, like a giant, irregularly patterned carpet. Many vantage points in the town, including the far end of the guesthouse's leafy terrace, promised our tiny irises vast landscapes. But our anticipation would often turn into disappointment as we found the city hiding under clouds of smog. If the mountain's mist did not block the view, the heat haze hanging over Beirut itself did the job...

But we could clearly hear the explosions. The creatures of war, like jungle creatures, had to rely on their ears more than their eyes. But we, creatures of war, also lost our mobility, and found ourselves stranded in one place or another. My eldest brother and sister had stayed behind in the besieged city and we worried about them. At night, we imagined the worst happening to them. Just like the nights in shelters, when the civil war first started seven years earlier, we couldn't see the violence but we could hear the explosions. The shelter offered safety, but at the cost of a strict sensory economy – hearing and no vision. This economy would play a major role in the life of my characters in *Tell the Running Water*, including the sniper who would command great cityscapes but would receive precious little sound, and the frontline fighter who would empty a magazine of bullets blindly, because the enemy would always be concealed by fortifications.

How different it was from my ancestor's adventures! Whenever I tried to imagine him fleeing Al Jazzar, I saw vast stretches of land, blue skies as infinite as oceans, open spaces which honoured his eyesight and never deprived him of clear vision. No wonder he reached India. As he rode east across the plains, through the rolling hills and mountain passes, he could probably picture India, months before he reached it. His galloping horse would have thumped the ground, sending wave after wave of echoes, which travelled ahead like perfect scouts and brought him back a flavour of the valleys lying beyond. There was no sensory economy at play there. Agency and abundant experience sent the world, in all its manifestations, coursing through my ancestor's mind, and bestowed upon him a rich vision. He was unlikely to find himself confined to bed. He was not made for shelters and idle talk in guesthouses. He did not listen to other people's stories and adventures – adventure was where *he* happened to be. The difference between my ancestor and myself, I decided as I turned in my bed and caught the smell of my own sweat, was that he knew where he was going. He could see ahead and I could not.

Brummana proved too expensive for us in the long run and, a few weeks later, my father decided to go south, to the village of Jibsheet where we could stay at my grandfather's house indefinitely. The South was by then fully occupied by the Israelis, the battle had come to a standstill around Beirut, and negotiations were under way to organise the withdrawal of Palestinian guerrillas from Beirut to Tunis in exchange for the lifting of the siege.

The trip was daunting. The coastline immediately to the south of Beirut was still an erratic battleground that had to be avoided. The only safe route south from Brummana ran through narrow mountain roads, roughly parallel to the coastline. On the way, we came across Israeli military personnel and armoured vehicles, seeing for the first time the enemy whose aeroplanes had dropped bombs on Lebanon and broken the sound barrier over its cities, so often and for so many years, we had almost ceased to believe Israel was anything but a colony of brilliant machinery put in place by unscrupulous American politicians. We had seen some Israeli soldiers in Brummana, but here on the road there were hundreds of them in full gear – tanks, armoured vehicles, trucks and jeeps. They appeared to be more vulnerable than we had pictured them and, perversely, there was something comforting about seeing them there, on the ground, rather than in the skies. Some had European complexions, others were dark-skinned and could have been from the Palestinian side, judging by their appearance. Also on the road were members of the South Lebanese Army (SLA) – a Christian militia set up by the Israelis after they first invaded in 1978, distinguishable from the Jewish soldiers by their darker khaki uniforms.

We crossed the Shouf mountains over potholed roads, snaking

through subdued villages, empty squares, encroached-upon pine forests, and unhealthy trees. Once we reached a point some twenty kilometres south of Beirut, far enough from the battleground, we headed west. My father drove slowly down a wider and steeper road towards the coast. And when, from behind a thicket, the Mediterranean finally emerged – deserted by boats and bathers, languid under the midday sun – its colour was the pale whiteness of a hypochondriac teenager.

Some thirty or forty metres before we reached the coastal road, the car started gathering speed dangerously. 'The brakes are gone!' exclaimed my father with frightening alarm.

Our Mercedes was now careering towards the T-junction and the SLA roadblock occupying it. At the last moment, my father managed to control the car and stop it, but not before it screeched and turned, right next to the road block, and certainly not before everyone in the car, all five of us, had anticipated that gunfire would put us out of our misery. These were the days before suicide bombing, which came two years later, making Israeli and SLA soldiers far more nervous. But even then, out-of-control cars rushing towards road blocks were not seen kindly by gun-toting men fighting a war.

A gunman wearing sunglasses stared at my father through the window then asked him to explain what was going on. Although gunfire did not materialise, we still expected some rough interrogation, and maybe even worse. After all, we were Muslims in what had now become Christian and Jewish enemy territory. My father was still recovering from the shock and needed a few moments before he could utter a word. But my mother was quick to tell the gunman about the softened brakes, in a slightly entreating tone, which her children, sitting in the back seat, secretly resented. The gunman did not acknowledge my mother, addressing my father again despite his silence. He checked our IDs, then asked my father to open the glove compartment and the car boot, and once he was satisfied that we were as harmless as we looked, he told my father to go back.

The Mediterranean, behind the gunman's shoulder, now appeared to be a tiny, distant version of itself, like an anonymous town on a map – the idea of a place rather than the place itself. No galloping horse or racing boat was likely to stir it out of its stillness or sound its depths. My father turned the ignition on and made a U-turn. Even if there was a point in arguing, at that stage, no one in the car had the strength to do so.

After hours of travel, we had, almost literally, driven into a wall. Why hadn't we anticipated all this? Why did we think that we would be allowed through the road blocks and the military convoys and the supply lines of the triumphant Israeli army? We had to blind ourselves to the reality around us, otherwise we would never have moved anywhere. Perhaps blindness, not vision, was the condition of escape and adventure. Perhaps if we knew where we would end up, we would never have left in the first place. Who knows, Ali El-Zein may have been planning an escape to the Hijaaz, or Istanbul or even Algiers, and might have ended up in India by chance. Did he outsmart empires or did he move within the limits set out by them? What kind of a hero would that make him? Although I would not easily admit it to myself, I suspected, even then, that the 'magic reality' of my ancestor's story might well turn into a dull illusion if I examined it too closely.

My father drove back and, on the way, decided to head for Beirut. There was an open passage between East and West Beirut and things had been very quiet in the preceding few days. We crossed into West Beirut and, although we were returning to a beleaguered city, we felt a great relief at re-entering familiar territory. The hundred metres of road which made up the crossing – between the National Museum on the east side of the city to the race-course on the other side – were full of sandbag walls and debris. The quietness was amazing given that fierce battles had taken place there only a couple of weeks earlier. Despite the destruction and hardship, there was a sense of relief in the city that the ordeal was over.

The hostility of strangers, I had just learned, could be as frightening as random shelling, air-to-ground missiles and the sniper's bullets. We had not travelled very far, had not been to exotic places but, at least, we were safe, and back where we belonged.

Things were to turn sour again. A month or two later, the newly-elected pro-Israeli Christian president was to be murdered by a bomb;

Israeli tanks were to cross into West Beirut despite the agreement which had seen Palestinians leave the city a few weeks earlier – apparently, Ariel Sharon could not resist the temptation of occupying an Arab capital-city, if only for a few days – and Palestinian civilians were to be massacred at Sabraa and Shaateela; Israeli soldiers were to be shot point-blank on the streets of West Beirut; the French and US soldiers from the multi-national force were to be blown up in suicide attacks which left huge smoke clouds mushrooming over the city. The new regime set up by the Israelis and the Americans would collapse two years later; seventeen thousand, Lebanese and Palestinian, civilians – a full half per cent of the total population – would be killed during the Israeli invasion...

Four years later, in 1986, I flew out of the country on my way to London to continue my studies. But sitting in my narrow, economy-class seat, not only could I not see the way ahead, my vision was hopelessly blocked by the seat in front of me. I was immobilised for five hours. The most basic of my eating, drinking and bladder needs had to be managed and timed, down to the minute. The distance I was crossing this time was respectable by my ancestor's standards. But had he been able to see me and overcome his amazement at the flying object, he might have sneered at this cattle-like mode of transport.

On that same day, my first day in England, by a strange turn of events, a policeman knocked on the door of my bed-and-breakfast room in Southampton at about midnight, just after I had slipped into bed. He addressed me with 'Sir', and asked to search my luggage because of 'all those terrorists coming from your country'. The bed-and-breakfast owners, a middle-aged married couple, had become suspicious when, on arrival, I had asked them for a nail or any pointed object I could use to force the lock of my suitcase, because I had lost the key on the way from Beirut. When we failed to open it, the owners suggested that we break the lock. But I decided, impatient as I was to go to bed, against anything of the sort before the next day. I was still hoping that, with a fresher mind, I might find the key in the morning. After I went into my room, the owners called the police.

As rude awakenings go, it wasn't so bad. I hadn't yet gone to sleep and, although I had read a magazine article on Omar Sharif and

Sophia Loren on the coach from Heathrow to Southampton, I knew that Arab men were not quite as popular as Italian women – even if I didn't expect the chemistry to work so fast. Besides, the bed-and-breakfast owners had been kind and hospitable. They had offered to pick me up at the Southampton coach station on Bedford Place, from where I called them on arrival, well after dark, even though they had no advance warning of my arrival and did not know me.

I was keen to explore the city I was visiting for the first time. As I walked through Bedford Place the next day, and saw the Indian and Chinese restaurants, the fish-and-chip shop, and the Turkish take-away, I must have been entertaining dreams of exotic travel and hospitality, not to mention wealth, success, gene-spreading and a glorious return. I was 23-years-old, after all, in Europe, about to do my Master's degree at University. There was a new white page in my life waiting to be filled, and the world was full of possibilities.

But I was further disenchanted a few days later, when I went to the police station to register as an alien, a word I had only come across in science-fiction movies – a point made by many migrants to the United Kingdom and the United States, I have since discovered. This had nothing to do with the bed-and-breakfast episode; I had been told by the immigration official at Heathrow that I was required by law to register with the nearest police station. Although back in Beirut, unacquainted as I was with bureaucratic English lingo, I had found the British word for a visa, 'leave to remain', a little obtuse – why not 'permission to stay' or just 'visa'? – I had failed to notice the reluctance subtly evoked by the words 'leave' and 'remain'. At Heathrow and, later at the bed-and-breakfast and the police station, I realised that, if I had counted on a refreshing anonymity in my new place of abode, on being a complete stranger, on some kind of new start, I was wrong. I hadn't become anonymous; I had been given a new, ready-made identity, a mass-produced garment which sticks to the skin. It wasn't so much anonimity as a stereotype; blind substitution rather than white page. As my aeroplane entered British airspace and thundered through the London sky, the nationality of my passport had billowed out and, like a mild but chronic illness, had colonised a small corner of my life.

Did Ali El-Zein carry a travel document? I am not sure. Nor do I expect that this detail would have survived, down the ages, the tale-making mill of my extended family. In fact, there was a detail in my ancestor's story which was sometimes mentioned but not dwelled upon by my relatives. Ali El-Zein was the treasurer of his overlord Nasseef Annassar, and may have ended up with a significant portion of his dead master's fortune as well as the bounty taken from the castle of Tibnine, or part of it, including taxes collected by the Ottomans. True or not, I like this detail. It injects a subversive element into the story. It could explain the open arms of the Indian king. It would certainly make my ancestor even harder to classify. Knight? Minister? Adventurer? Thief? Fugitive? Refugee? Or, real as he was, a figment of his descendants' imagination, the lands he had travelled, as infinite as their fancies?

What was missing from my ancestor's story were borders, highwaymen, distance, the duration of time, the economics of hospitality, red tape, travel documents, and the intriguing art of obstruction that is the road-block, the checkpoint and the immigration official sitting leisurely behind a computer screen.

I would hate to see my ancestor pandering to border guards, suppressing his pride and home-grown authority in foreign lands, concealing the source of his fortune from prying eyes, or getting stranded in a dull town because he or his horse has fallen ill. Yet the absence of these events puts him above other mortals. So I keep the possibility in mind. It brings him down to earth and allows me to entertain the thought that, although I went west while he headed east, although he travelled on horseback while I boarded a giant plane, perhaps we lived in the same emotional world after all. It is a little trick, a secret pact that I have with him. If we could see each other today, I like to think that he might see through my self-deception, might even nod or wink, in appreciation. After all, I have seen through his *own* deception – all those well-concealed imperfections – without losing my affection for him.

Jill Jones
A conjunction of bone photos

1. A sentence
'Please only open one drawer at a time
or the whole thing might collapse.'

But the surgery looks secure
though I can't address the ground.
Something grabbed my ankle
choking tendons and blood
and the sentence, formerly hidden,
is writ visible, risen through layers
from bone nudging nerves.
It says: the ground has fallen away
a long time ago.

The young doctor has a Christ
postered on the wall:
I am, I am, I am the way.
And you wonder what I am?
And where the ground went.
He wants me to make friends
with radiation.

My foot is placed
at various longitudes, latitudes
not freedom to move.
At each placement the tiny god
in the machine blinks

and some mystery in me is revealed:
I have a leg to stand on.
I am a machine of bone and flex.
Once or twice it seems
waiting for the bone photos
I am in pain but that disappears
into carpet, lost in public necessities.

The doctor reads me, his pen
follows a line across my instep
to my ankle. The sentence
is a good one, with mitigation.
No asprin, it thins the blood
I must be thickly grounded.
But it's also a dialogue –
I must elevate. This push-pull
ballet of cures
here underneath Dr Jesus.
I accept it like a lamb.
I am a way out of here.

2. A plate
Second surgery is labyrinth
astringent alcohol breath
dark paper gowns, the many rooms
where flesh becomes transparent,
an intimate kind of meat.

I am being made ready,
a plate must be got

on a second's outbreath,
perfect snaps, maps of my expeditions
conjunctions. maladjustments.
It's the core this time,
the spine's steps of bone
its mats of muscle, their tenderness
my pattern for this time.

I have to trust the machine
its straight steel limbs, electric veins
its gurgling inner works
and its flat square eye.

I will peer at the window
of it, search the contrast of it,
wonder at all that final stillness
the round hip joint, the slightly
left-leaning spine.
It is forced and arranged,
and strangely beautiful.
And it never stops the ache
or gags the years.

Jill Jones' third collection of poetry, *The Book of Possibilities*, was shortlisted for the 1997 National Book Council Awards, the 1997 *Age* Poetry Book of the Year and the 1998 Adelaide Festival Awards.

Barbara Brooks

Lil's Story

from *Verandahs*

Barbara Brooks is the author (with Judith Clark) of *Eleanor Dark: A Writer's Life* (Macmillan, 1998).

Remembering Lil

I asked my father about Lil, when I came back to Australia. When I came back from the grey city, from the city of ghostly marriages, after I left George. I asked my father about Lil because I remembered the stories he told us, and her poems that he read to us when we were kids.

I remember the valley full of German farmers who planted their crops by the moon, and Irish farmers who sent their kids into town to the convent. The kids sang songs about Catholics and Protestants, *Red white and blue, the Irish cockatoo...*

I remember the little wooden house with the red iron roof and the closed in verandah where Lil lived; now she was dead another cousin lived there and the garden was overgrown. It was on the road out of Moorollala, on the way to Gang Gang Creek where my father grew up on the old farm.

I remember that road. I remember that valley. The farms along the creek flats, the little wooden schoolhouse, the dingoes howling in the hills at night, the scrub turkeys rustling in the undergrowth, the deserted houses in the valleys. Concerts in the local hall, people singing and dancing and playing the accordion, huge enamel teapots and cakes on top of the long trestle tables and the bodies of sleeping kids underneath. I remember the farmhouse where my father grew up, at the end of the long dirt track that crossed the creek and climbed the hill, a wooden house almost invisible behind pepperinas and Moreton Bay figs. The turkeys roosted in the branches of the Pepperinas, and the dogs slept in the shade of the figs. What was it like inside the house? I remember lighting the kerosene lamps at night, and watching the spirits dance on the wall behind them. If you stood outside and looked in, the light was warm and yellow at the windows.

Women hiding inside houses

My father's widowed aunts lived in small country towns, in streets lined with dusty pepperinas and silky oaks and bunya pines. They grew old in grey wooden houses on stilts with the curtains drawn. I knew them all by name but now they blur together: Auntie Annie and Ruby and Gert, Ada and Elsie and Tilly, Milly, Mary and Dolly. Except Lil. Lil was out on her own. There were eighteen great aunts, but some had died and some lived too far away. They came from a German family who were farmers in the valleys east of the Great Dividing Range. They bought land near the mineral springs. These men and women were farmers, midwives, water diviners, teachers, storytellers, council labourers, factory workers, clerks, dreamers, and mystics. They worked hard, had a lot of children, planted by the moon, and almost lost their other language. They were survivors.

When I was a child, we lived in my grandfather's house, the house where Lil had brought my father up. Lil had died by then, but we visited the other aunts on Sundays. Climbing the splintery grey wooden steps to the front verandah, we hesitated at the front door and my father called out to them.

Anyone home? Elsie? Annie? Put the kettle on.

The words flowed down the hallway. Sun streamed through the coloured panes above the wooden front doors. Auntie Elsie or Auntie Annie came to the door in their floral housedresses, wiping their hands on their apron, smiling.

Vince and Frances, they said. *And your little girl.*

They were chunky women, short, blue-eyed and grey- or mousy-haired, with broad faces and capable workers' hands. They talked slowly and moved quickly, and faded back into the shadows. We followed them into the house. At first we were engulfed in a dark stillness at the heart of the house. It smelled of dead flowers and floor polish, camphor and old blankets. The kitchen smelled of cakes in the oven, and wood-smoke, and the bedrooms smelled of face powder and feathers. Everything stood still in these houses in the hot summer afternoons; everything was a long way away, like the photos behind glass of old weddings, dead uncles, children grown up and moved away, like the beds veiled with mosquito nets, like the conversations we children did not understand. Even the milk jugs were covered with tiny beaded nets.

I'll put the kettle on, they said. *We'll have tea and fruit cake. It's just come out of the oven.*

We sat in the kitchen while the adults talked and the kettle sang on the old wood stove in the galvanised iron stove recess, and the cut paper hanging over the front of the mantelpiece curled in the heat and turned brown with age, and flies settled slowly in the dangling fly papers. We held our breath in the middle of the house, noses full of dust, mouths full of marble cake. Tea poured out of the pot in a slow arc.

I dozed through the hot afternoons on lumpy mattresses on the back verandah, reading comics and magazines: the *Phantom, Pix* and *People, Man.* The adults talked in the kitchen, at the lino-covered table.

Pat says Percy's leg's playing up again...

That's not all that's playing up. I told her...

...kidney packed it in...too many Bex powders.

...those goats got out and into the yard and ate the legs off Ted's trousers on her washing line.

...I told Mavis the best thing to do with those goats was eat them...

They told family stories, talked family politics, who had fought with and stopped talking to whom, whose baby was born, whose husband had died; they talked about mysterious complaints and illnesses that took people suddenly and their insides were twisted and their colour changed and they faded away. The cats prowled in and out of the kitchen, and the tea-leaves flew over the verandah rail, and the dogs slept under the house in the shade. Nothing moved in those childhood afternoons. We floated in hot yellow sunlight, slow and sticky like honey.

My head was full of stories. The gossip of women in kitchens as they boil up soup out of bones and barley, as they endlessly stoke the stoves, and call the kids home before dark. The hand testing the stove, the arm holding the baby, the hip pushing at the door, the foot gently moving the cat. The axe striking ironbark in the woodpile, stroke after stroke, early in the morning.

Frost on the grass and fogs in the valleys, in a white and brittle winter light. The stories carried on breath light as ash.

Their history comes down through their bodies, past deaths, quarrels and reconciliations, years of not speaking much, a history of love and survival, of tears and jokes and secrets they shared. With each other but not with me.

Lil's story

My great aunt Lily grew up at Limestone but married a German miner from another part of the district. She was only eighteen, a girl who could play the piano accordion and sing, ride a horse around the rough hill country, and help deliver a calf from a pregnant cow. He was ten years older than her, a sleek dark-haired man with good manners who sang German songs to her. His name was Heinrich Froezt, and he told her his father had been a count whose family had been dispossessed. He had a suitcase full of music and letters on embossed paper.

Bloody count, my father grumbled. *He was out for the bloody count, if you ask me.*

Lil and Henry lived in the miners' camp at first; in one of six tin huts on the riverbank, with one tank and one cold tap for twelve adults and seven kids. Then they bought a house, two rooms and a lean-to, lined with newspapers and floored with wood and flattened kerosene tins. This was in 1921, in Queensland, in a coalmining town full of Welshmen who sang in choirs, voices harmonising, floating in the smoky evenings. *Men of Harlech ... march to glory ...* Lil planted a white rose by her door.

Henry hated the mines. Hard work, dangerous work, dull work. What else could he do? He didn't fit. He wanted to sing German poems, not Welsh hymns. Doubled up in the dark, deep underground, every day, his spirit cramped and withered and something stuck in his gullet. He started to go to the races every Saturday and always lost money. Lil told him he had to stop, but it was colour and life and movement and everything else was shadow; so he started going during the week, and he lost his job. Everyone knew about it except her. He still left the house every day at the same time. She found out from one of the miner's wives. *How did Henry get on at the races today?* the woman asked her one night. They were buttering scones for a concert at the hall. She knew as soon as she saw Lil's face she'd said the wrong thing.

I'd better go and see to the kids, she said, wiping her hands on her apron, and disappearing.

Lil walked home and sat on the verandah in the dark, with a pain in her chest, listening to the old miners coughing in the houses up the street, and someone playing a piano in the dark.

She didn't say a word when he came back that night, she lay in the bed as quiet and still as if she was asleep, but next morning she steeled herself. *Get out of my house*, she said. He packed his bag and took his hat and walked down the street. The dog followed him till Lil called it back. The winter mist was still rising from the hills like steam, and somewhere in the distance a church bell was ringing.

But it was too late. The bank manager turned up on the doorstep two weeks later.

You'd better come in, she said.

He was a stout man in a felt hat with a red face, awkward in her kitchen. She started to make a pot of tea.

Your husband mortgaged the house again, Mrs Froezt, he said.

She burned her arm in the kettle steam. The house she had made sure was paid off, out of his wages, every week. He had borrowed money against it, without her knowing, and lost it.

He was a bad lot, the great-aunts used to say. *A foreigner. A Kraut. Poor Lil, he done her down. Money burned a hole in his pocket. Followed the gee-gees. A kangaroo loose in the top paddock, they said later, with knowing smiles. Not the full packet of biscuits. A sandwich short of a picnic, a few bricks short of the full load.*

Lil sat on the verandah in the dark, every night, worrying. The women in the street leant over back fences and talked. Some of them came and brought cakes and jars of jam and asked could they help.

God helps those that help themselves, Lil said.

She sat and worried. But only for a week. Then she sold the house, paid back the bank, packed up and went bush with Norman, Elsie's husband, when he and his crew went out west droving cattle.

Lil was good with the horses and the cattle, good in the saddle, and she worked like a man. She went all round the west with them, for years.

Going back
I am the first who scratches the ground for pleasure, not survival, and grows flowers, instead of potatoes. I record rather than practice the arts that filled the days of my mother and her mother, and all the mothers going back into the shadows.
LOUISE ERDRICH

I went back, looking for the traces of Lil's story. Back to the little town, the valley full of derelict farmhouses. I found the farmhouse where she and my father and Fred lived, and stood under the fig trees and looked at the hills. Behind me, in the house, I could hear women's voices.

I have nothing but words. That's my line, not houses and children. My mother knocked down the kitchen wall so we could see out, and I grew up looking at the world, trying to describe it.

I dream about the voices of Lil and her sisters talking about the long walk to the top of the mountain, the early mornings in winter with frost on the ground and ice in the bucket of water, the way to bake bread, treat boils, kill chooks, and cure sick children. Inside my head, their voices blend with the voices of women I know in their kitchens, my contemporaries, talking about work, economics, relationships, about justice, bread, peace, children, about books and ideas. Telling stories still.

Somewhere in the mulga
What happened to Lil when she went out west? Out in the mulga, my father would say, or the brigalow country. It's all cleared now. A Danish migrant drove a tractor through it with a chain behind fixed to a heavy ball, smashing and dragging the vegetation behind him. He drove his

tractor out of the bush, down the main streets of dying country towns and across the plains, past the silos and the haunted windy padddocks where nothing grew but wheat and peanuts, across the range and into Parliament.

Tell me about Lil's poems, I asked my father.

I knew Lil took him out bush with her when he was a little boy, after his mother died.

My father laid down his cards. He played patience all night when he couldn't sleep for the pain.

A little while after my mother died she came and lived with us.

I wanted to read her poems...

I don't remember the poems much. She kept them for years but she hardly ever showed us. They were all about the starry skies and the cattle and her dogs, he said.

Lil lay in her swag and wrote poems about the sound of the cattle at night in the dark, shifting quietly, about the dogs panting under the trees at midday, about sleeping in the open under thousands of stars.

She wrote poems about freedom, not about loss.

A woman's voice, someone said, the mother tongue, a *language that hovers on the verge of silence, but also of song.*

Lil keeps disappearing

I look at her photo and try to imagine what she was like, but parts of her have disappeared. Lil keeps fading when I tell her story. She fades like the floral dresses the farm women used to wear. Did Lil wear a dress? When she went droving she must have worn pants. She disappears back into the house every time I call her out. The women of my grandmother's generation were all hidden in families and children and houses, they were the aunts in country towns, with faded cotton dresses and cakes in the oven and food on the table, in the stories that come down to us. But Lil was different.

I have to prise the details out of my father's memory to resurrect the tough, independent woman who had to let her husband and her house go, who slept in creek-beds and wrote poems about it, who took on another house and a silent man and a silent child and turned it into a life for them all.

Somewhere in Queensland

Somewhere in England, everyone is out. Somewhere in England in Brisbane, aspidistras, in memory of England, thrive in brass pots on tall wooden stands on long deep verandahs and someone sweeps crumbs from a dark green tablecloth in 1953.
PAM BROWN

Who were they, the couple in the oval-framed photograph hanging over the sideboard in the old farm house? The photograph that hung in our hallway, that long space that started in the light and ended in the half-dark, where I sat as a child and watched the sun move over the floorboards as the adults came and went.

He was tall with a brush of dark hair and a lean hawk of a face, and a big moustache. She was small and neat, with a handspan waist and a white veil. Fred and Tilly were my father's parents.

Tilly was only a little thing. She worked too hard, the aunts said.

Fred was a hard man, they said, then closed their mouths on the words.

Tilly was the second oldest of the sisters. She died when my father was a child. He could hardly remember her. When she fell sick, and went to stay with her mother, who put her to bed, it was no house for a child, there was noone to talk to except the dogs and the cats.

Fred was a silent man, no good with words. He sat in the corner of the dining table smoking his pipe. He had no idea how to look after himself, so there was no question of him looking after a young boy. It was as if Tilly had done it for ever. Divine right. In those days most men went straight from their mothers to their wives. Fred should have been able to look after himself. He selected the land. He camped in the scrub for months, just him and the dog and the horse, while he built a slab hut and started clearing the land. After he built the slab hut, the Chinaman turned up looking for work, and then they built the house, and for a while Fred lived in the new house and the Chinaman lived in the hut and made a vegetable garden and cooked for the two of them.

When Tilly came, she did everything. Fred opened his mouth to ask and Tilly was on her way to the kitchen, Fred came back from the milking and Tilly had tea on the table. She emptied the chamber pot that sat under the bed, she made the bed and smoothed the white bedcover from her glory box, she cooked breakfast, she salted and cured the meat, baked the scones, kept the stove hot, fed the chooks and planted flowers in the garden. She sang while she worked. She got pregnant and her belly swelled, and my father was born.

Then she grew sad, and developed aches and fevers; she went to bed, and six weeks after her mother came and took her away, she died.

Her kidney swelled her up, Lil said. *Like a balloon.*

Fred never said anything, but he suffered.

Fred sat in the kitchen with my father at night, silently watching the fire flickering in the wood stove. My father sat in the corner, half-hidden in the shadows, not knowing where to put himself. He talked to the dogs in the daytime, and followed his father around. He was thin as a rake.

A week later, while the others were still rocked by grief for Tilly, Lil came over on her horse and took the young boy away. Fred didn't argue. His face was long and gaunt, as he sat at the table, lighting his pipe. Lil talked and he nodded. She took my father out to a country of flat plains and big rivers, the Condamine, the Maranoa, the Diamantina. They rode all day, driving the cattle along the straight roads; the long paddock, as the farmers called the road edges, had some of the last grass left in the bad seasons. The boy rode behind her on the horse, slept beside her in the swag. They camped on a bend in the river, where the big white gums grew out of tall yellow grass, or beside the creek-beds where catfish and yellowbellies nosed around at night under the yellow water, where the birds came in relays to drink, first the parrots then the pigeons around sunrise, then more parrots, finches and honeyeaters at midday, galahs at dusk. Lil showed the boy brolgas dancing on the claypans, bouncing on their long stork-like legs, and bustards and emus in the long grass. When the boy was sick, Lil sat beside him, telling him stories, singing to him, reading him poems.

Farewell and goodbye to you Brisbane ladies...

She kept him for three months and then came back. Fred was out with the cows in the afternoon when they arrived. Lil and the child sat at the big kitchen table waiting.

The kid's got to go to school, Lil said to Fred, when he came in from the milking.

The house had grown cluttered and smoky, it fitted Fred like his boots, dirty but functional. She walked around, shifting things. She moved in to the bedroom off the verandah. They didn't talk about it, she just brought in her hessian bag of clothes.

In the morning she woke up to the sound of Tilly's turkeys and guinea fowl squawking in the low branches of the pepperinas. It wasn't even light, but she heard someone moving around the house. She got up, and went to the kitchen. Fred struck a match and flames rose from the paper and sticks, shadows flickered on the kitchen walls. He moved the kettle to the front of the stove. He took a sugarbag off the rack by the door and walked up to the cow bails, calling the dogs. There were strips of blue and lavender across the edge of the sky.

Fred had already started milking when she walked in. The cows were leg-roped, warm and breathy. She sat on a wooden stool, a piece of log worn smooth and polished by years of swivelling bums. She leaned her forehead against the cows side, remembering the smells and the shape of their udders, the texture of brown hide, and pulled at the teats. The warm milk spurted into the bucket.

When they finished the milking Fred sluiced the warm cowshit off the concrete with a bucket of water, and the cows swayed out of the yard and disappeared along the tracks they had worn over the edge of the hill. Lil fed the calves, dipping her hand into the milk and letting them suck her fingers. Their tongues were rough, like cat's tongues. She laughed.

By the time Lil walked back up the path to the house, the sun was up and the day had begun. She made tea and sat at the dining room table. Fred had covered it in clean sheets of newspaper.

My mother walked up to the top of the range once a week with a bucket of butter to sell, she said.

Sixteen miles up to the top, Fred said.

He put his pipe on the corner of the table and cut the bread. They drank hot sweet tea and ate bread and jam without butter. The boy heard voices in the kitchen. He came down the half-dark hallway in his pyjamas, towards their voices and the warmth of the stove. He stood in the doorway, uncertain, with his eyes screwed up against the light.

Come and have breakfast, love, Lil said, and she put out her arms for him.

Lil churned butter while the boy watched her. Flecks of yellow began to appear as the cream coagulated. She patted the small pieces of yellow butter together and drained off the buttermilk for the dogs, squeezed more white drops of buttermilk out of the butter, added salt, patted it into bowls and drew a pattern on top with a fork, the way her mother used to. She told the boy about her mother churning the butter straight after milking, and the four-hour walk to the top of the range, leaving before sunrise, walking in the dark, one foot in front of another, shifting a heavy bucket from hand to hand. About the clouds that lifted off the top of the mountain, and the birds that came out of the trees, the scrub turkeys and plovers that crossed her track.

In the morning, the house was quiet. The boy played around the roots of the big Moreton Bay figs, with the dogs sleeping and snapping at flies beside him. Lil swept the house, measured flour out of the sack for damper, set potato peelings in water at the back of the stove to make a yeast for bread later. The iron roof creaked in the heat, and flies crawled over the kitchen ceiling.

The net curtains hung between dust and sunlight, Tilly's clothes hung in the wardrobe. There were shadows in the boy's face.

Lil lit the copper and boiled the washing. Curtains flapped in the wind on the wire stretched between the trees, sheets tangled as she pulled them off the line. Lil might take off and float across the dry hills. The boy laughed at her struggling with the sheets. The dogs lifted their heads for a moment, then put their heads back on the paws and closed their eyes. Fred came to the door and watched.

The house at Gang Gang Creek

The boy stood at the door with his thumb in his mouth.

What's wrong? Lil said.

Are you going away again?

No, she said. *I'm here, OK?*

That kid is too quiet, she said to Fred later. *He never talks to anyone.*

He played on his own, or with the dogs, he looked at the hills and wondered what was on the other side. He watched his father, but they hardly spoke. Sometimes Lil saw Fred run his hands through the boys hair.

The boy has to go to school, she said. *I'll take him on the horse.*

He can go with the carrier, the man said.

The cream carrier picked up the cans from the farm gates every morning, hoisted them into the back of his truck, and jerked away down the dirt road, taking them to the butter factory. The neighbours' kids waited beside the cans. They rode in the back of the truck, crouching beside the cream cans, and jumped out at the corner where the track turned uphill to the little school house. The boy went silently to the gates every morning. In the afternoons he walked five miles home, stopping when he got thirsty, crawling through the barbed wire fence to dip his enamel school mug into brown water and drink from the waterhole full of mosquito wrigglers.

All day Lil and Fred picked tomatoes in the bottom paddock. They came up to the house before dark and found the boy waiting for them. At night, after dinner, corned beef and potatoes and cabbage, rice pudding with jam, and strong tea, they sat in the barn with kerosene lanterns and packed tomatoes into boxes for the market. The boy fell asleep among the boxes and hessian bags.

The farmers round here grew small crops, potatoes, turnips, tomatoes, grubbing out a living from goanna country.

Like Tilly and her sisters, Lil boiled up green tomatoes with sugar for tomato jam and with vinegar for chutney. They killed their own meat, sometimes, turkey for Sunday dinner, calves and pigs. The butcher in town would smoke a side of pig if the farmers didn't do it themselves. The women baked bread, or damper, as well as scones and cakes.

Once a month they went to Gang Gang Creek with its avenue of pepperinas down the wide main road. The boy went to the grocery store with Lil and looked at the shelves of kerosene lamps, boxes of soap, bottles of medicines, and jars of boiled lollies. Lil bought bags of sugar, sacks of flour, tins of syrup, packets of tea, a bag of broken biscuits, and tobacco for the man, who was at the produce shed buying corn for the chooks, fertiliser, a new vat for the separator, and kerosene. The shopkeeper gave the boy a handful of boiled lollies. The women in the town wouldn't speak to Lil. Did they think she slept in Tilly's bed?

Or did they just think she was odd? Country towns were tough when you sank right in, Lil said, tougher when you didn't.

Voices and silence

I came back from Europe to find home, and settled in the city. When I went to visit that country of dry creeks and poor farms to listen, the great aunts were all in the graveyard, mumbling in the dark. Behind me, in the house: silence.

What happened to Lil? Did she get married again? I asked my father.

She wanted to buy her house back, that was the only thing she talked about. I don't think she ever looked at another man. Some of the farmers came to visit, and stood around the kitchen looking like idiots. But she didn't take much notice of them and they soon got tired of it. She went out west again from time to time, and Norm must have paid her alright. Fred used to let her keep the money she got for selling the guinea fowl she raised, but she never earned enough money to get her house, he said. She lived with us. Later on she had Aunty Ruby's house.

Did Henry come back? I asked.

Lil went looking for him once. She didn't let on – I found out afterwards. She went back to the mining town and talked to her neighbours. He'd gone to live with Nellie O'Brien. They deserved each other. God almighty, my father said, she was a holy terror. Nellie had red hair and an Irish temper and when he lost all his money at the races she'd throw him out. Happened once a month at least. He'd camp somewhere else for a while, in somebody's sleepout, or in his car, then she'd take him back, and they'd have a shindig and invite all the neighbours and everyone from the pub and fill the verandah with bottles. In the end the old bastard got sick of it and came looking for Lil. That was after Ruby left Lil the house at Gang Gang Creek.

Did she take him back?

He lived in a blue wooden caravan in her back yard. He had a dog called Red, and he sat on the steps of the caravan in the sun, talking to the dog. Pure-bred blue cattle dog. Wasted, it never did any work, let alone got enough exercise, but he loved that animal. He couldn't give it any exercise, he couldn't do much. His lungs were bad, he had the miner's disease.

What was he like then?

They used to say he was a good-looking man when he was young, a flash dresser, a bit of a lair. I only ever saw him once or twice and he was old then. Thin as a rake and sallow. Sometimes we visited Lil and we'd hear him cough all night. I don't think I ever saw him in the house. At night sometimes she played the squeezebox and he sat with her on the verandah. He couldn't sing any more.

Did she still love him? I asked my father

Or did I? Would I have asked my father that, would we have talked about love?

References
Louise Erdrich, 'The Names of Women', *Granta* 41 (London, 1994)
Pam Brown, 'Colonial', in *This World This Place* (St Lucia, 1994)

Deb Westbury
Her Son's Keeper

1
The woman in the next house
is turning into my grandmother,
is turning into stone.

Behind the blue-green agate of her eyes
is the knowledge she protects
even as she dissembles.

But I've seen the candle, burning late,
and she must have heard my footsteps
passing by.

2
Suspicion hardens into certainty, into dread,
slowing blood and tongue, flesh and sinew,
crystallising old rage.

We wait for the truth
the way we wait for a storm,
to open all our windows and our doors,

to free her for that long run
on stone legs
to the sea.

Peter's Cowardice

(After Adam Cullen's painting of the same name for the 1999 Blake Prize)

Peter, of the stone,
in the crucible of dread
reduced to sulphur;
acid, ashes, stench.

Behind clenched teeth
you gag on it:
your eyes bulge
your tender membranes
bleed
with the shock of it,

betrayal
a blue pall descending;
the blue of nails
of manacles and spears.

You hunch your back,
you wring your hands against it.
Absolute as silence,
still it closes in.

The Tattooed Boy

It is said there was a moment
in the dock,
when her back was up against it,
she pointed the finger at him
to save her own, thieving skin.

O my mother

And it was he who wore the manacles
to Van Dieman's land

O my mother

On the ship, on his fifteenth birthday,
he had these words
tattooed on his skin:

O my mother

He learned that the heart,
like his captain's lute
was only hollow wood and string,
yet was somehow filled
with the music that it made.

O my mother

DEB WESTBURY

The words inflecting light
or dark upon the strings,
depending on the touch

O my mother

Music in the lute
heart in the body
body in the earth

Deb Westbury's new collection of poetry, *Flying Blind*, is to be published by
Brandl & Schlesinger in 2002.

Tom Carment

Illustrated Tales

Poco

The oldest sheepdog at Myola, Poco (who was given to Jacob when he was a toddler) began to lose weight and sicken. She could only just manage to shuffle around with a sideways list and lay most of the day by the house-gate panting. A few weeks before that she was still working, Geoff told me, not with a lot of energy but with intelligence. Geoff doesn't shoot his dogs himself, it breaks him up too much, and Poco he says was the best working dog he'd ever had – a ginger-brown kelpie cross. So on a Tuesday morning Jacob left his breakfast half-eaten and went out in his school uniform and sat there in the red dirt giving the old dog a hug. Later that morning Geoff and I went in the truck to Whyalla to take Poco to the vet and to see his father Mr Mills, who was slowly dying of cancer at home. Poco sat beside me on my flannelette shirt, so happy at the privilege of riding in the front instead of on the back tray.

I got Geoff to drop me near Whyalla Airport where I squatted down to do a painting of the factories seen across a small salt lake that was being whipped up by a blustery south-easter. The wind was so strong that I had to weigh down my hat, palette and paintbag with rocks. When it was done I walked back two kilometres to Hummock Hill where I'd arranged to meet Geoff, carefully gripping my small wet panel upside-down to stop it getting covered in wind-blown dirt. Chip packets were flattened against the mesh fence of the Aussie Rules field and floral tributes piled up against the fence of the cemetery further on.

When Geoff's truck pulled up I asked him how it had gone at the vets'. He pointed to a lumpy black plastic bag on the tray. Then we drove to the westernmost suburb of Whyalla where his parents had settled after leaving Myola. We rang the bell of a sixties' brick bungalow and Mrs Mills, a sprightly woman with a grey perm showed us in. Mr Mills was half-lying half-sitting in a special padded massage chair

ILLUSTRATED TALES

looking at the television: the Independence vote had won in East Timor and they were showing footage of Dili burning and women and children cowering in fright. Mr Mills could barely speak and gave me a polished soft hand to shake – a hand that must have been firm and horny not so long ago. The house was in the last block in Whyalla and from out the windows you could see the saltbush plains stretching off, in afternoon light. Geoff talked quietly with his mother for a while as his father kept watching the screen. I wasn't sure if he was really interested in Timor or whether he was just too tired look elsewhere. He'd been on palliative doses of morphine for some time.

The next morning back at Myola a front of high grey cloud came over and it began to drizzle. I put on my shirt to keep warm and it smelt of dog. Geoff grabbed a drum of fuel and drove out alone into the paddock behind the house. He spent an hour putting together a big pyre of twisted myall branches and placed Poco on it.

Mr Mills died two months later and was buried with a merino fleece draped over his coffin.

Caravan

On the way in to Kempsey en route to South West Rocks, with Fenn and Felix listening to their book tape in the back seat, I pulled off the highway to drive slowly past the house where a girlfriend once lived. It was back in the early seventies and her name was Lyn Reiby. The house is weatherboard and square with a high-pitched symmetrical tin roof, one of the oldest in South Kempsey – like a dairy farmer's place that the town had surrounded. 'Why are you slowing down Dad? This isn't South West Rocks,' said Felix in a querulous voice. There were no lights on (it was dusk) but the 60s' Viscount caravan was, as always, parked on the wide verge. There were a few old-style housefrocks hung up on a line under the verandah to dry, so I assumed that Mrs Reiby was still alive. If it had looked like someone was in I would have knocked, introduced my two little boys. When I last saw Lyn about fifteen years ago on a trip down the coast she said that her Dad was sick and would get up in the night to stomp around the house because of the bad circulation in his legs.

I used to be scared of Mr Reiby. He was a nuggety self-made

business man (in trucking I think) who didn't like me much and told me so. He'd read some of the letters that Lynn and I exchanged (several each week between Sydney and Kempsey) – mine full of pretentious adolescent self pity and long quotes from Dylan Thomas, and hers full of lurid accounts of high school, sex, drugs and fatal accidents – cars that shot off the bumpy riverflat roads, doing a ton.

The Reibys habitually took their caravan to Crescent Head for six weeks every summer, and in January of '72 Lyn invited me to come up in the train and stay with them there. I slept on a stretcher bed under their green striped annexe, with the sound of the surf pounding away on the other side of the lagoon. Crescent had the longest left-hand break on the coast.

And I remember one time on that holiday with great clarity: Mr Reiby was shaving over a white enamel bowl full of hot water with his safety razor in the darkened interior of the caravan (they always pulled down the venetians in the middle of the day). I was absent-mindedly watching this ritual when he looked up and asked me if I'd like to have a go after he'd finished. I was pretty smooth and hairless for a 17-year old – just a bit of bum fluff on my lip and chin – but nonetheless I said, 'Yep, sure.' Then he handed me the razor and stood and laughed as, in front of Lynn and her mum, I pointlessly scraped away at my soft chin. I hated him for that. Mrs Reiby told him to stop teasing me and he sauntered off with a bang of the flimsy screen door to the Country Club or wherever he was going.

Lynn told me that holiday how she liked receiving all my letters but that she just wanted me to be her 'friend' – she'd fallen in love with a local guy with broad shoulders, a job and a Valiant safari wagon. When he came in from surfing he'd buy a loaf of white bread, pull out the doughy centre and fill it with hot chips.

And now nearly thirty years later, as we rounded the bend in my station wagon (of a not disimilar vintage to the boyfriend's Valiant) I noticed, despite the fading evening light, that that the Reiby's caravan looked dirty – its windows were laced with glinting snail tracks, and curls of buffalo grass had wrapped themselves around its deflated tyres.

Boots

I had worn out my elastic-sided boots and was taking them to be repaired at Whyalla's biggest shopping-centre, called Westlands (the place where Bob Hawke in his 1990 election campaign called someone a 'silly old bugger'). Nico stopped me, saying, 'Don't go there. Take them to the old Scottish bloke. Here I'll find his address...Bill, that's his name. He's much cheaper – but he's on the juice most of the time.' And he made a bottle-tipping gesture with his thumb and fist.

Nico was going in for some wool-bale clips and gave me a lift in his truck: twenty kilometres along the straight road beside the ore line from Iron Knob, our passage marked by the metronome of metal telegraph poles, taller than the myall trees and saltbush roundabouts. A few kilometres short of town, just before the speedway, Nico veered off the bitumen onto a dirt track. 'Got something to show you – why we don't run sheep in these paddocks anymore.' After five minutes we came out onto a claybed and pulled up below the red ochre of a dam bank. 'Dad's father, old Andrew, sunk this dam in 1947 and this summer's only the second time it's been dry since then. Its real name is Koleroo Dam but everyone in Whyalla calls it Yabbie Dam.' We got out of the car and climbed the bank. The concrete tank was pockmarked like a wall in downtown Beirut and the water trough had been rammed and lay slumped in three pieces. The windmill, with 'Comet' stencilled on its fantail, was toppled sideways, its vanes perforated to lace by target practice. An upturned car wreck, a twisted shopping trolley and a mud-stained computer lay on the cracked dam floor. We took a piss on the dry dirt, Nico shaking his head at the destruction. 'If I paid you $5 for every virgin who's lost it out here you'd be a rich man.'

He dropped me at Bill's place which wasn't far from Westlands, in a street of small ochre-brick state houses, a bit the worse for wear, though not without their individual touches. When I dropped the boots off (entering through the back gate as instructed) he came out in a dirty white singlet and shorts. The backyard was congested with all sorts of forty-four and ten-gallon drums linked by bits of pipe which he told me collected every drop of water from his roof. There were two beds of shrivelled vegetables. He opened up his big back shed to reveal an enormous grinding and polishing machine dating from the 1940's – it must have weighed tons. He told me he'd once had a shop in Port Augusta and a shoe-store too. He liked to talk (and

I never mind having a Scottish voice wash over me). There are a lot of Scots in Whyalla, brought out to work in the shipyards and steelworks, many from the banks of the Clyde. Billy Connolly was a big hit when he did a show here (until word got out that he'd said in an interview that 'Whyalla's a great place to go for an enema', and now he is black-banned, not that I think he really cares). Old Bill inspected my boots with tremulous hands and showed me the bad stitching on the elastic gussets made by the previous repairer: 'My stitching doesn't waver like that'.

When I returned a few days later to pick up the boots he sent me out again to get the exact money, because he was 'skint' he said. When I came back he had a shirt on and his teeth in – very white with bits of bread caught between them. There was an HQ wagon in the drive roughly hand-painted in silver and blue with rust already starting to come through the paint. He told me he'd been D.U.I.'d and was coming off his ban next week. He'd modified the rubber on the roll-down tailgate window to stop water getting through to the bottom panel. It was done in a most complicated manner using shoe sole rubber and numerous screws and bolts to hold it tight against the glass. He asked me if I was married and had kids, and before I could reply he started telling me how he'd 'told the wife to fuck off eight years ago – best thing I ever did'. I interrupted and said thanks, I had to go. In fact I was off to see Elaine who lived a dozen blocks away and did tailoring in her spare bedroom. All the windows of Elaine's place have the blinds drawn and it takes your eyes a while to adjust from the glare outside and notice that the walls of every room are lined with pictures of Cliff Richard.

On the way there, at a set of traffic lights, an electrician's van (an ex-ambulance Ford 500) pulled up and burbled beside me. Its duco was completely covered with quotes from the Bible (King James version) and declamatory prophesies neatly painted in different styles and colours. On the driver's door I read: 'SATAN IS COMING – AND HE WILL BE ANGRY'. Later that day in Delprat terrace I watched a tubby man in blue BHP workclothes unload a sack of seed from a blue Volkswagen onto a blue wheelbarrow and wheel it out to a blue-framed cage of racing pigeons at the end of his drive. Whyalla is like that some days – you feel surrounded by people pursuing their obsessions.

There is a front fence in Essington-Lewis Street with all the notes of Rolf Harris's 'Tie me Kangaroo down Sport' cut out of sheet steel and welded onto the stave and bar lines of its metal frame. A Polish man used to run the fish shop nearby, but didn't eat fish. He said he didn't like it. 'Try the bream. It's good today,' he'd tell you. And Tom Tyce from Texas, a lay preacher from a fundamentalist sect of the Presbyterian Church, had a dream which told him to come to Whyalla and gather up a congregation. His flock was tiny if it existed at all, and he loved to come out to Middleback Station to muster sheep on his bike. He taught his two dogs to roll over and play dead when he pointed at them with a pretend gun. But he didn't wait around for Satan and took his family back to the States last year.

My boots haven't felt quite the same since old Bill worked on them. Perhaps he eased a little more leather out from around the soles, for even with two thick pairs of socks on, they're too sloppy. But the stitching on the soles and gussets is good – as equally spaced and unwavering as the poles along the line to Iron Knob.

Tom Carment is a Sydney-based artist, who has published a collection of art and prose, *Days and Nights in Africa* (1986).

Joanne Burns
chubby

the voice of the qawwali singer
lifts off your wig of poor listening
habits you meet with a stack
of ice cubes in an exploding
fridge spin across skies like
a valley rediscovering its dervish
wings the ceiling becomes
an empyrean of parachutes quivering
like the fountain of his chubby
throat he sings from the slender
disc above the bread board
like an accidental messiah and
the musak of the century takes to
its sickbed; arcane perfumes waft
over from the plastered walls your eyeballs
roll across the windowpanes like
surprise pearls you set fire to a
thousand travellers' cheques he
sings of the secrets in the ancient
library of your sleepy heart

qawwali – Sufi Muslim devotional music

how to sneeze in peace

the burden of dreaming, the bed a huge net dragging the monster octopus of story that lunges through the head at night: the corpulence of the drowning psyche. who, what, are these people, these shades, these feelings, places, likenesses, that tangle one up like a bad load of washing. this shamozzle of the long night.

tentacles shoot out new episodes, plots and subplots in the hours before dawn. who is the octopus – the dreamer or the dream. grubby stories, leviathan lore, cheap little anecdotes. you turn in the bed, and its creak documents another story. the glare, the smirks of strangers, familiar places, rearranged by the psyche's cruel interior designer. you know the loci by name but they look different. as if you are awakening from an anaesthetic.

in dreams irony does not exist, even suspicion, perspicuity is a struggle, you suffer physical pain if you try to break out of the dream. the dream and its fleshy, multifarious burdens insists you remain naïve, compliant, committed.

but for those who have been blessed with dust allergies there is a way out. if you find yourself near dusty spots in one of your dreamings try to get as close as you can to these sprinklings or mites. within breaths you will feel it coming. a huge sequence of sneezing that will blast you from your deepest slumbering, with a shower of clear ink, writing invisible gratitudes across the lightness of air.

JOANNE BURNS

peerage

his body a paradigm
of tattoo husbandry he
glowers on the street dreaming
himself to be an award
winning website hawks
the phlegm of his
rhetoric towards the ground
as he poises like some
ancestral reflex to peer
into a bookshop window
jeering as if it's a
vitrine in a fusty museum
till he sees a picture
on a cover looking like
himself with a front
tooth missing so he
fists himself through
then wanders along to
an internet café
where it's hotmail
time his night
vision goggles strapped
to a hip

Joanne Burns' most recent collections of poetry are *penelope's knees* (UQP, 1996) and *aerial photography* (Five Islands Press, 1999).

David Brooks

Napoleon's Roads

His vision, from the constantly passing bars,
Has grown so weary that it cannot hold
anything else...
R.M. RILKE, *'The Panther'*

David Brooks has published three collections of short fiction, *The Book of Sei & Other Stories*, *Sheep and the Diva* and *Black Sea*. His most recent book is the novel *The House of Balthus* (Allen & Unwin).

At first I thought they were wind-breaks, to shield the vines and villages from the Mistral, or else some charming custom of the particular area in which I found myself, a throwback to an earlier and nobler time. More than once in my mind's eye I saw some grand ducal or baronial carriage making graceful progress down one of these long, tree-lined avenues in the early autumn twilight. But no. Madame Elizabeth told me, when I mentioned them, that they were Napoleon's roads, the *Routes Napoleon*, and that he had had the trees planted to shade his troops, while on manoeuvres, from the harsh high-summer sun. And the idea had stuck. Even now, she said, almost two hundred years later, hardly a new road was opened that did not soon have, on either side, its avenue of trees.

All through the region they run amongst vines. In the winter the clipped stocks reach out for acres on either side of the avenues of trees like ranked armies being inspected by lines of silent officers, or else quietly waiting, before battle, for a signal. Watching them there is also something else, that you have also seen before – the ranked order, the long rows of stunted crosses, as if these too were somehow Napoleon's idea, or there had been an idea, a shape before all of it, running through Napoleon's veins.

At the *Jardin des Plantes* there is no panther, only a couple of aged lions in an ancient cage at an intersection of paths with a commanding view of the broad, central avenue. They do not pace, as the panther might, but sit at the base of their large rocks, looking out over the sparse winter crowd, with rheumy eyes that, it suddenly occurs to me, might well be half blind.

    Another day, walking back toward the fifth arrondissement, from the Gare D'Austerlitz, we pass the *Jardin* on the river side and find we can see clearly into the cage of wolves from the Cevennes. It is 4 p.m. The traffic is heavy on the Quai St Bernard. The wolves are relentlessly pacing out a large figure eight, over their small hill, down the other side, along the bottom end of the cage, back up the hill to cross the path they have just taken, then down on our side, along the fence, back up, crossing the path, down. Watching them, I am glad there is no panther, that he is out there somewhere, long dead, free of the cage. Paris is freezing. As we set off toward the hotel the wind picks up and an icy rain starts. I imagine the wolves pacing just to keep warm.

Napoleon's roads are very straight and very dangerous. There is little room to manoeuvre. Drivers in this country have a lust for speed, and for passing the car in front of them – a kind of wild impatience behind the steering wheel that is probably the inverse of their famous grace and civility in the office and drawing-room. They are *sauvage*, my landlady says, and will tailgate at high speed, pass in almost impossible places. With large trees every five metres or so, on either side of the road and only centimetres from the bitumen, there is no margin for error. Where in another country a slewing or swerving car might veer into an open field or ride up onto pavement, here there is only almost certain death, wrapped around one of Napoleon's trees.

Coming home from Montpellier long after sunset, nearing the turnoff, using low beam behind a car some four hundred meters in front of us, its light caged in by the long, straight avenue of trunks and winter branches, it is as if we are speeding through a tunnel far under ground, or perhaps a vein, an artery in the night. 'Do we have to take the turnoff?' my daughter asks asks me, 'Can't we keep going? I love driving at night.' As if, after all that, there would still be home at the end of it. Or this were home for the moment, this warm capsule, flying through the dark body of things.

A web – *une toile d'araignée* – with Paris at the centre. *Une toile abandonnée?* Or does the web still invoke the spider?

The first of the roads between the D32 and Puilacher, the one closest to Canet, is only one car wide but still has its row of plane trees along either side. To let past a car that is coming the other way you have to pull over to the very edge, almost into the ditch between the road and trees, or back up a hundred yards to the highway, running an even greater risk of ditching yourself. We call this road the stink road because of the large dam beside it, full of the foul smelling tailings from the winery. On warm days when the smell is worst we try to avoid the road entirely, or else quickly wind up the windows, drive along it holding our breath.

They are pulling up the road to Claremont in preparation for the Autoroute. Now, instead of the great trees between Canet and the Nebian turnoff, there are only the trunks of them, cut into segments, and the enormous, ploughed root-balls, almost lost, at sunset, in the gathering shadow below the pylons.

On the vast plain between Paris and the sea, the roads to Chartres are lined with tall poplars, bare winter branches interlacing high over the bitumen, the cathedral at the hub, stone branches in its nave and narthex just touching, as if the builders had been dreaming of poplars, or the tree-planters of the high gothic arches, the tracing in the rose windows that seem to remember the way the winter branches, interlocking over the roadway, are like a three-dimensional map of roads in the sky, seen from far off.

Late autumn, the harvest long over and the trimming and uprooting of stocks well underway, the stocks and cuttings and dead leaves raked into the ditches or piled in open spaces and set alight. But some of it is out of hand. Tonight eleven large blazes visible from the Paulhan turn-off alone, and the fire-brigades from Clermont, Gignac, Paulhan, Le Puget all out. Sirens everywhere.

And the police, driving slowly along the darkening vine-roads, looking for a culprit.

In London, up from the Languedoc and eating Lebanese at the Gallipoli Café, I try to tell my English friend about Australia. We are talking about Shakespeare and she doesn't quite see. She tells me about the great oaks and beeches and plane trees. I try to tell her how they line the roads, how dangerous and complicated this is, how they mark and shut out the countryside about them, but she can only see the trees, how ancient and solid and majestic they are, how nobly they mark out the land. Later, driving back to our borrow flat – past Picadilly, Trafalgar Square, the Smithfield Markets, all those old names – I remember what I should have remembered then: how the great oaks and beeches of the New Forest were cut down to build the ships that discovered Tahiti and New South Wales, how on the Federal Highway, between Goulburn and Collector, there runs an avenue of poplars ('*piboule*', Madam said – we are living on the Avenue de la Piboule – 'that is old *languedocien* for poplar') remembering the soldiers killed in Amiens, Arras, Gallipoli. Or how, beside them, someone has started to grow vines.

My daughter has an image that amuses her, of the Emperor, on his days off, with a shovel and a cart full of saplings, trudging along the roads between the grape vines, doing the planting himself. Did Napoleon get the armies to do it, we wonder, or was it gangs of prisoners, or perhaps of labourers, forced away from their vineyards for the job? And if prisoners, what kind would they be? Common criminals? Political prisoners? Prisoners of war? It's like the Great Wall of China, I tell her, and perhaps not; the different work sites, different regional commands, the building piecemeal, the intention to connect it all at last in some time far in the future. ('You start from Bezier, on the way to Pezenas; others will be starting at Montagnac, St Jean de Vedas, Gignac...

Car headlights, far back, in the rear-view mirror, like a large cat's eyes in the darkness, and I think, That's how they are, or we, coming and going, from Paulhan to Belarga, Canet to Plaissan, if seen from out there: the panther, pacing back and forth, behind the bars of the trees.

Approaching the Intermarché just north of Canet, along the short stretch of older trees before the river, we are passed by a speeding ambulance and twenty minutes later, coming home, find it again, with two others and a police van in a cluster blocking half of the highway. It must have happened while we were buying the milk and the cigarettes. One car, front badly crushed, is still on the road and the other, that had been trying to pass it, is as badly crumpled on its side in the ditch. There are enough people there already. I am concerned only to drive slowly past and cannot look, but my daughter tells me they are taking a bald man out of the car in the ditch, that they've had to cut it open to do so. The accident is just around the corner from the stink road and we take it into Puilacher, winding up the windows against the smell of it.

On a hill beside Plaissan is a dolmen, though you do not get to it from Plaissan but from Le Puget, up a long dirt track and then through thickets of some wirey brush I don't manage to get a name for. A depression, or trench, or wide grave, the earth held back by giant stones to create a narrow space for the body, though whose body no one can say: a chieftain perhaps, two thousand years ago. And around it – you can take in almost a full circle if you stand on the huge lintel – the roads, with their snaking, parallel lines of trees, in some pattern you would need a balloon to see properly. And perhaps, if you could, other hills, other dolmens. Nazca. A summoning. Except that the tombs remain empty, pieces of text, waiting.

Dogs on the road. Running towards me with no intention of stopping. A game of chicken. So that I have to slow down, pull to the side to let them pass, in their rush to get wherever they are going. Part of a hunting pack, lost, or on the scent of something, the rest of them somewhere out amongst the vines. Up in the hills they are hunting deer and wild boar, but here it is rabbits, quails bred for the purpose, released into the vines after the *vendange*, two weeks before the season starts. When you go out walking, they say, wear bright colours, stick to the paths.

The problem with a question is that it implies its own answer. The problem with an answer that it responds to a question. But the question that rejects its own answer? The answer that will not fit its question? The memory of the tidal flats about Mont St Michel, and in the fields beyond them the stands of trees, ranked, silver in the winter light, like fragments of roads long washed away, or that never came, answers to a question no-one ever got around to asking.
How do you write like sand?
How do you write like water?

... Artarmon, Clovelly, Clontarf, Vaucluse ...')

To see the other roads, the other trees is not easy. You must almost risk your life. Particularly if you wish to take photographs. You must pull to the side, half on and half off the bitumen, on the thin strip of unmown grass that sometimes runs between the ditch and the road itself, or turn on to one of the service-paths of the vineyards. Or else come to a dangerous halt in the middle of the road itself, hoping that you can be finished and driving again before the next car comes. Bearing in mind that while, when you're moving, you can think yourself the only driver on an otherwise-deserted road, when you stop you're likely to find that this is far from so, that within a minute, or not very much longer, a second car will pass, and then a third. Bearing in mind, too, that, unless you stop, unless you risk your life, you may never see, in that articulated sky-map of winter branches, a large crow landing, shaking the whole, or a flight of swallows darting through, straight from a meal among the vines.

I am beginning to drive like a Frenchman, my daughter tells me, taking greater risks, judging distances more finely, passing when there's no need to, driving at 120 in the 100 zones. I want to tell her about Rimbaud, his *'dérèglement de tous les sens'*, *'long, immense et raisonné'*. But it is not that. I have no excuse. The way, waking late at night, I can sometimes hear my blood, raging down its avenues. The way, not waking, I sometimes dream a dream of earliest childhood, in the Humber with my mother and father, somewhere between Belgrade and Zagreb, the rain, the long, straight road, the long avenues of trees. The heart like a creature pacing, inside the cage of bones. Things I cannot say, cannot retrieve.

Outside Canet, where the road narrows before the bridge, the great bruised trees, or by the Gignac crossroad in ghostly light, like scared men running, or the already-crucified, mile after mile. No unknown but we try to cage it, as if that were our greatest fear, the loose.

Driving in to town on a Tuesday evening, on the road toward Gignac, I become aware of a giant moon, and have to struggle to keep my eyes off it, to keep the car on the road. I have never felt the moon's power so strongly, so dangerously. All the way to the autoroute it comes and goes, strobing through the avenue of trees, slipping now behind a hill and appearing again, suddenly, through a cloud of vine-smoke. In Montpellier, safe amongst the buildings, I feel lucky to have survived — as if, very physically, something that had been pulling at me had at last let go.

How to say that these roads are about what is not road, this text about what it is not? In the apartment on the Avenue de la Piboule there is an aerial photograph of the surrounding countryside and the villages of *Les Six Clochers* – Puilacher, Tressan, Belarga, Canet,

Plaissan, Le Pouget – in such detail we can see the roof of our own building; the tree-lined roads like dark ribbons through the lighter quadrilaterals of the vineyards, the un-lined roads and paths amongst them a lighter and finer filigree. The *Routes Napoleon*, then, and the openness beyond them, the paragraphs of vines, whiteness.

The road outside Capestang, or over the river at Trèbes, above the ranked barges. There is a sudden turn there, as the road, that has been straight for five or six kilometres, enters the village and you cross the bridge – and calm, a moment's slowness after the highway speed, and the majestic trees bending in over the water, forming a great bower, and then the thin, winding streets, the café, the tabac, the boulangerie, before highway again, out through the acres of vines.

The plane and the poplar are fast-growing trees, but even Napoleon, planting them along his roads, can't have thought they would be tall enough to shade his troops the next year, or for several years to come. What was it then? Investment? Empire? Belief in the future? Each year, when they did go on manoeuvres – those who lived, those who survived – the trees were a little taller, a little fuller of foliage.

I imagine them singing as they marched, though perhaps it was harsher than that, only the occasional soldier, singing under his breath.

Thusday, 5.15 p.m., large moon over Campagnon, round and full and riding low over the scattered lights. Impossible to return the next night but there at the same time Saturday, with camera. But no moon. Have clearly miscalculated the rising times. Decide to pull off the road and wait anyway, to see. And within two minutes a police-car appears – I can just make out the 'Gendarme' sign in the half-dark – and moves carefully up beside me. One of them – there are three officers in the car – winds the window slowly down as I do the same. Does he think I have a shotgun? Matches?

'Un problem?'

'Non, pas de problem. ... J'attend un photo', holding up the camera, ' – de la lune...'

'D'accord', he says, calmly – not the slightest reaction – and they drive off.

God knows what they say. Maybe nothing. The moon, after all, is a remarkable thing. Even gendarmes watch it. Or might have – I think as I drive away – an hour ago, as they paced the D32, huge and dangerous, through the bars of the trees.

Photograph by Adam Geczy

Tim Richards

The Futures Market

Tim Richards is the author of three short-story collections published by Allen & Unwin: *Letters to Francesca* (1996), *The Prince* (1997), and *Duckness* (1998).

Mind Games

Maybe Simone shouldn't have called Lennon a twisted arsehole, but Andrew forced her to take extreme positions, and she began to enjoy firing these shots through his heart. Liverpool. No one in their right mind needed Liverpool. Hamburg and Abbey Road were enough. If Andy wanted to cream himself in front of George's first Strat, let him go to Liverpool. Simone was done with time-travel. She needed to take in some natural beauty.

The Beatles were never the issue. Simone couldn't have cared less whether Lennon was the true genius of his century or a snide misanthrope. For her, it was about coping with an otherwise intelligent man cursed with the need to take on his mother's high-school obsessions. How could you possibly start a family with someone who'd want to analyse and discuss 'Revolution Number 9' in his retirement?

After months living in each other's pockets, the break would do them good. Or so she argued. For Andrew, knocking back Liverpool was like a Muslim giving the finger to Mecca.

And no sooner had her train crossed the Welsh border than the guilts set in. She'd denied a pilgrim the chance to have his devotion validated. The poor bastard would have to beg strangers to take his photo in Penny Lane. Much as Simone adored the Beatles, she'd never embrace a world that proclaimed the currency and superiority of all things Fab. But as the landscapes she flashed through grew more spectacular, a desolation took hold.

Andrew was always map-man, and now she'd have to pretend she wasn't at a loss, desperately hoping that the wetness slapping her window wasn't the first sign of an unrelenting wet, nature's desire to quash her new freedom. Rain is never just rain. This rain was punishment for sadistic disloyalty. Her craven refusal to offer the hand that a Beatle-boy wanted to hold. Now it was certain to rain flat-chat for days.

The Switch

Other than the old song about having a lovely day there, Simone only knew Bangor via the Beatles. The newly psychedelic ones were meditating in North Wales the weekend their manager overdosed. They were shocked and stunned. And Brian Epstein's death would leave them to drift rudderless across the sea of unimaginable success. But none of this Bangor trivia was any help when a furious windgust put paid to Simone's best umbrella.

The lone traveller found a cheap bed and breakfast five minutes from the station. Though the Welsh were slightly easier to understand than the French, Simone had no idea why she was in Wales beyond her desire not to hear again how Paul consoled young Jude with a song. Maybe when the rain stopped, she could take a trip on the mountain railway. Mrs Evans soon put paid to those hopes. The railway was closed for winter. And this mist was nothing compared to how bad it would get in the next few days. So the traitor spent an evening alone in her room writing letters home which told friends and family what a fantastic time she and Andrew were having.

At breakfast next morning, Simone pulled back the curtain to find the water-world Mrs Evans promised. She knew that her actions were responsible. The sun wouldn't reappear until she'd fully undone her cruelties. She was searching timetables for the next train through to Liverpool when joined at the table by another guest, a stupendously large, middle-aged man who offered a nod and a shy smile before introducing himself as Ken.

Ken had the magician's gift for making food vanish. Several plates of sausages, eggs, and bacon disappeared without Simone seeing the man place food in his mouth. Her breakfast companion had refined the process of food consumption to such a level of elegance that he could cut, insert, chew and swallow during the natural pause between sentences, never once losing eye contact.

Ken was a Shrewsbury man, but he spoke with the plummy, educated accent of someone who produced radio arts documentaries. Though he'd never travelled to Australia, he did know one of Simone's English lecturers, Karen Williams, describing her as 'related by marriage' without detailing the exact nature of the relationship. No wedding ring. Simone saw Ken stacking on the charm, and she was sufficiently flattered by his interest to be curious how far that interest would extend. In the meantime, Mrs Evans delivered another plate of crisp bacon.

Questions. Simone was between degrees, unsure which direction to take. She'd spent three months visiting art galleries on the continent. Now she hoped to spend a few days here before reuniting with her friend in London. *Her friend?* An Australian she'd teamed up with when she arrived in London. A friend of a friend.

A kind of game, not using Andrew's name, studiously managing not to mention that this friend of hers was a boyfriend, a lover. A tease. Simone enjoyed Ken's melodic voice, and his quietly insistent gaze. The big man was smart enough to make his own surmises.

As she spoke about career hopes, Simone was reminded how little time she'd had to consider her future when travelling with Andrew. He'd taken up all the space she ordinarily gave to reflection and thought. Simone would tell her huge dining companion that she had no real sense of her future life, and needed to become much more focussed. She couldn't decide if she wanted to be an academic, a writer, or a filmmaker, and wasn't sure that she'd ever have the ability to fulfil those roles. Maybe she'd end up corralled by her inability to decide.

According to Ken, the important thing was not to let anxiety rule the show, or to make decisions for the sake of appearing decisive. Trust your most immediate passions and follow them wholeheartedly.

The future was certain to crush imperfectly formed hopes, so you had to let your resolve build gradually.

Ken managed to pass on this advice while a fried tomato and three sausages vanished from his plate.

Though Ken's tone was fatherly, and devoid of obvious sleaze, his gaze was unremitting. What would Simone the onlooker conclude if she saw her own father giving such close attention to a woman her age?

Not that Simone's father ever travelled to Paris to interview Beckett, Bunuel, or her own great hero, Eugene Ionesco. This Ken needed to be larger than life. He'd seen everything, read everything, and he'd met almost everyone whose name mattered to Simone.

The giant only neglected his plate when launching into literary and cinematic enthusiasms, and these almost exactly coincided with hers. His big jowls shook when Simone mentioned Robert Musil. The young scholar's declaration that *Love in The Year of Cholera* by Marquez was a favourite among all favourites brought a tear to the man's eyes. Ken had once flown to New York to interview Marquez, but illness forced a cancellation.

'Anyone who loves Marquez and Cortazar must read *Worthless Lives* by Manuel Primm. Primm does that great thing Marquez does. He tosses out as casual asides brilliant ideas that most writers would base three-hundred page novels on.'

Mrs Evans brought fresh toast while Simone searched her bag for a pen to record the book title and the name of an author she'd never encountered.

'And *Marginal Behaviour* by Michael Fouks. You must know him, he's an Australian.'

When Simone admitted that she'd never heard of her brilliant countryman Fouks, the man took her pen and paper and scrawled a list of a dozen authors and titles. None of the names were familiar. All, according to Ken, were crucial to any well-formed understanding of where literature was headed as it steered away from post-modernism. Simone heard her pen singing as Ken wrote.

'Oh, and Helen Bain, a new writer from Wick in the north of Scotland. *Unbelievable*. A little like Alice Munro. Not quite so elegant, but playful in surprising ways.'

Ken's list of must-reads would keep Simone busy for years. He made each of these books sound irresistible. Though she saw that the big man's outpouring of enthusiasm was in large part delight at meeting an attractive woman who shared his principal interests, she couldn't be certain that this was a tactic of seduction.

Simone couldn't read Englishmen. Men of any nationality for that matter. Andrew was relatively simple. Always happy to be enthusiastic about Simone, provided she was enthusiastic about him. Otherwise, bets were off. Now Simone found herself with mixed feelings. Big Ken would disappoint her if he made a pass, yet she would be equally disappointed if his obvious attraction to her wasn't charged with the man's characteristic hunger.

As Ken shifted attention from plate to teapot, Simone took the opportunity to draw the man out. He didn't strike her as the kind of person who came to North Wales for the walking or mountaineering.

She'd summed him up correctly. He wasn't that kind of person. Ken's ex-wife lived in Bangor. He came up every second weekend to visit his twin sons. The boys, young men of Simone's age, were in palliative care. Their lives had been cursed by a rare genetic disorder.

Rain lashed the windows, and Mrs Evans was heard rattling plates in the kitchen.

Simone was speechless. How could a man with two sons near death eat several hearty breakfasts? How could a father in his situation enthuse about the unrivalled qualities of obscure novelists? The man continued to pour his tea as if his remark had been a banal comment on the weather.

'I know what you're thinking,' Ken told her, 'but we've had twenty years to come to terms with the hand we were dealt. In the long run, you have to make a choice; to despise life, or to relish it.'

Even this struck her as glib, untouched by real feeling. Maybe the big man needed to see others feel in order to connect with the emotional world. Or maybe it was something much more complicated than Simone would ever understand.

Finally, the Australian told Ken that she couldn't imagine anything worse. The thing she feared most was the possibility of outliving a child. It was as if time was arse-about, running in the wrong direction.

The big man smiled gently and confirmed that's exactly how it was. Life was arse-about. Someone given too much responsibility had hit the wrong switch.

Simone never mentioned Ken to Andrew. After failing to make sense of Ken herself, she could hardly expect the boy stranded in timeless melody to get a handle on him.

Though still angry, Andrew was keen to relate the intensity of his Merseyside experiences, but now Simone lost interest in provoking him. The couple seemed to know their relationship would end somewhere between San Francisco and Melbourne Airport. Accepting this allowed them to be more affectionate than they had been prior to their Liverpool dispute.

'You realise the Beatles were staying in Bangor when Brian Epstein died?'

'No, I didn't know that,' Simone told him.

At Foyles in London, she enquired about the books Ken recommended. The shop assistant took the list to a female superior who pressed horn-rimmed glasses hard against the bridge of her nose and gave the colon-stressed wince of a passer-by asked to disarm a live bomb. Mrs Delaney knew none of the books or authors. Simone asked the assistant to check the computer, but the young man politely declined. If books were listed on the computer, Mrs Delaney would certainly know about them.

Several days later, during a stopover in New York, Simone made the same enquiry, first at Barnes and Noble, then at several more specialised bookshops. The same result. Computer records found no reference to any of the authors, let alone exotic titles like *The Abattoir at the Far End of the Futures Market*.

When another helpful assistant at City Lights in San Francisco returned waving empty hands, Simone had to concede that the big man's list looked dodgy. Amateur chimney sweeps were better known to the Internet than Manuel Primm, the remarkable author Ken situated somewhere between Marquez and Cortazar.

Perhaps the big man had greater need to hold Simone's attention than she realised. She couldn't pretend to have fathomed the depths of

Ken's behaviour that morning. *Invention?* Maybe those twins dying of a genetic disorder were no more tangible than the authors on the radio producer's list. Honey-voiced Ken was one of a breed of giants who took pleasure in devouring gullible young women for breakfast.

Left-Field Investment Strategies

Simone never would have imagined marrying someone so opinionated as Mark. People who didn't understand Mark often saw him as a dead-shit whose self-confidence was unshakeable as it was ill-founded. She knew that many of her friends considered her husband to be a bad investment.

For the lawyer, the Beatles were cordial passing itself off as Coke. Overrated. A bunch of sharp-witted pretty boys who should have gone to Hollywood. According to Mark, punk and new wave failed music in one respect only. Not arriving fifteen years sooner.

Simone now felt guilty defending the Fab Four against critiques she'd once made herself. Particularly when she thought of Andrew, who'd returned to live with his mum after his father's death. (This being the equivalent of choosing to camp in Strawberry Fields forever.) Yet Simone managed to see in Mark's brash assertiveness all the characteristic signs of denial. Her man was a frightened puppy. His whole persona was a confidence trick.

Having cottoned on to the rules of the game, she took pleasure stringing Mark along, a puppet-mistress who allowed her charge the illusion of autonomy. Mark could be made to do absolutely anything if his wife convinced him that he was calling the shots, that all her ideas were his.

Where did his surprising idea to call their unborn child Rose come from? Mark didn't know. How could his wife be certain he hadn't fancied a Rose? He'd never known any, the name Rose just struck him as a good idea and now he couldn't think of calling his daughter anything else. Simone would get used to it, eventually.

Yes, Mark was fragility itself, but Simone found his need to paper over vulnerabilities endearing.

Terrified of his wife's prehistory, Mark refused to look at old travel photographs, not wishing to encounter Andrew – 'that lanky dickhead.' Simone knew that Mark couldn't cope with the idea that she had known romantic excitement before meeting him, that she'd found other men to love, and that it might have been possible for her to live an equally happy life with someone else.

Unpacking after the shift from Elwood to Hampton, Simone found a box of papers she hadn't seen since she'd posted it home from Europe seven years earlier. Maps and guides to obscure museums. Tickets. Postcards. Programs. The front door key to a bed and breakfast in Canterbury. Notes written on the back of beer coasters. Even a forgotten Polaroid of her and an equally pissed Danish girl sitting topless in a Heidelberg Youth Hostel. (How Andy must have searched for that photo!) Among a pile of aerograms she'd received from friends, Simone found the useless list of brilliant authors and books big Ken composed in the breakfast room of a double-story terrace in Bangor.

And she would have thought no more about this list if her eye hadn't caught a name, that of the author Manuel Primm. What was it Ken had said about the South American's unusual sensibility? She couldn't remember. But Simone now recalled that this man Primm had just won a major literary prize. And two other authors on the list, Helen Bain and Miranda Murray, had attained sufficient prominence for their names to be known to her. Of course, Simone read nothing these days except books and articles pertaining to her doctoral thesis, an inspired attempt to relate the Myth of Sisyphus to the American film *Groundhog Day*.

So Ken hadn't pulled her leg after all. The big man's judgement was astute. She then recalled Ken's strangeness about his dying twins, and figured the boys must have passed on by now. Ken might have too. It just wasn't possible to sustain that sort of gusto at breakfast.

As Simone re-packed all the stuff into boxes that wouldn't be re-opened for another ten years, she placed Ken's reading list on a coffee table. Mark's birthday was coming up, and maybe she'd give him a book. Tired of sending threatening legal letters to DJs and samplers, her man needed a new outlet for his vast reserves of disdain.

Grotesquely pregnant at twenty-six weeks, Simone enjoyed the attention of shoppers in her new suburb.

No, so far as her doctor knew, there was only one child, though it felt like two football teams scrambling for a loose ball near goal. Yes, she did know the child's sex. *Oh, but why spoil the surprise?* Not her idea. A paranoid husband simply refused to let her keep anything secret from him.

Simone answered these same friendly questions when put to her by the woman who owned Kidna's Bookshop. This on her way to asking whether Kidna's had the latest novel by a South American author, Manuel Primm.

'Yes, *Worthless Lives*,' Barbara answered, pointing to an expensive hardback on the shelf immediately behind Simone.

When Simone suggested that *Worthless Lives* couldn't be the writer's latest work, she was assured that Primm's recent prize was for first-time novelists under the age of thirty.

Rather than try to make sense of this information, Simone gave Barbara Ken's list of hot tips. Most of these names meant nothing to the book woman. Not long ago, she'd had multiple copies of *Dream Life* by Miranda Murray, but she'd sold out. The book was on re-order. Though she read Helen Bain avidly, Barbara had never heard of *The Abattoir at the Far End of The Futures Market*.

The name that most intrigued the book woman was Michael Fouks. Fouks was a Hampton local who frequently came into the shop. The previous year he'd won a competition with his story 'Illusory Density'.

When Simone asked whether Barbara had a copy of Fouks' book *Marginal Behaviour*, she looked perplexed. So far as Barbara knew, the writer hadn't published a book. Just now, Fouks was writer in residence at Melbourne University, and she understood him to be using this time to finish a collection. She'd certainly ask him about *Marginal Behaviour* when he next came in.

Though Simone handed over thirty-five dollars for the hardback copy of *Worthless Lives* by Manuel Primm, she never gave the book to Mark, or read it herself.

In the past, impulses and sudden insights had taken Simone a long way. They'd once taken her to a bed and breakfast in North Wales. There she determined that life was much too short to get stuck in a vinyl groove half way through 'Maxwell's Silver Hammer'.

Simone now felt certain that one of the worthless lives Manuel Primm wrote so brilliantly about would belong to Ken, a charming, obese radio producer whose days were shadowed by a half-baked genetic transfer. Another of those lives was very likely Simone's own. Or a version of her life as she'd come to see it fifteen years hence. The South American's magical control of tense would bounce sentences off the wall marking the end of time.

As a post-graduate student at the same university where Michael Fouks was currently in residence, Simone could have approached the young artist to ask about his work in progress. But she was 'a woman with child', a woman who remembered the curse that had already befallen the unnaturally far-sighted Ken and his twins. To praise Fouks for the quality of his unfinished book, *Marginal Behaviour*, would be the equivalent of kicking sand in the face of a sleeping dragon. Or discovering too late your responsibilities with regard to a crucial switch.

James Lucas
Royal Hotel

A ute erupts from gravel skid,
no match for the drunken
matador who slaps the bonnet

off his hip. The bar
is shut. In my room a
straightback seat forced up

against a sawn-off downpipe,
the sealed-off ends of water
fawcets showing where

the hardware clerk ID-ed
the fittings with an inhouse
scrawl that says '60' or 'GO'.

Christmas, Kangaroo Valley

Even The Darkest Hour Lasts Only
Sixty Minutes says the billboard
at the Moss Vale Church: overlooking
Fiztroy Falls a hangover dictating
my best option is descent to land

where defunct tractor parts
are rusty but effective magnets
pulling holidayers into eateries
and Parisian Ladies of the Belle Epoque
hide their faces behind temporary

tinsel boas, as if they know softporn sepia
plus timing equals art. Outside I see
a servo owner's hung a hollowed half-log
right above the bowser. Even now this
planter trails the odd sear tendril.

Open Season

A cattledog drinks from a can, flanks vibrating,
tail the baton orchestrating bodyfat.
Conversely country music rides

a radio wave drawn-out dippy as akubra brims.
Hills I crested coming into town ran wire
fencing that resembled sheet music drawn freehand

by a drunk: small birds threading it at speed
produced no evening chorus. There were no cows.
The poem at this point might have headed

nowhere, or in various directions, but settled
in a carpark cum beergarden, saw the mascot
cattledog drinking from what was a paintcan.

See how form is following dysfunction?
The sky's an old tarpaulin. Music draws power
from a car battery, or we accept monoxide ambience.

Anything to fill the silence. Pizzey's *field guide*
to identify the birds I saw as wrens or finches.
Yokel spotfires lit to mark out riverbanks.

JAMES LUCAS

Elizabeth Bay Road

Fruit machines accept all cards for very punter
there's an addict doorframed, they punctuate the street
as in a Florence gallery when restorers airbrush out
aureole and child to foreground areolae puckered
for remedial teething, too pure or too stoned
for lewdness, this Beatrice-free opening
whose proven images are made not marred by copywriters'
truant and genius ink! And now commercial artists
bring the day to consciousness or coffee, at least sunlight
coaxes brown meniscus eyes that swill in time to waiters' hips
which anchor-leg a relayed pilgrimage from Kenya,
scent of Africa upmarket from U.S. Sailors
whose sleeveworn hearts are just the boon
a plein-air florist needs: Her birthmark
ups the stakes: should I tell you what she feels?
Or say a foil of jaywalk zebras plead panache
as if their skin complaint might be the next hot topic
for homeopaths? That kills the conversation
since you can't fit them on the side of a bus, or the back of a cab.

James Lucas has a PhD in twentieth-century poetry from Cambridge University and is an English master at Sydney Grammar School.

Antoni Jach

Strange Happenings on Via Silla

Antoni Jach is the author of two novels, *The Weekly Card Game* (McPhee Gribble, 1994) and *The Layers of the City* (Sceptre, 1999).

In my apartment building – via Silla 8, near the Vatican and metro station Ottaviano, Line A – there is something very odd happening. The authorities are excavating in our street, but that should have nothing to do with it. The warm spring nights have arrived, but that should have nothing to do with it. The Romans are linking arm in arm and wandering through the parks in the late evening warmth, but that should have nothing to do with it.

My neighbours are equally as curious as I am, and equally as perplexed. But we are all such busy people: professional people who work and shop and jog through the ancient streets of Rome in our Adidas runners and our golden Lotto tracksuits, and work and shop and sleep, fitfully. Just by chance we all happen to work in similar fields: we could be embraced under the term 'communications' – we work as publicists, public relations officers (like myself), journalists and marketing officers, and, oh yes, there is a professor as well, a difficult person to live with. Curious people by trade, we are all used to talking to other people for our living; our product though is sometimes nebulous...but I am beginning to digress.

The concierge is worried too, though she doesn't want to offend anybody; none of us do. We want to be able to get on with our lives with the least inconvenience. Everything we do is so tightly scheduled there is no room in any day for the slightest thing to go wrong. The owners of the building have been sent a fax, but they have informed us in a roundabout way (they will never put anything on paper) that they are not overly concerned and as long as everyone pays the rent it has nothing to do with them. We have formed a Tenants' Association – our first meeting was this evening – and we have agreed on a course of action...but I am beginning to digress.

What I am about to tell you is the truth. I witnessed it with my own eyes; and I am a reliable person. I have often been complimented on my reliability. I have won awards. I would not have obtained my present job – as the senior public relations officer for a respectable company that makes chemicals and plastics – if I did not appear to be trustworthy and believable.

And how could you possibly hope to represent the major polluter of the ancient city of Rome if you don't appear to be believable? My suits are French (Givenchy), my shirts American (Arrow) and my shoes are Swiss (Bally). I wear freshly ironed and lightly perfumed shirts with button-down collars, and ties – silk, floral, opulent. You will *never* see me casually dressed. I earn a lot of money, get pay rises regularly and shop on the via Veneto. I love shopping and cook well. My apartment is spotless. I keep a black Himalayan-Persian cat (whom I adore) with the most exquisite orange eyes whom I (ironically) call Mussolini...but I digress again...it's a bad habit of mine.

To get to the point though, something strange is happening in our apartment block. We are all feeling less secure than ever. I will tell you our problem: there is a family living in one of the two basement apartments – the one on the left as you go down the stairs.

But I suppose that is not enough information to impress you. There are many families living in basement apartments all throughout Rome I hear you say. Well, listen to this carefully. The family wear togas, they keep a number of slaves, and the head of the family writes on wax tablets with a stylus and makes speeches in Latin.

I know...I don't know what to make of this either. It is disturbing. All we want to do is be allowed to get on with our lives and make some money. Not too much, for that would be greedy, but just enough to be comfortable...Money isn't everything, you know...Though it does help, with all those little things in life. It's not that we've chased money, it's more that money has...well, been thrust upon us; though at the expense of time. Everything has to be so tightly scheduled: work, twelve hours; jogging, one hour; shopping, one hour; cooking, one hour...and before you know it, there goes the day. That's why we can't tolerate disturbances.

We are all perturbed. Life just hasn't been the same. At the back of our minds there is this nagging feeling that something is not right. The edges of happiness are mitigated by this new discovery. We have to get rid of them. We have decided on a course of action (which is unusual for us – we are so much better at simply discussing).

We don't know how long they've been there. We have had a string of concierges in the last year (there is neither heating nor air-conditioning in the concierge's tiny apartment), and while all of them have been contacted none have been able to tell us when the family arrived though our present concierge, Maria, says with a wan smile that the family has always been there, it's just that we the tenants have not noticed before. She says they ought to be allowed to stay, because they were here first. We say that they have to go because they pay less rent than us – as they live in the basement – and that they are disturbing our peace of mind. I brought up the point at our tenants' meeting that the ancient family was the worm in the apple of our present happiness. A sentiment which was applauded for its felicity of tone and the poetry of its expression and was agreed with by everyone; everyone, that is except for stubborn Maria.

It is a very disturbing thought: that we are living our lives on top of an ancient Roman family. It is hard to buy clothes, shop, jog and watch television (the big game is on tonight – Italy versus Holland in the finals of the World Cup – I mustn't miss it) while being aware of this.

Before the awareness of the ancient family we were living perfect lives: now we have become shifty and guarded with each other in the apartment building. Something has changed, but we're not sure why. If we get rid of the family we get rid of our disturbance and our lives can go back to normal. That's all we seek: normal lives;

undisturbed, uneventful lives – so we can maximise income.

I, and my neighbours, can see into the family's apartment by means of the porthole in the door. At nine at night, after work, shopping and jogging, I go down into the basement and stand in the darkness watching the family. It is better than television.

Peering in at the family I feel vaguely uncomfortable – like a voyeur. One of the slaves is teaching the youngest boy to write, the little girl is playing with her pet rabbit while the older boy is walking with a pigeon on his shoulder, the father is practising making speeches (perhaps he is a senator) while the mother is seated in a high-backed chair occupying herself with a distaff and a spindle; there is a statue of Venus in the corner, and another of Bacchus. When the father finishes practising his speeches he lolls on one of the embroidered couches eating grapes…That couch would be worth a fortune. (Maybe I could buy it from them at a low price.) The mother is burning incense and looks distractedly into the foreground.

A typical family scene, how pleasant, you might say. Not so pleasant if you have to live above them, I can assure you. Though I am curious to find out more about the family – especially now that I have been elected as the spokesperson of the group and it is thus my obligation to inform them – the ancient family – that they will have to leave their home.

But I can't stand peering in at them all evening because a) there are others waiting to peer over my shoulder, and b) it is time to have supper, and c) my cat will have been missing me all day and will become neurotic if I don't see him soon and comfort him, and d) I need to adjust the television set so that the picture will be clear for the big game, and e) I need to relax with a celebratory whisky (Glenfiddich, double malt) and enjoy the satisfaction of my first big pay rise for the year.

The pay rise was long overdue as the work I do is very taxing. How would you like to be the senior public relations officer for a large chemical and plastics firm that is chiefly responsible for much of Rome's pollution (especially now we have come into spring and the days are still and warm, with hardly any wind)? Can you see my problem? The worst thing is that I am more aware than most – as I have access to the appropriate information – of the amount of pollution our company is responsible for, and yet I'm paid, and paid handsomely too, to deny it all, to deny it totally, to deny it convincingly. Increasingly my boss has been urging me to lay the blame on our major competitor. I work long hours and I have to be so polite, so diplomatic, so even-tempered. I have to put up with personal abuse from journalists and I have to listen for hours to the 'lies' (usually true) that these journalists are spreading about the company. So you can see how richly I deserve the largesse that has been bestowed upon me.

But to return to the problem at hand: to live above an ancient Roman family is most disturbing. From my observations and my study of the classics I would say they are a family circa 50-100 AD. They are suitably well behaved but still they have to go, and I will go down soon, after another glass of whisky, to tell them the wishes of the group.

Our sense of well-being and comfort is disturbed by their presence. We are all professionals in this apartment block, with modern concepts of living, who all work very hard. What then is an ancient family doing beneath us?

The family is completely at home in its surroundings; it's like we are the outsiders now. Yet we pay our rent like good citizens, and our extortionately high taxes, and we keep the economy going by buying our fair share, or more, of the available consumer durables. The other thought, which has just crossed my mind, and which may have nothing to do with anything, is that the only inhabitants (couples and affluent singles) in this whole apartment block who have any children at all are the ancient family. It's an odd thought, but maybe the children of the ancient family will outlive us! Maybe the family will outlive us. Maybe they have always been there. Maybe long after our gold Rolex watches have rusted away the ancient family will still be there, living in the ground floor apartment, on the left as you descend the stairs. I have never felt more mortal than when thinking about the ancient family. None of us in this apartment block will ever have children; it's just not our style, we are *professionals* after all...Have you ever worked out the cost of children? Horrendously expensive! And the time involved!

I have managed to catch a glimpse of the floor of their apartment: it is covered with mosaics of fishes and cups of wine in blues and blacks and reds – sumptuous, refined, elegant. Those ancients had such exquisite taste! Such a sense of order and beauty. And yet the family still has to go. Their aesthetics won't save them. The smell of freshly baked bread escapes from their apartment in the early hours of each morning. Presumably the slaves are baking for the day to come. I have never heard screams of pain, so they must be treating them properly…It's so hard to get good help these days. (Maybe with my pay rise I could get Juliana to come an extra day?)

Though the one thing that comes to mind is that with so many slaves – there must be four or five – there would be no privacy. How would you like it if all your bodily functions were supervised? It must be rather crowded down there. Though no one is sure how large that basement flat is; maybe it is cavernous; it might extend in all directions. What a horrifying thought!

There are bowls of beaten silver standing on the mosaic floor (maybe I can buy them – I'll take my cheque-book) and there are burgundy and ruby-coloured rugs (I'll buy them too) on the tiles (maybe I could rent their apartment when they leave). They must be well off, with no need to work (obviously, as no one has ever seen them leave their apartment). They look so self-contained, so smug in their domestic way. It's unbearable – they simply *have* to go.

It is the strangest feeling when I arrive home late at night, having caught the metro to Ottaviano (I'm so glad they have finally put this line in – it feels so incredibly *modern* and *urban* to arrive home via the metro) to think while gazing out at the still, warm Roman night that I'm living above such a family…Maybe they are like us after all. Maybe all they want is peace and quiet. Unfortunately, I will have to disturb them. (It's nothing personal though.)

There has been a lot of excavation in Rome during the last year. The authorities have had to dig up the streets to put the new metro line – Line A – underground and they are still excavating. They have discovered ample evidence of ancient Rome but to the best of my knowledge they haven't yet discovered an entire family (let alone one that is still alive).

I will have to go and confront the family in a few minutes and, on behalf of the Tenants' Association, ask them to leave. At first I was reluctant to be the one chosen but then when it was mentioned that the elected representative might be able to purchase a few little nick-nacks I thought I would put my knowledge (fragmentary) of Latin to some use and provide a civic duty to the other tenants at the same time.

The meeting decided that we should not inform the media. We intended to until the two journalists present were so passionate in their opinions that other 'despicable journalists' would invade the privacy of the tenants in the most unseemly fashion that we decided the path of discretion was the appropriate one to take. We had discussed storming the apartment and forcibly ejecting the family but we have all noticed the gleaming array of daggers, swords, spears and pitchforks lying in the corner next to the statue of Venus along with the shiny, oiled, rippling muscles of the taller slaves and so we decided that 'communication' would be more appropriate, and in a room full of communication experts I was chosen. (I suppose I should be flattered.)

One more glass of Glenfiddich and then I'll go. I must get back in time for the big game though – not long to go now. Italy is doing well, we're in the finals again, we're going to win it again.

I peer out from my eighth floor apartment at the lights of Rome. Vaguely, through the polluted haze that my company has helped to create, I can see the lights that illuminate the exterior of the Castel St. Angelo. If I half close my eyes (blocking out the modern buildings that I don't want to see) then for a while I tell myself that this is exactly the same ancient city that the family belongs to. I am back in the first century AD, they belong to the dominant group and I am the intruder. But the moment passes quickly enough. I stroke Mussolini's sleek black fur (he spends all day cleaning himself) then choose an expensive shirt (freshly ironed today by Juliana, the little angel!) and an appropriate outfit to wear. I don't want to disturb the family unduly so I dress in an elegantly understated manner, as befits my station in life. I choose my favourite suit together with my best pair of shoes, as I want them to think well of me, and glancing back quickly at the ordered life of my apartment I begin to descend the stairs. I hastily check my Rolex; not long to go now.

It is quite dark at night on these stairs; the lighting is contained in cream shells that flute the light upwards; it is very beautiful but it means that it is difficult to see where you are going. I don't know what I'll say to these guardians of lost time but I feel confident that the right words will come at the right time. They might get violent, which is not something I would be prepared for. What a disturbing thought.

There are many stairs to descend. (It's almost like going down through the centuries, I think lightheartedly.) But what's this? The hair starts to bristle on the back of my neck; the heartbeat quickens; my breath gets shorter. I feel a touch of vertigo coming on as I look down the length of the ornate circular staircase…

Peering below me carefully I can vaguely perceive shapes coming towards me – human shapes, ancient shapes. It is the family! They are clunking up the stairs towards me. Here is the father leading the way – looking confident and relaxed. Behind him is his wife, looking serene. Then there are three children holding rabbits and pigeons with four slaves – two male, two female – bringing up the rear; each slave holds a loaf of bread and a wine pitcher. I stop where I am, hesitant to move. They are coming closer and closer. A metre away and I can hear the heavy breathing of the father; he passes so close to me that I can feel his sour, ancient breath on my face. He seems so benign, as do they all. I start to relax…After all we live in a rational world and there must be some meaning in all of this which will reveal itself at some later stage.

They all pass by me, without taking any interest in me whatsoever, and I follow. I want to see where they are going. They have passed by the seventh floor and now they are climbing the staircase up to the eighth floor and now they are standing in front of my apartment – number 13. (I'm not superstitious, after all we live in a rational world where normal things happen.) I graciously squeeze past them, unlock the door and let them in. They become quite animated, all chatting noisily as though they are going to a party. I can't really understand what they are saying; they are speaking too rapidly. I gesture that they should make themselves at home. Smiling all the while I offer them seats. They break the bread which they have brought. It is still warm. I taste a mouthful. It is delicious. I show my appreciation with animated gestures. The father is speaking to me loudly, forcibly. The others are backing him up with words and gestures. The slaves find a glass and pass me some wine which I drink thankfully, greedily. Everything is happening so quickly. I pass round the beer (Heineken) and crackers (local) then get a few more cushions for the slaves to sit on. They are all facing the television set. The chattering continues until the father waves his hand imperiously and everyone is immediately silent.

The father speaks directly to me, very slowly and loudly though with an affable tone as if I was a foreigner. He says, I am starting to make it out now, TEMPUS LUDO EST.

He gestures towards the television set. He repeats what he has just said. I work it out. He is saying: IT IS TIME FOR THE GAME. I look at my watch. But of course, it's just past nine. Time for the kick-off. It's a very important game. I have money riding on this game (a lot of money).

So I turn on the television. They are happy at this. We pass round the bread and wine and the beer and crackers. The game has been going for six minutes. Nil all. Italy is in attack. Antobelli has been given a corner. We all lean forward with excitement. We all watch with interest to see what will happen next…

John Bennett
Reaching Bedrock

Auburn, Sydney. 14.1. 2000
for Harry and Lucy

SWEET Auburn! loveliest village of the plain,
Where health and plenty cheered the laboring swain,
Where smiling spring its earliest visit paid,
And parting summer's lingering blooms delay'd.
OLIVER GOLDSMITH, *The Deserted Village*

Past the Turkish pizza and video shops

and the slow-paced women in head scarves,

past the citadel of units, out of scale with

your hot street, grass verged and wrought with iron.

We wait in air-conditioning watching the pilot

of *Lost in Space.* There's no Dr Smith

just wholesome cowboys wandering a moral maze,

dressing monkeys as aliens and killing Cyclops.

I open the gates so Sue can back their car,

guide a neighbour out of the way. 'Been

run over twice,' he mumbles, then rambles on

'the pirates are coming,' demented from the drink.

The Botanic Gardens are Sunday-busy,

we find a hill with shade overlooking 'the billabong'

and picnic while geese honk, chase each other

and race either side of a low wooden fence.

Harry and I spot a peahen trailing five spotty chicks
who whistle when we draw too close,
the women have found a red-bellied black
slithering on the edge of the site that backs onto

Duck River and a series of parks before you hit
the Clyde railway yards, Silverwater prison
and the industrial complex, smack in the centre
of a poisonous city sprawling west into the Mountains.

The kids head for the stepping stones, walking on water.
The 'Pool of Reflection' floats florid blue water
on a blue backdrop, Vietnamese wedding parties
are being processed and recorded a thousand times.

Back for afternoon tea behind the Federation house
in a garden rippling with corners, Tradascentia snakes
out towards the slide Lucy wants dusted of cobwebs
and spider skins before she'll demonstrate the art of falling.

Harry has climbed the ancient plum tree
withered and twisted as a mountain pine,
potato vine coils around with small white flowers
for barbs. He clambers down and swings

a geologist's hammer onto brick, smashing
the mould, then pounds the shards
to rusty sand, our constituent pieces.
He wields a tool to reach bedrock but

there's no such thing, only ways of being
in an environment. The Robinsons in space
pioneer every ecological niche, introducing
overly active imaginations and oversized boots.

If I have exhausted the justifications I have reached bedrock, and my spade is turned. Then I am inclined to say, 'This is simply what I do'.
WITTGENSTEIN, *Philosophical Investigations*, 217

John Bennett is currently undertaking a PhD, on a new Defence of Poetry, at Wollongong University; his second collection of poetry, *Field Notes*, was published by Five Islands Press in 1998.

Mandy Sayer

In Earnest

Hemingway's Short Stories

Mandy Sayer's recent books include her prize-winning memoir, *Dreamtime Alice* (1998), and the collection of short stories, *Fifteen Kinds of Desire* (2001), both published by Random House.

During the last three decades, the popularity of Hemingway's fiction has waned, especially with writers, readers, and women of my generation, whose feminist and post-feminist tastes lean away from what is perceived to be stories of violence, sport, and masculine authority. His women are weak and manipulative. He relies on exotic settings and situations to shoulder the drama of his stories. He is out-of-fashion these days because he was rumoured to be homophobic, anti-semitic, a bad drunk, a womaniser. Hemingway, it seems, only wrote of horse-racing, fishing, boxing, and skiing – and people have decided that it is better not to read him as the work seems so macho and dated.

In interviews, when I mention that one of my favourite short-story writers is Hemingway, invariably there is an awkward pause, and often a bemused reaction. Surely I would name someone more fashionable: Alice Munro, maybe, or Lorrie Moore. My reply is always that Hemingway's best work is important because he crafted a style and tone that approximated his ongoing themes and subject matter. For that alone he is worth reading.

'The dignity of movement of an iceberg,' he once remarked, 'is due to only one-eighth of it being above water.' This simple statement aptly reflects Hemingway's aesthetic and thematic concerns. He was one of the first short-story writers to pare back subjectivity and exposition to the extent that people had to read actively – indeed, they had to enter the narrative in order to fathom the seven-eighths of the story the author deliberately omitted. It is through his silences that Hemingway said the most, like a sulky, enigmatic child whose covert expressions reveal more than any number of clever words. 'A writer may omit things that he knows,' he said, 'and the reader, if the writer is writing truly enough, will have a feeling of those things as strongly as though the writer had stated them.' This technique is often referred to as Hemingway's famous 'objective' style, in which the point-of-view avoids analysis of a character's thoughts and feelings and instead creates external actions, images and settings that suggest the inner life of characters without explanation or commentary. As American author Frederick Busch remarked on the ending to *A Farewell to Arms*: 'He doesn't have to tell me outright that Frederic Henry weeps for his Catherine; the way he excludes the tears makes me taste them.' In this sense, the most minimal of Hemingway's stories are probably closer to the genres of poetry and playwriting than to the ornate prose of the century into which he was born.

He did, however, find his antecedents in the nineteenth century, primarily in Anton Chekhov, whose voice, if you listen hard enough, can be heard below the surface of Hemingway's prose. Chekhov was a master at using objective external details to convey complex emotional states, and employed understatement and irony to further the drama of the story. This rendering of the internal through the external, the subjective through the objective, is a technique that T.S. Eliot later described in terms of the 'objective correlative'.

This is one of the primary reasons Chekhov was hailed as the father of the modern short story, but what most critics and readers of his prose forget was that Chekhov was an accomplished playwright, and I suspect his discovery of narrative distance in the short story was as much a consequence of his experience of writing for the theatre as his desire to explore new narrative forms. His first two collections, *Tales of Melpomene* (1884), and *Motley Stories* (1886) were considered light and somewhat frivolous works by literary critics. It wasn't until 1887, when he published *In the Twilight*, that Chekhov attracted recognition as a virtuoso of the short-story form. It was also in 1887 that Chekhov's first play, *Ivanov*, opened. Chekhov appears to have developed the objective, 'dramatic' point-of-view in his short stories concurrently with his first works for the theatre. 'Subjectivity is a terrible thing,' he once said. 'It is bad in this alone that it reveals the author's hands and feet...Best of all is it to avoid depicting the hero's state of mind; you ought to try and make it clear from the hero's actions.' These are the words of a playwright rather than a prose writer, for the only tools the former has in order to convey meaning are dialogue, action, and setting – the three things both Chekhov and Hemingway concentrated on in order to suggest emotional and psychological undercurrents. Chekhov and Hemingway, I think, wanted readers to bring to the story what an actor would when performing a play script: engagement, interpretation, a layer of interiority in order to bring the work to life, a process during which the reader – like the thespian – becomes a collaborator in the making of meaning and experience.

It was Hemingway in particular who mastered, in prose form, the playwright's technique of conveying exposition through minimal dialogue, of 'showing' rather than 'telling'. Many of his settings appear to be influenced by the obvious limitations of the theatre: one scene, one symbolic background, whether it be the café of 'A Clean, Well-lighted Place', the railway station of 'Hills Like White Elephants', or the single train compartment of 'A Canary for One'. His most elliptical stories resemble one-act plays, comprised of dialogue, minimal action, and single settings that function as a thematic key. In 'Hills Like White Elephants', for example, a quarrelling couple sit on a railway station 'between two lines of rails in the sun'. In fact, the station is a junction, a crossroads of sorts, and perfectly represents the emotional crossroads of the man and woman who, we sense, will never be 'going in the same direction' after the argument that spans the story. Hemingway inherited the distant, dramatic style from Chekhov and, to a lesser extent, from Joyce. As Charles May notes, 'what at first seems merely a realistic depiction of ordinary physical reality communicates metaphorically what is, basically, incommunicable'.

Hemingway's iceberg theory extends even further than his choice of point-of-view and style, further than the clipped dialogue and spareness of his prose. Often, that which is incommunicable or unknowable is the very subject of the story, as if the protagonist is standing on that small frozen island and gazing into the depths of the encompasing water at his own terrible darkness. This is why 'A Clean, Well-Lighted Place' is one of Hemingway's best-known stories, and why he felt it to be one of his most successful. It is probably not much longer than seven-hundred words; it is a single scene, and in it very little 'happens'. The 'place' of the title is a Spanish café, and by the end of the story, the cleanliness, the light, and the order of the café provide a safe and comforting protection against the unknown – the darkness and danger of night.

There are only three characters in the story, an ageing waiter, a much younger waiter, and an old man who drinks brandy long into the night, as he does every night. The tension is mainly between the waiters: the older one doesn't mind keeping the café open; the younger one wants to close up and go home. The customer, however, won't leave and continues to order brandy. It is the older waiter who intuitively understands his need to stay every evening and get drunk in the bar, his need for 'a light in the night'.

The silent understanding that exists between the drinker and the ageing waiter is underscored by the opening dialogue, in which the young waiter comments on the fact that the brandy-drinker had tried to commit suicide the week before. When the older waiter asks why, the younger one says, 'He was in despair'. When asked what caused the despair, the younger replies, 'Nothing'. When asked, 'How do you know it was nothing?' the younger comments, 'He has plenty of money.' As the critic Carlos Baker points out, the force of the story is gathered through understatement, hints, the subtext of details and dialogue, and the transformation of 'the young waiter's mere *nothing* into the old waiter's Something – a Something called Nothing which is so huge, terrible, overbearing, inevitable, and omnipresent that, once experienced, it can never be forgotten'. The antidote to this Nothing that is Something is the small cocoon – the safe fraction of iceberg that stands above the sea of darkness – the place that is a clean, well-lighted café.

Death (*nada*) is at the heart of many of Hemingway's short stories, either literally or figuratively. I suspect this is why in recent times there has been a certain amount of confusion about Hemingway's work, along with the misconception that he only writes about bull fights, hunting, boxing, and the permutations of masculine heroics – all of which result in the protagonist stoically facing a violent and tragic end. A measured reading of his stories doesn't support this summary. Very few of them are, in fact, sports-related. Most appear modest and deceptively simple, relying on dialogue, patterns of detail and their underlying subtexts to create the drama rather than celebrate gratuitous violence. What many readers fail to recognise is that, even in the stories of violence, Hemingway uses sport as a narrative occasion to explore his literary obessession with the Nothing which is Something, just as he used the simple device of the waiters in the café of 'A Clean, Well-Lighted Place'.

The three stories I shall concentrate on in this essay – 'Hills Like White Elephants', 'A Canary for One', and 'The Short Happy Life of Francis Macomber' are concerned with the complexities of male/female relationships. In these stories the *nada* concept is realised through breakdowns in partnerships – death comes in the form of separation, divorce, or simply a couple's inability to communicate any more.

Following Chekhov's dictum that the short story should begin in the middle of things, each opens in a drama that has begun long before we are admitted into it. There is an unspoken 'it' in all of them, a buried subject that the characters talk around but do not directly address. 'The Short Happy Life of Francis Macomber' begins with: 'It was now lunch time and they were all sitting under the double green fly of the dining tent pretending that nothing had happened.' Set in the wilds of Africa during a safari expedition, the mysterious 'it' is not directly explained until a quarter of the way through the story. The experience of reading the story up until that point is one that evokes a certain voyeuristic quality, as if the reader were eavesdropping on some vastly personal subject, and if he listens hard enough and picks up enough clues the private information will be revealed.

Hemingway begins similarly in 'Hills Like White Elephants'.

After the two characters have been established in the symbolic setting of the Spanish railway junction, the man, who is never named, remarks, 'It's really an awfully simple operation, Jig…It's not really an operation at all.' In 'Hills', Hemingway pushes his elliptical style further and the characters never directly reveal what 'it' is. The conversation progresses: 'It's the only thing that has made us unhappy'; 'If I do it you won't ever worry?'; and, '…once they take it away, you never get it back'. A close reading of the story reveals, entirely through inference, that the man is trying to persuade the woman to have an abortion; she in turn does not exactly refuse or agree, her main desire is for the man to want what he does not, to find Something in Nothing. This idea is recapitulated in the title, which is lifted from a seemingly casual observation the girl makes, that the hills near the station look like white elephants. White elephants, of course, are either associated with totally useless possessions or a possession that is a liability because the expense of keeping it far outweighs its value. After the girl begs the man to drop the subject ('Would you please please please please please please please stop talking?'), Hemingway can't resist invoking the *'nada'* concept in the last line of the story: '"I feel fine," she said. "There's nothing wrong with me. I feel fine".' Nothing is exactly resolved, but by the end of the story we know that, figuratively at least, these two won't be travelling on the same train for very long.

In 'Canary for One' the Nothing that is Something is not revealed until the last line of the story. An American couple is travelling between Cannes and the Gare de Lyon in Paris, sharing a compartment with a partially deaf woman, also American, who carries with her a caged canary. Through seemingly insignificant dialogue the woman reveals that the canary is a gift to her daughter, a kind of consolation prize for the Swiss man the girl had wished to marry. The mother forbade the union because, as she maintains, 'American men make the best husbands.' The woman soon discovers that the couple themselves are American, and throughout the story she twitters away at them more frequently than the bird, particularly about the virtues of American husbands. The train compartment functions symbolically as a kind of cage confining the three characters, all of whom gaze out at the world through the window. The point-of-view of the story is a very distant third-person singular, from the American man's perspective – though typically the fact that he is narrating is not revealed until almost halfway through the story when he remarks, 'For several minutes I had not listened to the American lady, who was talking to my wife.'

The story begins with an image of domestic comfort: 'The train passed very quickly a long, red stone house with a garden and four thick palm trees with tables under them in the shade.' Soon, this image is undercut by another, more sinister sight of domesticity, which foreshadows the last line of the story: 'As it was getting dark the train passed a farmhouse burning in a field. Motor-cars were stopped along the road and bedding and things from inside the farmhouse were spread in the field.' A similar juxtaposition is created between the very fast train the three are travelling on – which the older woman is convinced will crash – and the image the man observes just before they arrive in Paris: 'We were passing three cars that had been in a wreck. They were splintered open and the roof sagged in.' At the end of the story, the older woman walks away down the platform with her canary, convinced the couple she is leaving is happy because they're both Americans. The last line of the story, however, reveals that the couple's Nothing (what the narrator has failed to tell us) is definitely Something: 'We were returning to Paris to set up separate residences.' The line functions as a dramatic punch line – deadpan, ironic. Most of the story, it seems, will happen after it has ended, as the events in the narrative impact on the future of the couple.

Hemingway's various techniques for communicating the incommunicable have a lot to offer writers at any stage of their careers. Not to read him because he's too macho, too violent, or too sexist is to miss out on a consummate craftsman who honed his work into a precise marriage of style and subject matter. He was a writer who made silence sing, who found a way to disturb readers by what he didn't write, and for that alone would-be authors should be intimate with his work.

Of course, I'm not always comfortable with his manipulative women, his emasculated men, his tragic heroes, but I admire and have been inspired by the way in which he wrote about them. Instead of placing a blueprint of feminist or Marxist theory on top of his work or, even worse, not reading him at all, I decided to have a dialogue with Hemingway's stories in three of my own, inspired by 'Hills Like White Elephants', 'The Short Happy Life of Francis Macomber', and, to a lesser extent, 'A Canary for One'. I wanted to speak Hemingway's narrative language so that I might invert and play with the values it contained.

Employing his signature iceberg technique, in which seven-eigths of the story is known only to the writer, I wrote 'Still Life' as a way of conversing with 'Hills Like White Elephants'. In an unnamed Sydney beachside café, a couple discuss a serious problem they share without ever directly naming it. Just as the hills and what they resemble in Hemingway's story provide a metaphorical key to the subject – the unborn child – in 'Still Life', the objective correlative here is the beach across the road, usually a favourite beach for surfers, though on this particular day the sea is uncommonly flat and still.

My couple, too, is in transition, as they have been travelling by bus from northern New South Wales and have stopped off in Sydney for the afternoon before continuing on to Melbourne. Their relationship is also in transition, and seems to be going down (heading south) rather quickly. In my story, however, it is the woman who broaches the delicate, unnamed threat to their union, the *nada* that lurks between them. After ordering lunch, she remarks to her lover, 'Maybe if you went to see someone…It's pretty common, you know…More common than what you'd think.' When she receives no response, she adds, 'I could go with you…We could go together.'

The 'it', however, remains elusive, drawing more and more attention to itself because it is never named. The man tries to distract the woman from addressing the *nada* by remarking that 'the surf might get up' and later they could go for a swim. The woman replies, rather testily, that it has been predicted that the surf will not get up today and thus there is no point in swimming. The two talk around the subject and gradually, through inferences and verbal slips – 'Maybe it's psychological'; 'It affects us both' – it is revealed that the woman is trying to talk the man into seeking medical help for his impotence – a condition that is realised symbolically in the beach across the road that has no surf.

The inspiration for this story came not only from 'Hills Like White Elephants', but also from the American painter Edward Hopper. I was always drawn to his paintings for the same reason I loved the short stories of Hemingway – he composed figures centred in auras of mystery, and gazing at them afforded the viewer a certain voyeuristic experience. Hemingway makes you feel as if you're eavesdropping all the time; Hopper's gift is that he makes you feel as if you're watching something you shouldn't be. He positions the viewer as a Peeping Tom, and you find yourself gazing at the usually hidden tensions between men and women, without ever knowing the cause. Hopper's images speak of an unnameable loneliness and isolation, and in paintings like 'Hotel by a Railroad', 'Hotel Lobby', and 'New York Lobby' the loneliness is not individual only, but an expression of disconnection between two lovers – articulated through their tense bodies and expressions, in the ways in which they always turn away from each other. In this sense, Hopper also communicates the incommunicable. Hopper's preoccupation with the confined spaces of hotel rooms, lobbies, and cafés is a visual equivalent of the spacially-limited railway stations, bars, and trains that are the signature settings of Hemingway's stories.

I've often felt that the painting that best reflected Hemingway's aesthetic was Hopper's 'Nighthawks', which was also his most famous. In many ways it can be interpreted as a visual relative of 'A Clean, Well-Lighted Place' and 'Hills Like White Elephants'. For this reason, when drafting 'Still Life', I decided to have a print of 'Nighthawks' hanging on the wall of the beachside café. Approximating Chekhov's and Hemingway's third-person distant narrative point-of-view, the narrator describes the famous painting:

a man and a woman were sitting up at the wooden counter of an American diner. The man looked like Humphrey Bogart and wore a suit and hat. He had a cigarette between his fingers. The woman, also smoking, was pretty and wore a red dress. They were both drinking coffee. It was night... There were two other figures in the painting. An attendant in white behind the curved wooden counter. His lips were parted, as though he were answering a question the Bogart look-alike had asked. The fourth figure sat at the other end of the counter with his back to the viewer. His suit was the same greyish-blue as the first man's, the one who sat with the woman in the red dress.

The couple in the 'Still Life' story find themselves in a startingly similar situation: they are the only people in the café apart from the waiter and a man dining nearby. Since the couple are unable to address directly the cause of their own personal *nada* – the man's impotence – they both use their individual interpretations of the painting as a way of talking about what they cannot say. Each makes predictions about the couple in the painting as a way of second-guessing the other's intentions and beliefs:

'They look serious… They've been having an affair. See the way she can't look him in the eye?'
  'She's contemplating her cigarette. They've probably just had sex.'
  'Is that all you ever think about…The woman in the painting…
she's going to leave him. She just hasn't found a way of telling him.'
  'Maybe if you didn't drink so much – '
  'Don't you think…that he's trying to talk that woman into something she really doesn't want to do?'

The couple continue to argue about aesthetics as a way of articulating the unspeakable. The man maintains he loves the way Hopper 'leaves just enough out to make it interesting', how everything is 'just below the surface', while the woman, frustrated by what is left out, by what cannot be said, maintains that 'even when he paints a couple, there's always this huge distance between them, like so much hasn't been said.'
    The man distracts the woman by continuing to suggest that 'the surf might get up', despite radio reports predicting the opposite. The woman comments, 'You know I don't like swimming if there's no surf'. In this story, like 'Hills', nothing is resolved on a literal level, but the reader hopefully senses in their silences that their union, like that of the couple in the painting, will never be the same again. 'Still Life' employs many of the objective techniques of 'Hills Like White Elelphants', but slants the story toward an opposite, more 'female' point-of-view: it is the man who has changed physically, not the

woman, and it is she who tries to persuade him to restore their former – but unattainable – harmony. 'Still Life' is not so much a feminist revision of 'Hills' as a second voice to it, a literary dialogue.

My thoughts about Hemingway and literary dialogues have had an influence on other short stories in *Fifteen Kinds of Desire*. 'The Drover's Wife', for example, is a narrative improvisation on the other Drover versions – first authored by Henry Lawson in 1892, then reworked and parodied by Murray Bail in 1975, in a story which 'dialogues' in turn with the painting 'The Drover's Wife', by Russell Drysdale. I've also reimagined several fairytales – all set in Sydney's red-light district Kings Cross, which functions as a contemporary version of Grimms' deep, dark woods. The story 'Ash' is a reworking of 'Cinderella', in which the protagonist is a seventeen-year-old boy, who is still a virgin. Ash is forced to work as a receptionist in his stepfather's brothel after his mother dies. In 'The Best', which is a reworking of 'Snow White', the same boy is expelled from the brothel and his step-father's home after he is discovered stealing from the till. In order to support himself he becomes a transvestite prostitute on William Street. His life is threatened by an older, more experienced transsexual hooker on the same block, who was considered the best and the prettiest, until seven English backpackers take pity on Ash and cart him back to their nearby hostel. In 'Beau', which is a rewriting of 'Sleeping Beauty', a mother of three boys is hit by a car and goes into a permanent coma. 'Scarlet' is a reworking of 'Little Red Riding Hood', in which the protagonist is the eleven-year-old daughter of a heroin dealer who lives in Kings Cross. Scarlet has been taught how to mix heroin and inject it into her mother's veins in the event that her mother is too strung out to do it herself. Instead of being a cautionary tale about a naive girl too young to protect herself, it becomes a parable that makes a virtue out of knowingness: the danger and corruption with which Scarlet has been raised proves to be her best defence during her walk through the 'woods' which are the threatening streets of the Cross.

My dialogues with the original stories and fairytales are inspired by the spirit of revisionism, although, unlike the revisionist fictions of Angela Carter or Margaret Atwood, my references to the original texts are unobtrusive; sometimes, I've been told, they're not apparent on a first reading. The stories in *Fifteen Kinds of Desire* contain no direct quotations or replications, but invert and play with the subject matter of the 'master narratives'. With these stories, I do not see myself as arguing with the original texts; rather, the conversation is between me and the ways in which women and men have been imagined. Much of what we communicate to one another remains underneath the story-line, there in the silences that Hemingway taught me not to fill.

Reference is made in this essay to the following works: Ernest Hemingway, *The Fifth Column and the First Forty-Nine Stories* (New York: Scribner, 1938), and *Death in the Afternoon* (New York: Scribner, 1932); Frederick Busch, *A Dangerous Profession* (New York: St. Martin's Press, 1998); Anton Chekhov, Letter to Alex P. Chekhov, April 1883, in Louis S. Friedland, ed., *Anton Chekhov: The Short Story, the Drama and Other Literary Topics* (New York: Milton, Balch, 1924); Charles May, *The Short Story: The Reality of Artifice* (New York: Simon & Schuster MacMillan 1995); Carlos Baker, *Hemingway: The Writer as Artist* (Princeton: Princeton University Press, 1952); Mandy Sayer, *Fifteen Kinds of Desire* (Sydney: Random House, 2001).

In researching Hopper's work in order to write this story, I should not have been surprised to find that Hopper was a huge fan of Hemingway, and wrote to him frequently.

Hugh Tolhurst

A Little Madness

Manic-Depressive Illness and Poetry

Hugh Tolhurst's first collection of poetry, *Filth and Other Poems*, was published by Black Pepper in 1998.

Fear of an as yet imperfectly understood disease, the tuberculosis which took John Keats' life in 1821, led to the burning of all the furnishings in the small room overlooking Rome's Spanish Steps in which he died. Literary shrines like the Keats-Shelley Museum are rare in the Antipodes, and this visitor wandered with interest and care through the rooms where portraits, busts, framed letters and glass-encased manuscripts celebrate the lives of Keats, Percy Bysshe Shelley, Mary Shelley and George Gordon, Lord Byron. The room in which the death mask of Keats sits remains more sparely furnished than the rest, though it contains along with the sketches of the dying poet, the certificate of his qualification as an apothecary. Pausing in this room, I found myself thinking of another as yet imperfectly understood disease which affected all four of the literary figures honoured in the Keats-Shelley house. At the milder edge of the spectrum of manic-depressive illness is a condition termed cyclothymia, and the poet Keats who described himself as possessing a 'horrid Morbidity of Temperament' was a cyclothymic young man who may have experienced, if he had lived for a few years longer, the progression of his temperamental condition into the more pronounced

209

'bipolar II disorder' or the 'classic' manic depressive illness, 'bipolar I disorder', the illness which affected Lord Byron, Percy Bysshe Shelley and Mary Shelley. In her *Touched With Fire: Manic-Depressive Illness and the Artistic Temperament*, Kay Redfield Jamison (who is both a John Hopkins Professor of Psychiatry and a St. Andrews Professor of English) gives reasonably detailed evidence to support the diagnosis of each of these literary figures, along with many other well-known poets, writers, painters and composers.

Depression as an illness seems to have been much more widely understood in recent years, and the subject of educational campaigns for greater community understanding in various countries. The apathy, lethargy, hopelessness and loss of pleasure associated with major depressive, or unipolar, illness are gaining wide currency as symptoms of illness to which less and less stigma is attached. Mania and hypomania (mild mania) are less well understood. One result of this is that, as Jamison's most recent book *Night Falls Fast: Understanding Suicide* notes, patients with bipolar II disorder 'are frequently misdiagnosed as suffering from depression only'. This misdiagnosis may occur with as many as one third of sufferers of manic depressive illness according to Jamison, and as 'anti-depressants, if prescribed alone…can precipitate mania and, occasionally, highly agitated and potentially suicidal mixed states,' it is a misdiagnosis of grave concern. Were manic states and particularly the milder hypomanic states of manic-depressive illness as well understood and recognised by both doctors and the community, one might hope that fewer individuals with manic depressive illness would be misdiagnosed, and that less fear and stigma would be associated with manic depression. An irritability and agitation lying underneath an extended period of depression may be easily missed, and the brief mild manic states of bipolar II disorder can easily appear both to the sufferer and to others as ebullience in recovery.

In *Touched With Fire*, Jamison describes these manic states:

Unlike individuals with unipolar depression, those suffering from manic-depressive illness also experience episodes of mania or hypomania (mild mania). These episodes are characterised by symptoms that are, in many ways, the opposite of those seen in depression. Thus, during hypomania and mania, mood is generally elevated and expansive (or not infrequently, paranoid and irritable); activity and energy levels are greatly increased; the need for sleep is decreased; speech is often rapid, excitable, and intrusive, and thinking is fast, moving quickly from topic to topic. Hypomanic or manic individuals usually have an inflated self-esteem, as well as a certainty of conviction about the correctness and importance of their ideas. This grandiosity can contribute to poor judgement, which, in turn, often results in chaotic patterns of personal and professional relationships. Other common features of hypomania and mania include spending excessive amounts of money, impulsive involvements in questionable endeavours, reckless driving, extreme impatience, intense and impulsive romantic or sexual liaisons, and volatility. In its extreme forms, mania is characterised by violent agitation, bizarre behaviour, delusional thinking, and visual and auditory hallucinations. In its milder variants the increased energy, expansiveness, risk-taking, and fluency of thought associated with hypomania can result in highly productive periods.

These hypomanias and manias are episodic, as are the depressions associated with manic depressive illness, lasting days, weeks or months. Importantly, in terms of medical and community misapprehension of the illness, they are separated by periods where no symptoms are evident, periods of good health, and these periods may last days, weeks, months, or years. It is possible to speak of sufferers who cycle quickly (there are individuals who have the misfortune of all four seasons in one day) and slow-cycle manic-depression, yet these are generalisations which can mislead as the illness rarely works like clockwork; a sufferer on a slow cycle might be free of hypomania and mania and depression for five or six years, then experience bouts of each within a twelve-month period. Alcoholism and drug abuse are exceedingly high among individuals with manic-depressive illness: one reason for this is the impulsivity of hypomania and mania, but another is the possibility of a sufferer hiding the condition behind another more obvious problem (it is still the case that in many circles less stigma attaches to alcoholism or even drug use than to mental illness). Alcoholism and drug use tend to worsen the progress of illness, and greatly increase the risk of suicide of the sufferer. Often disturbed sleeping patterns and, in particular, periods of insomnia, are the trigger for hypomania and manias; for this reason cocaine, ecstasy, and most particularly amphetamine use are fraught with danger; moderate use of marijuana on the other hand may slow alchohol intake and also have a soporific effect, and I would suggest (though I know of no studies) that many sufferers of manic-depressive illness find it helpful.

The average age of onset of manic-depressive illness is eighteen years and this is markedly earlier than that for unipolar depression, which is twenty-seven years; manic-depressive illness sufferers are also usually from the upper or professional classes; though there are exceptions both in terms of age and social status. Men and women are equally likely to suffer bipolar disorder, where unipolar depression affects twice as many women as it does men. Classic manic-depressive illness is found in about one per cent of adults where a further two or three per cent will suffer bipolar II disorder or cyclothymia. These rates are less than those for major depression of the unipolar variety (five per cent) but they may be increasing. An interesting passage in Kay Jamison's memoir of life as a psychiatrist with manic-depressive illness *An Unquiet Mind* (a feature film adaptation of this is in the wind with Hollywood) is suggestive of the prevalence of manic depression in senior ranks of the military. Romantically involved with the late Colonel David Laurie, a psychiatrist in the British Army Medical Corps, she tells the story of how (after he'd been told of her illness), her lover set out to reassure her 'in his rather systematic way', partly through dinners with serving senior officers of the British Army (and their wives) who also had manic-depressive illness. *An Unquiet Mind,* and also Jamison's study of suicide *Night Falls Fast,* suggest that she is not alone among medicos, or psychiatrists, whose healing careers coexist with managing the healer's own manic-depressive illness. Scientists, lawyers, politicians and all the other professions have higher rates of manic depression than the general population figure of one per cent; to my mind the reason why the rate among poets is exceptionally high (even compared with other artists), is in part that poets are by and large the black sheep of professional families. Controversy does attach to linking poets and manic-depressive illness, not least to the statistic quoted in Jamison's *Touched With Fire,* that sixty-one per cent of poets suffer manic-depressive illness, yet maybe this would die a little if we had accurate statistics for the rates of manic-depressive illness among say surgeons and admirals.

Touched With Fire deals largely with historical poets and fascinates both in its reading of literary history and in the different shades of understanding it lends to the works and lives of prominent artists, particularly poets. A feature of the book, unusual among literary studies, which relates to the hereditary nature of manic-depressive illnesses, is the plethora of genealogical charts showing the family trees of poets and artists. A blacked-in square or circle indicates respectively a male or a female family member with clear manic-depression, a dotted square or circle indicates cyclothymia, a crossed figure denotes a relative whose death was through suicide. Among the Byrons, Tennysons and the family of Virginia Woolf, manic-depression, cyclothymia, depression and suicide are quite widespread. Of Alfred Lord Tennyson's six brothers who lived to be adults, only young Horatio 1819–1899 is left blank, though this seems cautious given his 'strange personality was legendary' and he had the distinction of being described as 'rather unused to this planet'. These charts with their various choice details of contemporary description speak volumes for just how common it is for a manic-depressive individual to marry another, or to marry someone cyclothymic or depressive. This 'assortative mating' results often in volatile, pressure-cooker relationships. Furthermore, where the child of one manic-depressive parent has a twenty-eight per cent chance of inheriting an affective disorder, where both parents have affective disorders and a least one has manic-depression, three children out of four will inherit an affective disorder.

There is something both extraordinary and perhaps profoundly luckless about the lived reality of 'assortive mating'; partners of those with manic-depressive illness need the patience of saints often at those times when wife, husband or lover is blowing up into manic behaviours, and also must face the bewilderment of the person who shares their bed breaking down into depression and staying there. In sexual terms, intensified heightened sexuality one month and famine the next is something that can take a little getting used to in a lover. The assortative attraction between sufferers of affective disorders being strong, the person from whom saintly levels of understanding are required is very often battling their own mood disorder simultaneously. 'She/he would have to be mad to go out with him/her' is a statement of considerable banality when attached to relationships in which love and manic-depression are both present. Into such explosive unions are born children who must learn to live with interesting parents, and who themselves carry the genes which make mood disorders of their own highly likely. If you are yourself affected by manic-depression, you are also almost certain to know difficult life situations where someone close is suicidal, where someone close must be coaxed into a temporary holiday in a mental health facility, where someone you love is falteringly making small steps back into (irrationally terrifying) everyday life. Before you are thirty, you will have an ethic for interventions in the mental health-care arrangements of others, and also an ethic for the intervention of others in your own.

Over-compensation for profound feelings of inadequacy, guilt or shame, are often what lies underneath, what underpins, hypomania or mania. Both the hereditary nature of affective disorders, and the pronounced assortative attraction in relationships, tend to provide many a difficulty of the bewildering variety; manic overcompensation (for all that it may, as grandiose, seem arrogant or self-obsessed) is normally rooted in impotence before the suffering of others. As Jamison notes in *Night Falls Fast*, the depression which usually follows an episode of mania (which is a period of pronounced suicide risk) lasts around four months in most circumstances, however, where a death or serious illness in the family preceded the climb into the manic, the recovery time triples to eleven months. Those who suffer from depressive illness or manic-depressive illness are fifteen to twenty times more likely than the general population to commit suicide. In manic-depressive illness, the times of recovery from profound depression or from manic periods constitute one kind of high risk, while the possibility as the disease progresses of experiencing 'mixed states' where manic and depressive elements of mood coexist simultaneously provide the other. These mixed states are often at the watershed between the two poles of the disease and are periods of high energy and fast dramatic swings of mood. To be both profoundly depressed and jumping out of your skin is an extremely difficult experience and in terms of self-slaughter an extremely dangerous one.

Whether a prolonged, bleak, crushing period of depression is associated with unipolar or manic depression, it is a truism (rather than a tragic freakish circumstance) that the sufferer emerging once more into the light may commit suicide. Utter depression permits thoughts of suicide but rarely the will to go through with the act. *Night Falls Fast* is very acute on this point – the return of the will, a feeling that the depression through which one has just lived could not be borne again, a feeling of being a burden to others: these plus the availability of means can be quickly fatal. That it is true of the different forms of mood disorders points, as Jamison suggests here and there, to the binarism between unipolar and bipolar being flawed beyond the level of useful generalisation. Which is to say, that 'mixed states' may be implicated in the vast majority of suicides, even when unipolar depression is to all other intents and purposes a correct diagnosis. To put it another way, when the great pleasureless grey world suddenly releases the sufferer from a life without any form of joy, whose mood would not swing up perhaps too quickly somedays, perhaps with elements of depressed thought, depressed feeling still embedded? Jamison is a strong advocate of the mood-stabiliser lithium for its anti-suicidal properties (and these properties seem to apply even where it does not lend stability of mood). Though I'm about to point to lithium's shortcomings in another context, in the context of the depressed individual entering a phase of recovery I'm totally in favour of it as a brake on suicide. Life is precious, and even those creative individuals who find lithium hampers creativity should, with an awareness of its efficacy as a break on suicide, put their objections to one side when it is administered because the patient is believed to be in a transitional phase to which suicide risk adheres.

Quoting from a 1970 and 1979 study on the effects of lithium on the productivity of writers and artists, Jamison in *Touched With Fire* reports that, 'The overwhelming majority indicated that their productivity while on lithium had either increased (fifty-seven per cent) or remained the same (twenty per cent)', which (though it says nothing of quality) vindicates the idea that lithium can indeed be liberating for writers and artists with manic-depressive illness. Anecdotal suggestions make me think a study of poets alone might give figures of a less promising nature, however, as Jamison further reports, 'Approximately one-fourth (twenty-three per cent) reported a decrease in productivity, and a significant minority (seventeen per cent) stated they had stopped taking lithium due to its adverse effects.' It's not stated, but I take this to mean 'adverse effects' on the quantity or quality of artistic production, and thus see the reporting indicating that one in four writers and artists who suffer manic-depressive illness find lithium throws out their creativity with the bathwater, and most of these won't take it. Author of the 1979 study, M. Schou, is reported by Jamison as having 'noted that lithium might affect inspiration, the ability to execute ideas or both', and as stressing that, 'artists and writers clearly vary in a number of important ways, including severity and type of their illnesses, their degree of dependence on manic periods for artistic inspiration, and individual sensitivities to the pharmacological action of lithium'.

Schou speaks of 'their degree of dependence on manic periods for artistic inspiration' and I think 'degree' is well chosen, for most artists living with the illness do tend to link creativity with the up-periods. Hypomanias and even the less extreme manic states fuel creative fires; a decreased need for sleep is combined with pronounced combinatory thinking, an increase in intellectual functioning and an elevation in mood; these can be times of artistic breakthroughs because the realm of the possible seems larger in a hypomanic state. Of course, the artist must resist the likely simultaneous rise of a desire to go out and blow the rent on alcohol or drugs, but hypomanias, as mild mania, are full of the possibility of finally getting some work done. Across pretty well all the forms of artistic expression, boldness and expansiveness are seen as positives, and the intensity of works essayed in hypomania or even the beginnings of mania are permitted boldness and expansiveness. Even mixed states can in their radical ambiguity and their fraughtness spark flashes of artistic brilliance. The radical productivity of these times can see six months work produced in a weekend; it's not the side of manic-depressive illness that artists want to give up. For some, and I'd venture that with poets it is more than 'one-fourth', lithium does involve losing these times of heightened artistic facility and productivity. Of course many poets have no affective illness, and many who do find lithium works for them, but if Shelley had lived under a medical absolutism that insisted all manic-depressives should be on lithium, he may never have said that 'poets are the unacknowledged legislators of the world'. I've heard that very absolutism uttered by a psychiatrist at a fellow artist's Mental Health Review Board hearing as an argument against the restoration of her liberty, and I do not like it.

Lithium is still much in use as a lifetime medication for manic-depressive illness, yet a significant minority of artists with the condition do find it has for them such adverse effects on creativity that they won't take it 'for life'. I don't think that there is anything 'non-compliant' about an artist refusing the medication on these grounds, and it is not a rare problem with lithium; if it is true that six out of ten poets suffer manic-depressive illness and that one in six writers and artists refuse lithium because of its adverse effects, then we are talking about one in ten poets finding lithium unsuitable. Lithium saves a lot of lives, and Kay Jamison is right to praise it and point to its anti-suicidal properties. Nobel Laureate James D. Watson is quoted in the blurb of *Touched With Fire* – 'an emphatic analysis of the creativity that emerges from a little madness and the horror from too much' – and I think where Jamison writes of lithium, that 'emphatic' can be seen as cutting both ways. Valproate and other anti-convulsants are becoming more common in the treatment of manic-depressive illness, and beyond *Touched With Fire*, in her more recent *Night Falls Fast*, Jamison again points to the anti-suicidal properties of lithium, yet qualifies her emphasis:

The clinical problem is complex, however. Not everyone who has depression or manic-depressive illness is suicidal. If a patient refuses to take lithium or does not respond to it, anti-convulsants provide an important and often more agreeable treatment alternative. Lithium is effective in preventing suicide only if patients are willing to take it and if they respond to it. Not everyone will take it. Not everyone will respond to it.

Sufferers of manic-depressive illness have an extraordinary sensitivity to seasonal changes in light. Manias and hypomanias tend to occur in autumn and spring when fluctuations in light are greatest. The grim side of this is that late spring and early summer are the annual peaks of suicide, manic-depressive illness being very often the background to suicide. This isn't to say that sufferers go up and down with every season; the episodic nature of the illness might, however, follow the flow of an autumn hypomania, a spring mania and a black summer in one year after a few years of uninterrupted good health. Various graphs in *Touched With Fire* show that artistic and literary production tends to peak in autumn and spring and to fall away sharply in winter and summer. These might seems surprising charts to contemporary readers, yet they probably strike a true chord with many artists and writers: the poet who like W.H. Auden always writes by electric light with the curtains drawn, is still unusual.

Jamison's chapter on George Gordon, Lord Byron, is one of the longest in *Touched With Fire* and pleases with researched detail, such as the story of the night Byron's daughter was born, with the father downstairs cutting off the tops of every soda bottle in the house with his sword. Readers can enjoy *Don Juan* less guiltily for the understanding of the poet who struggled long and hard against severe manic-depressive illness. It was Auden who called *Don Juan*, 'for all its faults, the most original poem in the language', and read against the life understood as being a constant battle with the illness that made him 'mad, bad and dangerous to know' his considerable achievements, especially the long poem, can be perhaps more fairly appreciated. Neither his mother, nor his great uncle nor Lady Caroline Lamb were what you might think of as easy to know, as heredity and assortative mating tends to make the case with many sufferers. The unkind picture of his wife in *Don Juan* (though he denied Donna Inez was an 'elaborate satire on the character and manners of Lady Byron), is interesting to peruse after reading *Touched With Fire*. Annabella Milbanke somewhat before divorcing Byron on the grounds of his insanity is quoted: 'The day after my marriage he said, "You were determined not to marry a man in whose family there was insanity…You have done very well indeed," or some ironical expression to that effect, followed by the information that his maternal grandfather had committed suicide, and a cousin...had been mad, and set fire to a house.' Now, however odd this may seem as something said the morning after marrying someone, it isn't a story without a history. Three years earlier in 1812, the heiress Annabella Milbanke had turned down a proposal (presumably politely) from Lord Byron; she had also that year turned down Peninsular War hero General Sir Edward Pakenham on the ground that 'All the Pahenham family have a strong tendency towards insanity'. That rather damaging rejection tended to get quoted then (as it does in biographies now) because Sir Edward was the brother of Lady Wellington and as a grandson of the first Baron Longford, Thomas Pakenham (1713–1766), he had a lot of important and powerful relations in Ireland and in England who didn't think of themselves as having 'a strong tendency towards insanity'. Remarks like Annabella Milbanke's can easily cause wide offence; this writer too is descended from Thomas Pakenham, and like Sir Edward Pakenham his first cousin, my great great great grandfather had his Dublin address IN Rutland Square. I'm sure she'd have been safer on the Pakenham line, but I too can see the irony of her having married Lord Byron.

Touched With Fire gives in an appendix a list of poets 'with probable cyclothymia, major depression, or manic-depressive illness' and the only Australian listed is Adam Lindsay Gordon. Gordon committed suicide the day after his *Bush Ballads and Galloping Rhymes* was published. Yet, other leading Australian poets, including Les Murray and Bruce Beaver have written of struggles with depression or manic-depression. The rising generation of poets is not without individuals affected by such difficulties, and the next generation will doubtless include manic-depressive poets. In recent years a career in Australian poetry has become more difficult through major publishers ceasing to publish contemporary poetry; it's a literary culture where poets are seen as difficult individuals at home though among English language poetries Australian poetry is seen as quite vital internationally. It can be something of a dog's life, the life of poetry, and for many the early onset of manic-depressive illness arrives simultaneously with first recognition as a poet. I can't help thinking that the stigma associated with affective disorders is implicit within the marginalisation of poetry within Australian literary culture. When I encounter young poets of talent attempting to start careers, with no equivalent prize like the *Australian*/Vogel Award for Fiction to aim for, and with few interested publishers to aim for, well, I tend to wish them better pay and better conditions.

Works by Kay Redfield Jamison: *Night Falls Fast: Understanding Suicide* (Picador 2000), *An Unquiet Mind, A Memoir of Moods and Madness* (Picador 1996), *Touched With Fire: Manic-Depressive Illness and the Artistic Temperament* (Free Books, 1993).

Lucy Dougan
White Clay

In high school
she moulded a man
and a woman.
When the work
got her palms
tight and dry
she was learning
something about touch.

The anatomy was all
wrong said her teacher,
but pinching muscles
and curves out of
nothing felt good.

The man lay along
the woman's back.
The girl stroked the slip
from faceless starts
to uncertain ends
and found a word
that softened her inside.

Another girl
called it fucking.
She tested this word
against the raw silk

limbs she had shaped.
There was no congress
between form and sound.

Boys looked at her now.
(Had they looked before?
She couldn't say.)
They were curious
to know if her fingers
would be patient with them
like white clay.

Art classes taught her
the true nature of bodies.
Although they started out
cold and ended hot,
they could not be counted on
to do what her hands wanted.

Lucy Dougan's first collection *Memory Shell* (Five Islands Press, 1998) won the 2000 Dame Mary Gilmore Award.

Judith Beveridge

Writing Home

Poetry from New Zealand

Jenny Bornholdt, *These Days* (Victoria UP, 2000)
Paula Green, *Chrome* (Auckland UP, 2000)
Anna Jackson, *The Long Road to Teatime* (Auckland UP, 2000)

Judith Beveridge has won the Dame Mary Gilmore Award and the NSW and Victorian Premiers' Awards for her two collections of poetry, *The Domesticity of Giraffes* (1987) *and Accidental Grace* (1996).

Of the several New Zealand poetry books which I have looked at recently, the most interesting are those which have set about exploring the spaces that constitute and reconfigure ideas of home. Perhaps it's not without coincidence that these books are written by women, as women might be more readily inclined to define themselves in relation to family and kin, and through the occupation and management of domestic space. Certainly, for all these poets, family is a central focussing force, and integral to the idea of 'home'.

Language and the senses are bound up in ways often taken for granted. Both are sources for feelings of belonging. Poetry, through the precision of its enactment and embodiment of what we experience and perceive, is the language that's most apt for exploring notions of home and belonging, for locating the areas most open to our vulnerabilities and affections.

Part of Jenny Bornholdt's charm in *These Days*, is humour and her ability to observe and capture the ordinary details which make up her life. Home is revealed as being constantly 'in process', created day-to-day by events that are often peripheral, yet which still impact greatly: the world of appliances, of escaped pet rabbits, of workmen and repairmen, of the round of chores and routines which can sap energies:

You say *giddy*
giddy giddy giddy
giddy and very soon
you are and you fall
right down.

Bornholdt's poems are very much concerned with naming, of putting detail into place, of using incident and anecdote to reveal the nature of the everyday. Yet it's often in what's implied by her poems that the nature of home is most potently revealed. The demands of family are nowhere better indicated than in 'A rabbit in danger', ostensibly about a pet rabbit being bailed up under a car by two dogs:

Your rabbit is under the car, the dogs' owners explained.

Oh. Jasmine's mother looked weary. *I'll go and make her special porridge, she'll come inside for that.*

Shall we stay and make sure she doesn't go onto the road?

No, replied Jasmine's mother as she turned and walked through the gate. *I've just about had enough of that rabbit.*

The last line is wonderful for the way in which the frustration gains in force from those emphatic 't's. Home is predicated by the momentum of the everyday, by the movement of incremental processes that keep us tied to the small, the mundane, despite our lives being carried on by surges over which we have little control: the passing of time, the progress of pregnancy, birth. Bornholdt has a well-tuned ear and eye for the small, revealing incident:

> Cricket balls release the scent of lavender.
> Leaves visit. The kittens Smokey and Molly play on the
> footpath. Jasmine the rabbit eats breakfast. An elderly
> woman, getting off the bus after a fast ride, says *I feel
> a bit like Elvis, I'm all shook up.*

Though Bornholdt's uncomplicated sentence structures produce clarity, as a reverse effect they do make for poems which are often technically shallow. Figurative images are not favoured. She prefers her images unmediated, unjuxtaposed – and thus she restricts her tone. If language points to or names, then nouns are the most functional part of language. The noun is the source of the image, and naming confirms the world. In *These Days* Bornholdt is principally concerned with the process of naming, of fixing tangible points: the poet as nomenclator.

I would have prefered a poetry with a richer, more varied use of other elements of speech: the adjective, for example, is not much employed by Bornholdt in this book. Many poets become afraid of adjectives because they are perhaps the first parts of speech to betray incompetence, and it is preferable to cut them out or to convert them into a noun, or noun-phrase. As Ellen Bryant Voigt says in her essay 'Rethinking Adjectives' from her book *The Flexible Lyric*: 'Because of its subjective nature its presence in the poem is the hardest to earn; craft does not put it there so much as vision, intuition, temperament, perhaps even character.' Adjectives are sourced from the senses and thus help to put the poet's stamp on the poem, they supply tone and feeling and also music.

In her desire to be straightforward, Bornholdt often sacrifices music and the rhythms that would be gained from varying a poem's grammatical behaviour, though at times, as 'In waiting', she does achieve an elegant poise:

Here's winter coming up
the valley, the last
of the monarchs sailing
past the hillside's glossy pelt
of flax.

Farewell summer.
Farewell autumn.
We marvel at the seasons
and how persistent, through
all of them, the ivy
is, slowly dragging the washing
line earthwards. And how persistent
this child is, also heading
earthwards, yet turning back
again and again. Your body
too persistent, longing for
memory to kick
into gear and relieve
this ache – dull – like
the soft thud of passionfruit
striking the ground.

However, to my mind the poem should have ended on the word 'ache', as it would achieve more resonance, opening its meaning out, rather than closing it off; for me, the sound image ('soft thud') doesn't successfully translate over into touch.

But Bornholdt, throughout *These Days*, does give the reader grounded, convincing disclosures. Home is not at all idealised in her work, but attested to with both vulnerability and strength, born from the effort of finding and maintaining an authentic orientation within the broader, illimitable world.

Home, for Paula Green in her four-part book *Chrome*, is more an essence, a tone, a flavour evoked through the touchstone of colour. Yellow, red, green and blue represent repectively her self, her mother, her father, and poetry. Her book is an exploration of mood, memory, past and present, image and abstraction, the boundaries of self, place, and the way in which these can be given resonance. Green's work is fluid and heavily nuanced. The emphasis is not on incident, or story as it is in Bornholdt, but rather on suggestion, atmosphere. Her lines meld into each other lyrically rather than narratively, meditately rather than dramatically:

syllable by syllable I decorate myself
rhymed with grapefruit or saffron fuelled

by the clutter of paper honey open wounds
the walls are home to artworks

audible noise the whole year round
routines that dwell in our place

the bare wood the connections
between art and artifact splendid

I carry tokens of my existence
buttery verse culinary herbs cadmium yellow

the lightness of work on a new scale
the lungs or bone or blood or water
(from 'Yellow')

The poet in *Chrome* endeavours to live inside her language, to render her images, at times, with an epiphanic quality. As much as anything, the poems seem to be about the nature of poetic reality. Boundaries are difficult to define, and the poetry enacts this, the lines constantly shifting between the tangible and the abstract, constantly playing off nimble conceptuality against gravity and substantiality:

I am at the starting point
home to a precious stone

past and future
basking in a vast present

here, an intimate chair
here, a blue chair

here is the empty bed, ultramarine
here are the flaking chairs, duck-egg blue

here is the winter window sill
here are the straw tables

little wonder at levitation
a possible flight into a huge beautiful leaky realm

disguised as a bird
a heroine in the plumbago air

in the hue of ambiguous depth
in the tint of distant hills

and so, the poet unwinds
unwinding the powder-fine substance of home
(from 'Blue')

This produces wonderful results, but at other times it leads to little other than a windy lyricism, too elusive to mean much: '*I am enclosed within cyanic space/ occupied and occupying/ the absurd truth/ the necessary truth/ setting tasks beyond hope/ about full and dripping breach/ binding the blueness/ conjectural and manifold/ where am I?/* where am I?/ *waiting to give speech/ to the ice-bright blue.*'

    Green is not afraid of adjectives. Indeed, it is her use of these qualifiers that give the book its innovative scope, and which amplifies and unmasks the feeling. In 'Red', the section dealing with her mother, so much comes through just in the crucial implications her adjectives are able to supply: 'the bottled daughter/ the strawberry daughter...my mother in a pinch of light/ grown on placenta and orchard fruit/ in her torn heart/ red wounds and crimson lake...with her longing she fans/ a beetroot flame, the boiling legends'.

    Taking her cue from film and painting, Green, with a great deal of subtlety and skill, builds her work less from discursive and expository elements, and more from elements that appeal directly to the senses, those tools for gathering presentational information. Each of the four parts of her book – Yellow, Red, Green, Blue – have their own musical key. Each takes its tone from the visual or presentational use of the specified colour. Yet Green's lines are often elusive, and remind me very much of French poetry for the way in which the language seems to be one of essences, of nuances, for the way in which an image comes into being, then dissolves. Her lines resist the pull of the tangible, and progress more through innovation and intuition than through the need to be grounded or resolved:

I am a dance without wind
I am a shroud without plangent moon

what I have said so far
dissolves in fierce pigment

a streak of sunlight on a peacock blue floor
makes itself at home with compelling lightness

yet the burden is hidden in unbearable weight
like some heavy thing in deep water
(from 'Blue')

At times, the effect is sheer enchantment, at other times I'm not always convinced that the English language can carry such totality over into poetry as French can, 'where,' as Octavio Paz wrote, 'the world becomes writing and language becomes the double of the world.'

However *Chrome* is the most interesting and original of these three books, and Green's construction and prefiguring of ideas of home much more complex and elusive. She takes language on board in a way that is essential to any understanding of a sense of belonging; 'home' being made and constructed by language, which is not simply a tool to describe, or locate it. Thus, the last section 'Blue', in which Green uses the suggestive possibilities of that particular colour to uncover or filter a sense of poetry, illuminates a space in which writing can find measure and embodiment amongst change and unsubstantiality:

I write this attached to all objects
bedding down in the spree itself

profoundly moved by blue
the colour of the shadow of a southern moon

drawn into the far-off
the bliss of space, a slightly deeper blue

I write to make room for breath
wavelengths of reality and dream

Chrome is a magnificent attempt to explore the material and immaterial dimensions of 'home'.

Anna Jackson in *The Long Road To Teatime* uses a less poetic, yet still intimate voice to convey a sense of belonging. For Jackson, it's principally family — both immediate and distant — which provides the locus for an understanding of home. The first poem in the volume 16 Pakeha Waka is a potted family history, ranging from 1860 to the present day. I'm doubtful that the first sections hold much interest for the reader because of the content and the reporting style: 'One of my sixteen waka arrived in Auckland in 1860/ the *Ellen Lewis* from Nova Scotia, and on board/ my great-great-grandparents, John and Flora McDonald.' The poem does, however, pick up resonance later, when Jackson locates her own presence and that of her present-day family along the narrative continuum, the idea of *waka* (Maori for boat) beautifully and poignantly transposed:

Our daughter was born at last, in New Zealand,
at home, in the bath, on the 7th of February

after a Waitangi Day of contractions.
We called her Elvira — a Spanish name

meaning fair one — foreigner — Pakeha.

At sixteen months, she still rows herself
about on the floor, bottom-shuffling.

Not a walker, but a waka –
my waka to the stars.

Important to this book are the concepts of journeying and arrival. The section 'The Long Road to Teatime' recounts an imaginary journey the poet makes with Dante as he leads her down into the darkness before she can 'rekindle [her] affair with the sun'. It's an intriguing, imaginative poem, full of humour and bound to appeal especially to other poets, as it becomes finally revealed which category of human beings lies at the very base of the inferno, (below even the murderers and child abusers): 'I open my mouth to ask Dante who they are,/ but no words come./ Then I know these are the traitors to their calling./ Here the artists who gave up painting, the poets/ who were too busy teaching, are sealed/ in their silence.'

What is delightful about this book is Jackson's ability to be both 'artless' and 'literary' within the same poem. She writes with appealing clarity, the tone almost naive, yet with loads of stylish humour. The sections 'Breakfast with Ruffy' and 'Mealtimes at the Bookhouse' are beautifully achieved in their use of voice and form. The poems convey a sense of domestic closeness, of kinship, innocence and rapport. The characters she imagines having tea or coffee with (Katherine Mansfield, Viktor Shklovsky, Marianne Moore, Gudrun and Ursula from D.H. Lawrence's *Women in Love*) are rendered with empathy and concision. Jackson writes a language which, though often simple and unadorned, is also at times clever, flexible and playful.

There is more versatility of tone and rhythm in Jackson than in Bornholdt, though less linguistic fluidity than in Green. Verbs have a predominance of place in this book, the events presented by way of action rather than description, weight being given to the dynamics of interaction.

There's a great sense of contentment and reposefulness in Anna Jackson's concept of home. The poems have the feeling of being written around a large kitchen table, to which many people come and partake of the company and home cooking. Indeed, in 'Tea with the Timorese', various people *do* come — not only the Timorese victims, but also members of the Indonesian military. Again, Jackson uses humour to propel the political import of the poem. The domestic setting takes the concerns out of a broad arena and puts them into the familiar and everyday, humanising and highlighting them. Jackson uses 'home' as a venue for the political to be watched, scrutinized, discussed. The speaker appears almost naive, too polite and commodious to confront the General, yet her poems can still be disarming:

Should I have raised the issue of the massacre
in East Timor with the General? I passed
him a bagel and asked Johnny to stop kicking
his chair. The General spread cream cheese
and jam on his bagel and Simon poured him coffee.
But when I introduced him to Simon, Simon's eyes
narrowed. He asked the General, 'so how
do you feel about all the kids who died?'

'They weren't kids,' the General replied.
('Bagels with General Panjaitan')

By the end of *The Long Road to Teatime* home, as much as anything, is tone, texture, courtesy, sociability. It is also the site where identity is most fluid, most protean. In Jackson's work, home constantly reconfigures life's processes by laying bare essential roles — parent, spouse, daughter, son etc. Home is made up of the relationships by which we define ourselves and others, and by which others define us.

Each of these three books — *These Days*, *Chrome*, and *The Long Road to Teatime* — while finding their points of belonging within the New Zealand landscape and cultural milieu, also mark out territory that universally crosses into the familiar. Home is not simply the places we inhabit, but also the places and relations that we imagine. The mind and senses meeting together as poetry.

Brendan Ryan

John Forbes

Collected Poems (Brandl & Schlesinger, 2001)

Brendan Ryan's first collection of poetry, *Why I Am Not a Farmer*, was published in 2000 by Five Islands Press.

When I first saw the cover of John Forbes' *Collected Poems* I was momentarily silenced by the photograph of a younger Forbes, sitting in a café, smoking pensively, as if contemplating the future before him. The John Forbes I had known was a single man in his forties who lived in a shared house in Carlton. The surprise of seeing a younger Forbes on the cover of his *Collected Poems* immediately raised the question for me – Is this the John Forbes we are to remember? Is this the self that is both absent and vulnerably present in Forbes' poems? The photograph does create a playful relationship between the self, depicted on the cover, and that a reader may find in reading the poems. Forbes loved to satirise and critique the idea of the self as 'a centrally defining principle' in many of his poems. In fact, his humour in poems like 'Melbourne', where he urges himself to 'Be a caricature,/ John, and not a cartoon,' and 'Self Portrait With Cake', prevents Forbes from taking the self too seriously. He deplored poets who created their own myths through the projection of idealised selves, yet he wasn't averse to exploring national myths through a collective persona – see 'Europe: a Guide for Ken Searle', 'Anzac Day', and 'Watching The Treasurer'. The images of John Forbes in the poems may be illusive to some, yet what will be recognisable to many readers is his combination of wit and intellect in producing poems which challenge our way of viewing our selves.

I was a student of John Forbes in a Creative Writing Diploma at RMIT in 1989, and later on a more personal level at his house in Carlton during 1994-95. Much of the advice and help Forbes gave to me in those days still resonates with me. His influence upon my own writing was like a skills coach in an AFL side. Forbes was the person you went to when you needed attention to technique, philosophy, and energy. He encouraged me to read a wide range of other poets, and in doing so, helped me to take the capital P out of my poetry. Later, I took part in workshops with Alan Wearne, one of Forbes's closest friends, who had an uncanny knack of knowing which poets could be of help to me, and whose teachings were like an AFL team coach giving much needed pep-talks at three-quarter time.

One of the most instructive things Forbes said to me was to make your lines radically different from each other and to let the reader fill in the gaps. This basic tenet of contrast and connection lies at the heart of much of his poetry. In his poems he continually brought opposites together – high and low cultural references, imagery, formal and colloquial language – as a means of creating tension between the lines, and perhaps between John Forbes the person and the reader.

An early poem that announces Forbes's use of comparison is 'Admonitions', written with the almost mythical Mark O'Connor. The poem begins: 'The happiest of cannonballs/ is a burger/ a labour of love walking naked'. While the humour in these opening lines can be read retrospectively as suggesting Forbes's facetiousness, the poem lacks a paraphrasable sense, and so challenges the reader to find or make the meaning. His juxtaposition of imagery, questions and information defies traditional subject-based readings of the poem. The reader cannot help but become engaged, both positively and negatively. Alan Urquhart makes the mistake of attempting to make literal sense of this poem when he asks (in *Westerly*, no.3, Spring 1997), 'How can cannonballs be happy or have any personal feelings?' Such a reading misses the humour inherent in the poem, and the point that Forbes was experimenting with how language can be structured, and in turn structures each of us. By bringing together opposites in imagery, disrupting syntax and challenging the reader to become engaged in the construct of the poem, Forbes was preparing the ground for a style of poem he would continue to write throughout his career.

There is a poignant echo of 'Admonitions' in a poem from his last book *Damaged Glamour*. 'Admonition', written without Mark O'Connor, is a more sombre poem beneath its playful surface. Like other late poems it is notable for the way life experience has seeped into it as subject matter. The poem is a playful rebuttal of emotion, and yet the second last line, 'That's Grace enough this mild autumn day', alludes to Frank O'Hara's lyrical epitaph – 'Grace to be born and live as variously as possible'. Although Forbes is ironically depicting an iconic self here with his references to Greek gods, A.D Hope and a slightly romanticised inner city lifestyle which suggests a vulnerability to emotion, the tension between the apparent ill-health of the narrator and the iconic self reveals the weight of lived experience – something missing from the earlier poem.

Like 'Admonitions', 'Ode To Tropical Skiing' is another example of the open-form poem that Forbes wrote throughout his career. The ode is arranged across the page, lines and imagery juxtaposed, as he contrasts the exotic with an everyday hedonism: 'Enjoy the ice-cream, Gerald/ the sun sparkling/ on its white frostiness/ is the closest you'll ever get to St Moritz/ racing up the tiny snowfields on the side of a pill'. Had this type of poetry been written in Australia before? Possibly so, in the declamatory tones of Ern Malley ('We will be wraiths and wreaths of tissue-paper/ To clog the Town Council in their plans./ Culture forsooth! Albert, get my gun.'). And while the poem is of its era, it is unpredictable, energetic and at times surreal. However Forbes was far from a surrealist looking for images to reflect the troubled psyche. He was more interested in the energy disparate imagery can suggest in a poem. Towards the end of 'Ode to Tropical Skiing', Forbes' customary lopping of literary seriousness appears in his satirical reference to Shakespeare – 'where I compare thee/ to a surfboard lost in Peru'. Forbes said in an interview that he found this image of a surfer riding a wave in the Pacific and landing in the Peruvian Alps poignant rather than merely comic – a point to be considered when coming across the many references to high and low culture in his poetry, since occasionally Forbes's humour doesn't translate for readers searching for an identifiable realism in his poems.

While Don Anderson, in his introduction to the *Collected Poems*, rightly suggests that a range of poets influenced Forbes, the importance of American poetry cannot be underestimated. As he says in 'To the Bobbydazzlers' (reminding me of a K-Tel Greatest Hits album of the 70s), it was American poets who saved him from the 'talented earache of Modern/ Poetry'. Ted Berrigan, John Ashbery and Frank O'Hara were the poets to influence Forbes the most. Berrigan was a poet of the everyday, whose poems could be alternately experimental, open to experience, bardic and intimate. Occasionally, Berrigan's poems suffer from a subjective sentimentality, especially when they're about friends in New York. But like Forbes, Berrigan was a bower bird in the contemporary world, borrowing lines from newspapers and other poets, and creating collages where the poem becomes a thing of itself, a lived experience which keeps the reader alert. Perhaps Forbes' closest imitation of Berrigan is in 'Ode/Goodbye Memory' from *Stalin's Holidays*, where the repetition of the phrase 'goodbye memory' is scattered as a motif throughout the poem. 'Goodbye memory & goodbye/ to the sheets held against hot windows/ on days when the morning's blue intensity so crushes me.' Berrigan's 'Farewell Address', taken from his 1970 collection *Buffalo Days*, has goodbye repeated in a similar pattern throughout it, except unlike Forbes' farewell to the apparent saving grace of memory against the hedonism of the body, Berrigan's poem is an intimate farewell to the parts of a house he has lived in: '& Goodbye first floor. Goodbye kitchen, you were a delight; you/ fed us morning, noon & night.' While both poems capture the disclosure a farewell often gives, Forbes' poem is more metaphysical and Catholic than Berrigan's, especially with the division he suggests between the mind and body.

The open-form collage poem was only one type of poem Forbes wrote. His Ashbery imitations – 'Four Heads and How To Do Them', 'Topothesia' (based on Ashbery's 'Clepsydra') and 'Phaenomena' – all point to a philosophical interiority where the subject of the poem is dislocated and yet contained by the intimacy of the relationship between poet and reader. What are these illusive poems about? Again, Forbes is pulling the reader in to see a function of language as being to structure our responses. Language for Forbes was not something like a window scraper that you pick up and use, but rather something that structures you.

>   And
> if we glance back at the panorama (and you can bet
> we will) which our fatigue and cigarette smoke frame
> into well earned images of self esteem that border on
> wonder at our avoiding the issue
> ('Topothesia')

While these poems may lack quotable lines, they possess a meditative calm produced by the evenness of the language, and by the desire to reflect on the possibilities such poems create in the reader's mind. Also, the idea of a definitive self was, for Forbes, almost always a construct to be satirised and questioned, a cue he seems to have taken from Frank O'Hara.

The influence of O'Hara can be noted from the first poem in the *Collected Poems*, 'Oranges'. O'Hara actually wrote a long poem about oranges titled 'Oranges: 12 Pastorals', which Forbes might have been referring to at the end of his poem. O'Hara was known for his poems of gay life in New York in the 1950s and 1960s, and of his friendships with various American Abstract Expressionists, and his chatty, conversational poetic style is tempting to imitate. O'Hara also had a wacky sense of humour, evidenced in such poems as 'Ave Maria' and 'Poem (Lana Turner has collapsed!)'. This must have appealed, as O'Hara's sense of humour and importantly his timing seem to have been taken up by Forbes – 'A Loony Tine in the rumpus room packs/ Them in. It wakes up the wisdom tooth/ Our guide, philosopher and friend' ('A Loony Tune'). Or:

>   You
> celebrate your indifference
> with a packet of lollies

or a Ton-Ton Macoute
haircut. It's almost
pure debauchery, as prayer
is for example
('Ars Poetica')

Some critics might argue that here Forbes is being merely silly or comic for effect. What is the function of humour in a poem where meaning isn't transparent? Is it merely a humour of aesthetics? Yes and no. As a poet of experiment and technique, Forbes was making connections between opposites to create humour and irony within the directions language took him. He has said in interviews that he would often begin a poem with a line and add another, and then see where the poem took him. He rarely started writing with a preconceived idea of what he was writing about. This is why the reader often discovers what a Forbes poem is about, rather than being told in the opening lines what to expect. His poems are funny because the reader is surprised or caught off-guard by the reference to a Ton-Ton Macoute haircut or, as in 'Winter Olympics', 'where being on TV means success', Ronald Reagan's voice presented as a pinnacle of a kind of bland happiness, while a reference to The Everly Brothers fades the poem into a nostalgic joke. Like the often hilarious similes Forbes scattered throughout his poetry, his humour is driven by the associations he makes within his poems. Call this energy, timing, the result of wide reading, a razor-sharp mind, or simply his preference for humour over seriousness, Forbes kept his poems alive by constantly being aware that they were constructions.

Poetic influence isn't always easy to locate and in one sense it only matters what the poet does with his influences. Writing out of an American poetic style, Forbes seems to have hit his mark with the collections *Stalin's Holidays* and *The Stunned Mullet*. In these collections, he comes into his own as a poet writing 'public' poems about Australian culture, history, drugs and death. While these poems are more subject-based than his earlier poetry, Forbes' language draws its energy from the random associations and criticisms of 'Oz culture' that he squeezes into the poems. 'Frames snap in the cartoon air./ Is prevention better than cure? Is Canberra?' All this in 'The Joyful Mysteries', Forbes' playful reference to a Catholic prayer associated with the Rosary commemorating Christ rising from the Tomb.

Forbes' urging me to write about what you don't know, to discover what your poetry is, was a maxim he used repeatedly in his own poetry. In fact, the opening lines of his poems typify the challenge he often gave to himself – 'Lips bruised blue' ('The Stunned Mullet'), 'Subtract me from the motions of my body' ('The Poem on its Sleeve'), 'It's fun to take speed' ('Speed, a pastoral'). His poems often went through thirty or forty drafts, which suggests why he wrote few bad poems. His meticulousness pays off with poems from this period, many now regarded as classics – 'Stalin's Holidays', 'Watching the Treasurer', 'Afternoon Papers', 'Drugs', 'Europe: A Guide', 'The History of Nostalgia' and 'Love Poem'. In these Forbes has perfected his satiric style. His tone is confident, his intellect restless, and despite what some critics have said in the past, the poems end at just about where you wouldn't want anymore. 'Yes, this/ was the decade known as the 'Eighties' where,/ stunned by the speed of capital you thought/ 'What a horrible tasting pie!' ('The Corrosive Literal').

These poems from the late seventies and eighties seem to have had an influence on a generation of younger poets. Of the mainly male so-called 'generation of 68', Forbes and Robert Adamson appear to have had the most influence on younger poets. You can see Forbes' influence in Adam Aitken's juxtapositions of Asian and Western values, and the combination of energy and form in Cassie Lewis and Emma Lew's poetry. Hugh Tolhurst and Ted Neilsen borrow heavily from Forbes stylistically while updating his view of Australia, and Kieran Carroll's explorations into Australian suburbia are as funny and poignant as Forbes' satires on a TV life in the suburbs. Perhaps Forbes' poetry is more relevant to this generation, proud of its popular culture, and yet sharp enough to see through the facade of that culture's permanence. In the future, his poetry may experience a backlash – he has always had his detractors, he does not yet enjoy the popularity of Bruce Dawe on VCE school lists – yet the influence of Forbes on younger poets will endure because his poems are made from the surprise and energy of the contemporary world.

The later poems, from *Damaged Glamour,* continue Forbes' explorations of politics, of Sydney as an iconic entity, popular music, Art, with references to actors and minor philosophers such as Willard Van Ormond Quine, who is worth including in a poem for his name alone. One of the main developments Forbes was making in these poems was to include more lived experience in his poetry, to speak openly of himself, as in 'Lassu In Cielo', where he writes from a residency at Loughborough University in England. While he is hardly confessional, the main change seems to be an awareness of the vulnerability of the self, both in a political sense in poems such as 'Ode To Karl Marx' and 'Anzac Day', and in a personal sense in 'Love Poem', 'Entartete Kunst' and 'Poem For Greg Forbes'. One of Forbes' weak areas was in writing about love, and poems such as 'The Harbour Bride' and 'Europe, Endless' rely on female stereotypes to represent a slight intellectual point. As Gig Ryan suggests in her foreword to the *Collected Poems*, Forbes preserves an Old Australia while satirising it, and I wonder how relevant this version of Australia will be to future generations brought up with Game Boy, global chat rooms, and the politics of Eminem. Still, the last poems includes classics such as 'Sydney Harbour Considered as a Matisse' and 'On Tiepolo's Banquet of Antony and Cleopatra', a poem that would look fine beside the actual painting, or piped through headsets for visitors to the National Gallery in Melbourne.

One of the abiding memories I have of Forbes occurred after one of our tutorial sessions. It was peak hour on a Friday and we were walking around the corner from his house in Carlton onto Princes Street. The traffic was banked up in a gridlock. I think we were talking about a poet when all of a sudden John did an impression of pogoing to 'Suzy is a Headbanger' on the footpath. Drivers were looking over at us. Other pedestrians were turning their heads. I remember thinking: here I am with a man in his forties dancing to the Ramones in peak hour traffic. People get arrested for this. Not John, he was as personal and unpredictable as his poems.

Martin Duwell

Contemporary Australian Poetry

Calyx: Thirty Contemporary Australian Poets, edited by Michael Brennan and Peter Minter (Paper Bark Press, 2001)

New Music: An Anthology of Contemporary Australian Poetry, edited by John Leonard (Five Islands Press, 2001)

Martin Duwell was the editor of *Makar* and its associated publishing program; he teaches at the University of Queensland and has written extensively on contemporary poetry.

From the distance of this new millennium, the general shape of post-war Australian poetry looks clear enough. We tend to see the fifties as a landscape divided between academic poets and poets fostered by Douglas Stewart's *Bulletin*, in turn challenged by a younger generation, especially from Brisbane and from Melbourne University, but of surprisingly diverse character, collected in Hall and Shapcott's *New Impulses in Australian Poetry* in the mid-sixties. The seventies seem now essentially a battleground between the New Writing group collected in John Tranter's *The New Australian Poetry* and a reaction, lead by Les Murray, involving figures like Robert Gray, Geoffrey Lehmann and a group of younger poets. The eighties saw that simple binary opposition complicated by the arrival of feminist poetries, multicultural poetries (especially the discovery of a great, previously unknown, Australian poet, Dimitris Tsaloumas) and black poetry in English (initially with poets like Mudrooroo and Lionel Fogarty). The first and last of these poetries have brought with them interestingly contentious theory.

The extent to which these outlines are accurate is another matter. Sometimes distance in time does show patterns more clearly, but equally it is possible that, through the general process of forgetting, only the dominant shapes of the landscape are visible and a lot of intriguing and important poets are simply edited out for the sake of convenience and consistency. Whatever the case, it is indisputable that anthologies rather than individual collections have given us some sense of what is happening, and so one turns to these two anthologies, Michael Brennan and Peter Minter's *Calyx* and John Leonard's *New Music*, for clues as to what happened in the nineties and thus to what is still happening. The former is very much a book built around poets, especially those making their debuts in the nineties. It omits crucial figures like Anthony Lawrence and John Kinsella and is really a book of contemporary and provisional process rather than calm, retrospective judgement; it is, to make an analogy from an earlier period, an *Applestealers* rather than a *New Australian Poetry*. *New Music* is much more a snapshot of the decade (an image used in the introduction), including brief samples of nearly a hundred poets whose dates of birth are separated by sixty years. There is a lot of acceptable prejudice in favour of the young and new and, in keeping with Leonard's practice, they are arranged in reverse order to the conventional scheme so that the poems of the youngest poets come first.

On the surface the introductions strike very different notes. Leonard's is, at least in part, concerned with some fairly old-fashioned formal observations and the high culture/low culture distinction. But both share the idea that the nineties is a decade of bridges and tunings rather than excluding poetic ideologies. According to Leonard, the new poets 'evade categorization' and 'a new spirit of eclecticism is abroad'. The editors of *Calyx* describe the quality of the poetry, as 'energetic' and 'significant', but when it comes to describing the nature of the poems, the language gets more desperately metaphoric: 'meetings', 'conversations', 'constellate', 'space', 'mapping', 'contact', 'trajectories', 'alignments', 'demarcate', 'interactions' and 'hybridisations'. The emphasis, in this introduction, is on poetic scene rather than individual poets and their achievements, and the crucial fact about this scene is that, though it engages contemporary life, it should not be seen as one with 'an exclusive, generational poetic'. Both books convey the sense that the poetry of the nineties is a poetry after the great poetic revolutions. It is marked by what the *Calyx* editors call 'recombinant poetics', by hybridisation and respectful interactions, rather than the narrower horizons that Chris Wallace-Crabbe marked out as the essential feature of the fifties, or the oppositional poetics of the seventies and eighties. This is a surprising and almost modest view of a decade's new poets, certainly a long way from the Oedipal melodrama of most poetic history. It also sounds like the position of people for whom editing journals and presses, as well as their own writing, is a formative experience. To be a viable editor one has to publish (and thus be committed to) poetries that are different to one's own.

Because many if not most of these books' readers will be looking for a sketch map of what is happening and will want as much help as they can get, *Calyx*'s choice of an alphabetical listing for its poets is a bit frustrating. It makes for some nice patterns, but they are essentially accidental, as when the anthology is inaugurated by Adam Aitken's 'Saigon The Movie', set outside Australia and elegantly assertive:

James Bond flies into Phuket, which he pronounces
Fukit and this announces the demise
of the colonial era.
My mother sits on the Left Bank harvesting rice.

It concludes by the more defeatist, elegiac mode of Adrian Wiggins' two poems, set in Sydney at the site of Australian poetry's greatest elegy:

There a city leapt lightly from the ships,
pegged itself to the rocks and persisted, picked up

its registers: birthing, dieing, marrying –
at night the harbour buoys wink out
but not in memoriam, not for you.

One pattern that suggests itself as significant in Calyx, though it is probably a tension played out perennially in poetry, is the opposition between attention-to-the-world versus attention-to-the-medium. One could try to set up a spectrum with poets like Coral Hull and Peter Boyle leaning towards an apprehension of aspects of the world (or, at least, producing a poetry clearly inspired by and attached to the world) and poets like Javant Biarujia, Louis Armand and perhaps Peter Minter up at the other end. But these are crude parameters. 'Attention to the world' can mean many things ranging from social activism to an interest in culture to a desire for an unmediated apprehension of reality. 'Attention to the medium' can vary from an interest in poetry as a self-contained signifying device to language to an attention to the ways our minds are wired and, eventually, to ways in which reality is mediated.

As though to emphasise the crudity of this approach, it is immediately apparent that those poets who focus on the world demand to be arranged in terms of those who focus on relationships and those who focus on sensory apperception – that is those for whom the world is a human experience (or at least a populated landscape) and those for whom it is a rather more solipsistic one. On the left are poets like Felicity Plunkett, Adrian Wiggins, Jane Gibian and Cassie Lewis, and on the right, perhaps, a poet like John Mateer. Those who might be said to focus on the medium itself also can be very different poets. And in the centre is the poetry of Peter Boyle (one of the more widely published poets in the collection) for whom poetry, in the words of a ghostly interlocutor at least, points in both directions: 'And what you place on the page/ is mostly read by no one and/ what you value in the way the words fall/ or run together/ pointing outwards to the world/ and inwards to a private reticence,/ is something not explicable to others.'

Among *Calyx*'s surprises are the poems of Nick Riemer and Noel Rowe: what are we to make of a sudden efflorescence of intense religious experience in an essentially un-religious national culture? The fact that Noel Rowe is deprived of a biography is, I hope, an editorial glitch rather than a mystic's denial of the ego. In a sense these overtly religious poems derive from pre-, proto-, or non-poetic experience (depending on your aesthetics or theology), but they too can look towards community (Rowe's 'Perhaps After All He Hasn't Gone' and the second part of his 'Magnificat') or, like Riemer's 'An Oily Rag', towards a more solitary and isolating experience. His 'Sunset: Macdonnell Ranges, Central Australia' recalls, for a brief moment, the Lowell of 'Skunk Hour' – 'The sky's not sitting right' – but that is probably the right sort of reference for religious angst. Riemer's poems are very uneven and this one is no exception; it has a marvellous beginning – 'heavy birds / swivel overhead' – but a finish that won't trust the scene the poem describes to convey its own unease.

It is also surprising and pleasurable to feel that what are essentially epistemological or cognitive positions can be emotional ones for poets. Louis Armand's 'Psychopathologies of the Commonplace' does the epistemological despair of poetry and the life of perception well:

but what does it matter to have been, here or there? the same
narrative of disappointment in the eyes of everyone ...

But when in time
we are left to the dumb-show of our shadows' diminishing
how will we know which of those meanings
ever concerned us?

And there is also Michael Brennan's 'The Imageless World' which has a tone of – to me at least – surprising nostalgia for a universe run on pre-Nietzschean, pre-postmodern lines:

Radiance slips from us,
there is nothing
inside our words

contained within
the groundless world
and its struggle

of limits and beginnings...

What
to praise but

endurance,
the ceaseless purpose
of meaningless things.

Less surprising is the power of the Emma Lew poems, written like intense dramatic monologues from inside a situation we are never sure of (to distort a line in her poem, 'Marshes', we know the language but we don't know the country); the quality of the Alison Croggon poems, written as though to prove that large statements can still be made as long as you are confident enough; and the stylish meditations of Luke Davies which always seem anchored in a physicist's sense of the universe, rather than a philosopher's.

If *Calyx* balances attention to the world with attention to the medium, the selections of *New Music* clearly favour the former. In a book of nearly a hundred poets only twelve of *Calyx*'s thirty poets make an appearance; there is no room for Luke Davies, Kate Lilley and Adrian Wiggins let alone the headier reaches of Louis Armand, Javant Biarujia and Arthur Spyrou. (Nor, incidentally, is there room for Rowe and Riemer; Leonard's nineties are very secular.) And yet, as I have suggested, one of the strengths of *New Music* is its lengthy focus on young poets; it is just that they are often from outside the Sydney/Melbourne axis. You read more than forty pages of poetry before arriving at John Kinsella, and most of these early poets are worth their introduction; they tend to be writers either close to producing their first book or with a single small collection behind them (John Mateer is an obvious exception here). With the limited number of poems offered it is impossible to make judgements about their staying power but a number (including, randomly, Elizabeth Campbell, Cassie Lewis, Rebecca Edwards, Brett Dionysus and Lidija Cvetkovic) are poets whose later careers look more than promising.

As Leonard says in his introduction, anthologies of contemporary poetry are a 'sorting on the run' and there must be an element of rapid, almost instinctive choice about the process. It is complicated by the relatively brief exposure that the work of individual poets can receive. You get a strong sense of what the editor thinks was happening in the nineties but it is at the expense of a sense of what individual poets are doing. True, some poets seem represented by strong recent poems: Peter Rose, Judith Beveridge, Anthony Lawrence, John Forbes and Jennifer Maiden are cases in point, though no doubt they might have (or have had) feelings about the poems chosen which contradict mine. Others seem much more puzzling. To take examples where I know the books from which the selections have been made: Adam Aitken's 'Changi' is a fine poem from *Romeo and Juliet in Subtitles*, but 'The Corrosive Littoral' has always seemed one of the weaker poems. Is it included because its different mode – *faux* science-fiction – is an example of a minor mode of the nineties? At any event the six-poem selection of Aitken's work in *Calyx* gives the reader a much more accurate sense of what the poet, himself, is doing. For similar reasons I'm not sure that the Adamson selections from *The Pepper-Mill* are well-advised, the stronger Adamsonian poetry of the nineties is reduced to a single poem.

There is one factor in the composition of both *Calyx* and the first eighty-odd pages of *New Music* that scholars of the future will want to know more about. This is probably the first generation of Australian poets to have an extensive exposure to tertiary creative writing courses, both as students of such courses and, later, teachers. The brief biographies of the poets in both books obscure the exact degree of participation – reasonable enough since neither anthology is designed to pursue this question. But one would like to know more about the effects of this new *gradus ad parnassum* since it marks a radical change in literary culture and has been put in place comparatively recently. It is interesting also to monitor the crucial magazines and presses for these younger poets and to register the importance of Black Pepper Press and Five Islands Press. It is probably no accident that the second of these, run by Ron Pretty, has its origins in the University of Wollongong's impressive writing program.

And then there is the question of poetic mentors. It is difficult to be specific about the younger poets of *New Music*, but the poets of *Calyx* make their debts very clear. Twenty years ago one might have predicted that John Tranter or Robert Adamson would be likely to be the essential reference points for this generation of poets. While their work is clearly there (one of Adrian Wiggin's poems overwrites an early poem of Adamson) the figure who stands squarely behind *Calyx* is John Forbes. He is evoked by single words ('asymptote' from 'Love's Body' appears twice); by a dedication (in Tracy Ryan's 'Holywell'); by a repeated phrase ('the woman of your dreams' in Dipti Saravanamuttu's

'Lumination in Budapest' and by the openings of poems by Kate Lilley, very Forbesian in their simultaneous assertiveness and ungraspability: 'The waterfall attracts its share of losers' or 'quarto doesn't last a weak crush lingers / like a festival of moss / the clerk of all passports takes me round...' Clearly the benevolent ghost of John Forbes haunts the poetry of the generation that followed him. Even Armand's 'Perpetuum Mobile' is a meditation on the Australian littoral in a way that recalls Forbes' 'On the Beach'.

These two books provide a complementary overview of the last decade and should be bought and read together. The larger question remains as to what sense a combined total of nearly five hundred and fifty pages of poetry can give us of poetic activity in the nineties. At one level, the selections bear out the implications of their introductions: the nineties are a respectful decade, a kind of reconstructive phase after the horrors of poetic civil war, East Timor after Indonesian rule. Everything is about connections and interactions, across gender, national and generational boundaries; it is all civilised, accommodating and unarrogant. This seems fine except that it is hard for me to repress the sense that the results are worthy but just a fraction dull. One of the things literary history teaches us (if it can teach us anything at all) is that sometimes poetic changes are made violently and under great pressure. In preparing John Tranter's *The New Australian Poetry* for its new, digital existence, I have been rereading that major anthology of the end of the seventies. Although as its publisher, I am undoubtedly biassed, I also feel enough of the distance of time to look at it calmly, retrospectively and with very low expectations. It is a shock to me just how lively a book it is, what a pleasure it is to rediscover and how well it survives the passage into a calmer poetic decade. Some of this derives from factors that *New Music* and *Calyx* cannot benefit from – really substantial representation, for example, allowing the inclusion of long poems – but the essential difference must lie in the milieus from which the books derive. For all its confrontational quality, the seventies, the decade of the 'poetry wars', produced an outstandingly and consistently interesting body of poetry that the nineties, on the basis of these two anthologies at least, would be hard-pressed to match.

Greg McLaren

Blowing Dandelions

Calyx and Contemporary Australian Poetry

<blockquote>
Greg McLaren is a doctoral student in Australian literature at Sydney University; his poetry collection *Everything Falls In* was published by Vagabond Press in 2001.
</blockquote>

An anthology ought to show what is being thought about poetry in a given place at a given time, and to facilitate debate about its context and contents. *Calyx* fulfils these criteria. I have difficulty making the anthology hang together, though, a difficulty that seems to lie in the editorial criteria for inclusion. There's an awareness, but possibly too self-conscious, that 'anthologising in any context can only ever be the result of partial, processual visions, and anthologies on the whole best function synthetically rather than analytically.' There is a distinction between avoiding partiality on one hand and indecision on the other, which seems to be papered over. The criteria for inclusion are almost impossibly vague:

While our initial focus was to collect work by poets we had recently published and encountered creatively, we soon broadened our scope to include other poets who also started publishing widely in the 1990s. In discussing our processes of selection we agreed that a poet's age would be of no consequence and that the anthology would seek to represent material from a range of localities.

From such starting points it becomes perfectly valid to include or exclude practically any poet.

Despite the disavowal, the bulk of *Calyx* consists of 'younger' poets, those under, say, forty years of age. This leaves it at risk of appearing as an anthology of younger, emerging poets, in which role it is satisfactory, but little more; or else as a snapshot of where Australian poetry 'is', in which case it fails by the exclusion of major contemporary poets. It might appear to suggest that to be 'contemporary' is to be young, a move that potentially disenfranchises much compelling poetry. Among the surprising absences, I would include writers of the calibre of Nicolette Stasko, Jordie Albiston, Lisa Bellear, Louise Crisp, Lionel Fogarty, Cath Kenneally and Peter Rose. These poets represent distinctive poetic stances too often missing from the anthologies of the last ten years.

One of the striking features of *Calyx* is the proliferation of Language poetry. In his *Landbridge* anthology, John Kinsella includes the Language project under the umbrella of 'linguistically innovative' writing, but the fact remains that the movement derived its impetus from political/poetic considerations in the U.S. in the 1960s, 70s and 80s. It is hardly innovative any longer. As Kevin Hart notes, in the U.S. 'language poetry…became the new formalism'. I share Hart's criticism of Language poetry: 'with hindsight language poetry seems so academic. People shake their heads and wonder why it once appeared so liberating, so cool.' Sigi Curnow writes that 'Language' poetry 'takes "language" as the subject of a poetic practice whose concern is with the linguistic operations that determine our sense of reality'. Ann Vickery takes this further, insisting that when it is '[no] longer a mere tool to represent what is real… language is seen as the constitutive fabric of reality'.[1] But while language is certainly a constitutive component in our articulation of what we perceive as reality, it is not the sole means by which we engage with experience. Vickery's perspective suggests there is nothing we can 'meaningfully' engage with that is outside the scope of language so defined. Language might no longer be a human artefact: rather, people become linguistic artefacts. Vickery, citing Charles Bernstein, suggests that Language poets alone are capable of making language work in a different way: 'in language-oriented poetry, reference escapes the one-on-one reflection to an object, and words are multivalencies rather than reflecting back a single perception.' The assumption that the multivalency of words and images is a quality exclusive to 'language-oriented poetry' is simply nonsensical. It cannot seriously be argued that Language poetry has invested poetry or language with these qualities in the last few decades. The poets and theorists of the Language school may have found new ways of articulating what has always (already) been present in language and its operation, without having 'discovered' what they consider to be new. There are limitations in the field of what Language poetry is capable of.

In *Calyx*, in Kate Fagan's work, for example, the field of reference is ambitious and vast, but little value is given to the specific, concrete instances in which the problems the poems take issue with actually occur. There is little attempt at persuasion: we are meant simply to trust the poet and her argument. I find this deeply unsatisfactory. The ideas Fagan works with are straightforward enough, but there seems no engagement or interest in the ways these ideas might make themselves apparent. Because meaning, like the self, is assumed to be fugitive and utterly subjective, what the poems' implications are, what they might 'mean', go unaddressed: 'what is it about narcissism/ that suggests/ only deserved loss as an option,/ when detailing the space/ of conflict/ is possible/ and exquisite?' ('Return to a new physics'). Her poetry does work when read in parallel with Peter Minter's 'Morning, Hyphen': there's a formal and theoretical link that bears investigation. Michael Brennan also explores this territory, but his poem 'The Imageless World' embodies the concerns of theory without discarding a context for its theoretical assumptions. Rather, it works through the image, something that Fagan and Armand for example don't generally manage. Brennan intuits the danger of giving the idea more importance than the idea's application, of the poem then becoming a mere statement of ideology. There is a concern with what language points to (and what is radically beyond language and 'self') when he writes of 'a need/ to love something/ stronger than ourselves'.

Otherwise the poem, so intently and sometimes exclusively concerned with how language operates, and feeding upon itself and its own theories, without references external to text, becomes solipsistic and narcissistic. There's little sense of the Language-influenced poetry here consistently addressing the crisis of language in the context in which it becomes a crisis; even less how writers might actually proceed past the fact of language's problematic nature.

John Kinsella, a champion of Language writing and theory in Australia, wrote recently that 'the real engagements with Australia-wide poetry and poetry-scapes come via a writer such as Coral Hull [and her] moral investigations of people's relationships with animals'.[2] Hull is atypical of many of the poets in *Calyx* in that she breaks through into what is beyond the textual: to compassion, disgust, visceral anger, surprising equanimity. There is a strong tendency toward the ethical that is not obviously dependent upon the meta-narratives: she's an exemplar of a possible postmodern ethic based on recognition of community and the need for that community to be safe for all its inhabitants. In *Landbridge* Hull wrote: 'I want to tell it like it is, then have something done about it'.[3] Against this, the Language poetry view of ethics in a textual dimension — writing ethically — begins to look pale, superficial and passive. In *Calyx* Hull's been done a disservice, represented by a mere seven pages, while poets who currently seem less significant receive greater space. Her work gains strength through accumulation. The three poems here, while not atypical of the range of her work, are insufficient to suggest the breadth of her capabilities.

Hull is not the only poet in *Calyx* working from such an ethical perspective. Peter Boyle is one of the few showcased at sufficient length. His material is quite different to Hull's but he has a similar concern with the social, creating a web of associations which draw in a widening and deepening sense of connection. 'Child on Smoky Mountain, Manila' moves from the specific poverty of Manila ('He eyes the fishbones') to the broad reach of global capitalism and, implicitly, our part in it ('slow trains grind their cargo/ of foodstuffs for Japan'). In this poem also Boyle makes a link between writing and the ethical that is far keener than any of the poets whose primary interest is in the politics of writing and linguistics: 'No matter how thin the poet/ wants to get/ his lines/ they will never be as thin/ as this/ child's/ wrist.'

Boyle's poems are not generally 'set' in Australia, but their engagement with European and displaced European cultures works parallel to patterns of displacement widely dispersed through

Australian history and literature. His drawing on various cultural traditions, as in Hull's poetry, demonstrates the significance of connection. We might also place the poetry of Adam Aitken and Dipti Saravanamuttu in this context, since both work within a poetics of political and formal inclusion that exceeds the tag 'postcolonial'. Margie Cronin's interest in the Latin Americans ('A Fiction Reprised (retelling Borges)' and 'Women of the Sky') and Russians ('Note to Anna Akhmatova') operates powerfully in counterpoint to Boyle's. Although her work has an international and historical sweep (see her poem for Tibet, 'where the word for body is baggage'), the local is also of great significance. Cronin's excellent and moving poem 'The Cuan' celebrates the personal and particular while mourning its loss, closing immaculately: 'And on this weekend away my mother cries/ And pays for everything'. The plotting of these webs of relation between the local and the global marks an ethical engagement with what it is to live as an Australian now, and these poems are reminders of the community in which we live and of which we must be a part.

These sort of correlations – between poets; between the global and the local; between the general and the specific – can also be seen in the poetry of Nick Riemer and Noel Rowe. Riemer's work, and that of Luke Davies – was for me the real surprise packet of *Calyx*. His poems are striking in their evocation of a value inherent in the space and place that they render. It's a poetry that allows linguistic theory, a postmodern aesthetic and 'nature' to meet in productive, collaborative ways. Desire for 'meaning' and the erasure of meaning inherent in language collide: 'Whenever/ you understand,/ you're on/ our own./ There's no/ such thing as/ language, I / sort of hope' ('Glary Days'). Riemer's use of language evades stasis and mere 'representation' while engaging the reader in what his poems are 'about'. Linguistic considerations (as in 'Same' – 'Your pencil/ turns into letters') find embodiment in landscape and the processes of change at work in it: 'The river gets wider, flows more deeply,/ still through the same layered landscape' ('Afterlife'); 'A breeze picks up, obliterating every footprint' ('Sunset: Macdonnell Ranges'). This play with impermanence, absence and time continues in Rowe's work. The first poem in his selection also has a particularity that assigns an implicit value to what is observed: 'There was fear, yes, but also/ faith among familiar things' ('Magnificat'). The absence and space that for Riemer is as physical as it is figurative ('There is no more inside./ The distance is the distance.'), is embodied in Rowe's work as loss, as in 'Perhaps After All He Hasn't Gone': 'perhaps after all he hasn't gone/ so far away/ but is still coming home/…heading towards the dairy he knows/ isn't there anymore'.

Luke Davies' work, on the other hand, abounds with both presence and scientific rigour. It's no joke to say that God is everywhere in his poems – in 'Flowers', 'From Theory to Pulse', 'History of Violence' and 'Passage of Time'. Davies melds the religious abstract and the concretely scientific, deploying the general and the particular: 'the bee,/ which is abundance, with its fat belly, drones/ into my life. Meaning I am at the mercy/ of greater forces. Meaning because joy is limited/ it is infinite' ('Ezekiel'). The 'greater forces' here are certainly not the sole province of religion. What would normally pass for a religious humility comes from awareness of the scientific: the speaker can 'feel the planet swing through space: oxygen/ a reprieve, atmosphere the illusion of a comfort zone'. Davies perfectly embodies the problem of theory and how to make use of it: 'the first postulate of relativity, and I believe it, says to me/ there's no such thing as place. But here I am. It's nice to sit a while.' ('From Theory to Pulse').

There is impressive work in *Calyx*. Adrian Wiggins' 'Milsons Point' is an update in miniature of Slessor's 'Five Bells', and his take on Adamson, 'Acting Would Almost Kill It/ A Gambol' is amusing. Michael Farrell's work owns at times a surreal energy that meshes well with Jane Gibian's poems. Her 'Poem for Dissolution', 'Poem for Retrospection' and 'Poem for Distraction' form a dynamic, considered sequence which, with the excellent '(sky harbour)', acknowledges the processes of flux while addressing the need to find a way to live 'postmodernly' in a world that seem to evade being pinned down ('the universe/ becomes cornerless once more'). Emma Lew is one poet who benefits from a generous selection, though she might have read better if not preceded by Hull: her poetry doesn't have the same visceral buzz, though it has its own *post-sequitur* chaos which revels in the dissociative. The typically postmodern ploy of dismantling the divide between popular and high culture is meat and three veg to Kate Lilley – her

'Nicky's World' is one of *Calyx*'s highlights. It contains a whole web of relationships and associations, even if they depend on a working knowledge of *The Young and the Restless*, and owe a small debt to John Tranter's cocktail-sipping genre poems. It's a nice coincidence, one of many in the book, that Lilley's pantoums, like Hugh Tolhurst's ('In the red') set up the US and Canada as a significant, nearly mythic Other.

As Brennan and Minter suggest in their introduction, the poets in *Calyx* are involved in 'a number of new meetings and conversations'. These conversations need to be listened to in relation to what has gone before. The poetry of J.S. Harry, for one, is engaged in a sharp, clear-eyed and wide-ranging analysis and interrogation of language, perception, art and its place in the world, and possesses a preternatural style and humour notably lacking in *Calyx*'s Language-influenced poets. Harry, Adamson, Tranter and the late John Forbes might all be seen as exemplary postmodern poets. Harry and Forbes in particular, continually undercutting the speaker's 'self', without devaluing the poems' concerns, show up the younger writers in terms of their practical understanding and ironic deployment of the theoretical positions the latter are so earnestly interested in. Adamson is another who investigates the status and operation of language in relation to meaning and yet ties these postmodern concerns to place and body and history. Possibly the most interesting aspect of John Kinsella's work is the way in which, in his anti-pastoral poems, he has made an effective engagement with the environment and the ethical from his Language-poetry influences. This ethical engagement is a continuing preoccupation in Australian poetry. That many of the poets in *Calyx*, divergent in their approaches and methodologies, are concerned with the balance between how to write and how to be ethical is encouraging. Is is hardly a movement, even less a new direction, but what it does demonstrate is the depth of poetry's ability to respond to how we live.

---

[1] *Sydney Morning Herald*, Spectrum, 27 January 2001, p.6; 'Language Poetry and the Academy', *Meanjin,* 1, 1990, p.171; 'Beyond Strictly Verse and Pulp Diction', *Salt,* 9, 1996, p.130.
[2] *Sydney Morning Herald*, Spectrum, 20 January 2001, pp.1, 9.
[3] *Landbridge*, ed. John Kinsella (Fremantle Arts Centre Press, 1999), p.179